My Lady's Secrets

Also by Katy Moran

Game of Hearts
Wicked by Design
Scandalous Alchemy

My Lady's Secrets

KATY MORAN

An Aria Book

First published in the UK in 2024 by Head of Zeus Ltd,
part of Bloomsbury Publishing Plc

9 7 5 3 1 2 4 6 8

A catalogue record for this book is available from the British Library.

ISBN (HB): 9781035914241
ISBN (E): 9781803280202

Typeset by Divaddict Publishing Solutions Ltd.

Cover design: Micaela Alcaino

Printed and bound in Great Britain by
CPI Group (UK) Ltd, Croydon CRO 4YY

Head of Zeus Ltd
First Floor East
5–8 Hardwick Street
London EC1R 4RG

WWW.HEADOFZEUS.COM

To Lucy and Alec, who could not be less like the Butes.
Thank you for giving my imagination somewhere special to fly

On 11 May, at the hour of five o'clock in the evening, Spencer Perceval, the prime minister of the United Kingdom of Great Britain and Ireland, was SHOT DEAD by John Bellingham, a Liverpool merchant with a grievance against the government.

The Globe
12th May 1812

'More of these damned Scoundrels must go the same way and then the poor people may live.'
'This is but the beginning'

Samuel Taylor Coleridge, quoting
interviewees in *The Morning Post*

Part One

If I should meet thee after long years,
How should I greet thee?
With silence and tears

Lord Byron, 'When We Two Parted'

1

Cressida clung to the wisteria vine and set one foot onto the first-floor balcony railing, trying to ignore a spine-cracking drop to the walkway below. Her chest heaved with exertion. The soldiers who had pursued her across London could only be moments away. Of all the places she *really* didn't want to get caught breaking into, Fife House was top of the list: home of Lord Liverpool, Secretary of State for War and unofficial government spymaster.

Oh, hell. With a swift exhalation, Cressida shifted her other foot onto the balcony and relinquished her grip on the twisted wisteria trunk, only then allowing herself to jump down into the balcony itself, which was dominated by a large, unshuttered window that had been left ajar. *Breathe. Just breathe.* For a moment, she crouched amid a drift of bruised wisteria petals with the sulphuric stink of gunpowder still in her hair.

Cressida's pursuers had been close behind ever since she'd

shaken off her guards in the aftermath of a bone-shaking explosion at the Port of London. All were officers. Exactly the sort she did her best to avoid.

Sometimes, in Cressida's barefoot and often drunken years with first the British army and then the French, she had exchanged information for coinage or rum: perhaps the positioning and morale of troops, whether their supply wagons were stranded on the wrong side of a ravine. Sometimes, there was a price to pay for that.

Cressida got to her feet: as ever, there was nowhere to go but onwards.

Lady Liverpool was entertaining this evening: the room beyond the balcony blazed with candlelight. It was quiet, though: good. Her ladyship must have kept her guests corralled downstairs. Cressida brushed down the green satin skirts of the evening gown she'd stolen before the siege, filched from a French commandant's wife in an ancient Spanish walled town, where the night was heavy with woodsmoke and the scent of charred herbs. She tucked a stray ringlet behind her ear, raised the sash window and stepped into the quiet of Lord Liverpool's library, accompanied by a sudden volley of barking so loud it rent the air.

Cressida caught her breath, making the usual rapid assessment that had saved her life on more than one occasion. Bookshelves reached all the way up to the embossed ceiling; blazing candlelight picked out gold lettering on leather-bound spines. Two footmen in powdered wigs and gold-laced blue livery stood by an imposing fireplace of rose-pink marble, imprisoned by a bear. Cressida stood very still, breathing in the acrid, animal reek of a creature in distress even as the bear whipped around to face her, letting out another volley of excited barking. It was a dog, of course, the size of a small pony.

Cressida held up one hand, palm outwards. 'Stop at once. Oh, what nonsense.'

The dog stood easily three feet high at the shoulders and leaped at Cressida with such weight and force that it took some effort to steady herself. Hairy paws landed on her shoulders with staggering force, and Cressida had to gather her strength to remove them, one by one.

'*Sit.*'

Recognising a true mistress when he heard one, the dog settled back on his haunches, shaking his great ursine head with a spray of saliva. Cressida turned her attention to the footmen, who had by now scrambled to block her path to the door; these were men trained never to forget a face. They knew, after all, who she was.

'Lady Liverpool is not at home to visitors.' The taller footman smirked, even as the sounds of distant merriment drifted into the room from downstairs: wild laughter, a concerto.

His colleague sneered. 'Out the way you came, milady, unless you're wishful for us to call the Runners. Scotland Yard is just across the way, after all. That or we can march you out through the servants' quarters: we always do like a bit of light entertainment below stairs.'

The dog – a Newfoundland crossed with a mastiff, perhaps – let out a low, rumbling growl that Cressida felt through the soles of her feet.

'Oh, I don't think we need create a spectacle, do you? Are you going to open the door or not?' Cressida asked, gently. '*Come.*' This last directive was issued to the Newfoundland cross, now at her side, and together they left Lady Liverpool's footmen to concoct their excuses for being outmanoeuvred by a fallen woman and a dog.

At the top of the wide marble staircase, Cressida rested one hand briefly on the dog's vast shoulder as he waited at her side, quivering with anticipation.

'Come on then,' she said. 'I'll take you to his lordship.'

The Newfoundland whined with longing, the object of all his desires now within reach. Cressida knew by the time they both reached the foot of the stairs that her command over him had wavered. A pair of large gilded double doors had been thrown open, and here the babble from within grew ever louder. Cressida breathed in the scent of over-warm bodies and champagne breath. There was still time to run away from all this, not that she had anywhere to go, no other choice at all in fact. Silence descended. With the dog at her side, Cressida walked into Lady Liverpool's drawing room.

Somewhere, someone dropped a glass of claret-cup, and the bright burst of broken glass rang out. Cressida caught sight of familiar faces from her youth, people she had known, and some she'd even liked. Those closest to her turned their backs in a flurry of shivering ostrich feathers and shimmering silk. It was to be expected. Cressida smiled as the dog left her side, bounding towards one of the side doors, spraying drool and now unstoppable. Cressida followed in his wake, looking neither right nor left until her companion let out a crescendo of excited barking and surged into the side-chamber, knocking aside an acne-ridden young footman like a single painted ninepin.

Cressida followed her companion into a room with an embossed ceiling and panelled walls hung with portraits of people and horses, all framed in heavy gilt. She shut the door behind her at speed, which was just as well. A dark-haired young man of about her own age was vigorously swiving a slight woman bent over a chaise longue. Her skirts were pushed up around her waist and Cressida just had time to register a head of cropped fair curls and a cry of shocked indignation, which would have been maidenly had it not emerged from the lips of Lady Caroline Lamb. Someone had drawn long brocade curtains across the tall window that faced out onto Whitehall. This did little to muffle the tail end of a riot: broken glass and hobnailed boots upon the paving-slabs. Out in the street, someone was singing one of the new rebel songs, lauding General Ludd in a reedy falsetto. With one final workmanlike thrust George Gordon, Lord Byron pulled away and turned around to face Cressida. His fine lawn shirt was in fantastic disarray, both his dark eyebrows raised, his face flushed with spent desire and that wary, irresistible smile upon his lips. Lady Caroline whirled around, yanking down the fragile skirts of her gown. Her eyes narrowed as she recognised Cressida. One word was enough.

'*You!*'

This was too much for Cressida's companion, who bounded forward to greet his master, both paws upon his shoulders.

'Show some propriety, Timothy.' Byron laughed, tucking in his shirt and everything else back into his breeches with his one available hand as he fended off the dog with the other.

'I thought you said you wouldn't get another after Boatswain?' Cressida demanded, as Byron buttoned up the fall of his breeches, one-handed. He ignored Caroline, who was white-faced as she retied her garter, her large, expressive eyes glittering with unshed tears.

'Oh, Timothy's not mine,' Byron said. '*Down*, you wretched thing. I'm just looking after him.'

Caroline poured herself a brandy from a decanter on the side table and flung herself onto the chaise longue, canny enough not to storm out of the room while she still looked unmistakably like someone in receipt of a flyer.

Byron spread his hands out wide in a gesture of helpless confusion. 'Dare I even ask what you want, Cress?'

Cressida smiled. 'I need to get out of the country before they hang me.' She hated this part: 'And a loan of a few hundred or so. I won't trouble you again.'

'You chose a fine time to come home. It's a damned thing when the Prime Minister can be shot dead in the House of Commons.' For once lost for words, Byron gesticulated at the window. Outside, rioters howled an approximation of 'The Cutty Wren'. Rebel songs meant one thing when all was said and done: a fine crop on the gallows.

'Whatever happened to that boy who wanted to build the world anew? Revolution is neither tidy nor convenient,' Cressida said.

Byron frowned at her, then shot a quick glance at his mistress, before switching into effortless French. 'Darling, I suppose it'd be a fool's errand to mention Greville at this point?'

Cressida laughed, recalling the mob of siege-crazed

British soldiers advancing on her in an ancient Spanish town, forcing her to back up against the bloodstained, crumbling wall where they had shot French survivors.

Step away from the lady. Achingly recognisable, the voice had come from behind them all.

She'd known him immediately, even with the familiar lines and planes of his face darkened with gunpowder, and even in the dusty, bloodied dark green uniform of the Rifles, not dressed for the balls or country houses where in truth he had always been so bored and restless.

She recalled odd details that flew upon her like hornets in a rush of memory and sensation: how Greville hadn't been wearing his fur-plumed shako helmet and how the dark waves of his hair were crusted with sweat and blood but touched gold by the sun, the dark gaze that had once been full of humour now scorching with slow, deliberate hatred right down the length of her body.

Thanks to Greville, she was still alive.

Thanks to Greville, she had been arrested for treason, brought back to an England on the brink of revolution to face what passed for justice these days, and as of this afternoon was now a fugitive on the run.

'*Cressida!*' The panic in Byron's voice brought her sharply back to the present. 'I'm going to regret this – listen: the Season's nearly dead and buried. I've received more invitations to house parties than I know what to do with, but I've accepted your cousin's. Meet me at Drochcala? It would be wiser to discuss this another time.'

He wasn't wrong. A selection of Lady Liverpool's burlier footmen had advanced into the room; she couldn't afford to be marched through a drawing room like some kind of criminal. Instead, she followed Byron's gaze to the window that gave out right onto Whitehall itself and sketched a mocking curtsey, which he returned with an equally unserious bow. Then she ran.

2

Not half an hour before, Lieutenant Colonel Lord Greville Nightingale snagged one of Bessy Tot's small tables in the taproom at the Oxford Arms, deep in the environs of the Devil's Acre. Greville had taken off his shako, but he was still clad in the dark green officer's tunic and the grey breeches of the 95th Rifles: he hadn't been home since the *Princess Sophie* docked at the Port of London that afternoon. He felt an odd sense of dislocation: everything about the Oxford was familiar, from Bessy's weary smile and dishevelled red ringlets to her husband, Thomas, leaning on the bar, exchanging quips with a stripling street-walker in a satin gown that was so big she'd pinned it clumsily across the bodice. It was all a world away from the war he'd left behind in Spain: campfires, siege trenches, mud and rubble, the permanent bitter taste of gunpowder in his mouth. His uniform and evident rank drew suspicious glances from Bessy and Thomas's patrons: riots had exploded all over London since the prime minister's assassination less than twenty-four hours earlier, and still no one knew whether that fatal shot fired in the House of Commons was the first of a full-blown revolution.

Greville could have done without it: God only knew he'd had no desire to come back to England at all and yet, courtesy of his extremely estranged wife and his oldest friend, here he was. He sat at a table near a leaded window with a clear line to the door, his body thrumming with a soldier's awareness even as he stretched out his long legs, crossing them at the ankle. Bessy brought the gin and he dropped the coinage into her outstretched hand without even returning her smile, a rare lapse of courtesy. Greville saw only Cressida in the ruins of a Spanish town, clad in a gown of spoiled silk, her face bloodied, her fingers and her lips black with gunpowder, tangled auburn curls loose around her shoulders, with that fire in her dark eyes he had never forgotten, not in all these years.

Greville drained his gin; he should have told Bessy just to bring the tin jug and have done with it.

Major Lord Arthur Lascelles of the Peninsular Corps of Guides walked into the Oxford then, all blue superfine and exquisitely polished top-boots. Raconteur, childhood companion and devious expert in military intelligence, evidently Lascelles had at least found time to change since his ship docked, just hours before Greville's. His hair was arranged with a stylish element of en deshabille, the ironic tilt of his smile exactly the same as it had been in the overheated London salons of their youth. With a swift glance around the gloomy reaches of the tavern, Lascelles lowered himself into the chair opposite Greville, letting out a small sigh. By rights, Lascelles ought to have laid himself open to attention from cutpurses, but no Devil's Acre thief would make the attempt on him.

Lascelles beckoned to Bessy for porter and she bustled across the room in her best gown of grubby glazed calico. Her eyes widened with alarm at the expression on Greville's face; she refilled his glass without a word and retreated.

Lascelles sighed. 'The court martial's over, Grev. You could be on furlough in Lisbon with a girl on each arm.'

Greville smiled in such a way that even Lascelles flinched; after boarding the *Sophie* in the heat of a white-hot fury, he'd had two weeks at sea to consider the wisdom of pursuing his errant wife and Lascelles back to England. 'Is that really all you summoned me here to say?' Greville leaned back in his chair and allowed the glass of daffy to swing gently from his fingertips as he raised it in salute.

'No,' Lascelles said. 'It's not even the half of what I have to say to you. You could literally have escorted Cressida out into the hills after catching her on the wrong side, given her a horse and never laid eyes upon the wretched hellcat again. That siege and the aftermath was chaotic and hardly the British army's finest hour; no one would have been any the wiser. Instead you arrested Cressida and then beat the Guards officer who apprehended her, in territory we'd just recovered from the French, into a bloody pulp, earning yourself a court martial in the process. He was a baronet's son: you can't thrash men like that into next week without consequence. Now your wife is my problem. Why?'

'I don't care who his father is. He would have forced her before he cut her throat and I would have done the same if he'd tried it on any woman.' As for the rest, Greville had asked himself the same question at sea, multiple times, and found no satisfactory answer. He was also uncomfortably aware that his own rank in society was what had swung the court martial in his favour.

'Don't give me that look,' Lascelles went on. 'If it's also because on some level, Greville, you couldn't leave Cressida a second time, go back to Spain.'

'Give me a good reason why I should not also beat you to a bloody pulp. Sir,' Greville said.

Lascelles gave Greville his most disarming smile. 'Because I pushed that ogre Arbuthnot down the stairs at Winchester when he questioned your mother's virtue?'

Greville watched him. 'Keep Sylvia's name out of your mouth. *You knew.*' He measured out each word. 'My wife has been following the army with no protection and no honour, living among the camp followers and surviving God knows how, for years, and *you knew*.'

She'd run away after a night Greville preferred to forget, disappearing from London society like campfire smoke on the wind.

'What are you going to do with her?' Greville spoke with a calm he wasn't even close to feeling and drained the last of his gin.

Lascelles gave him a steady look across the table. 'You captured Cressida in territory we'd taken from the French. *She was on the wrong side, Greville.* She was lucky not to be shot, hanged, or otherwise quietly disposed of, and that's before we even consider her father.'

Greville stared back. 'The less said about Rosmoney the better.'

'I agree, but having a criminal for a father won't help her now.'

'Did it ever?' Greville demanded.

Lascelles spoke with restrained calm. 'The whole country is on the brink of revolution and the Prime Minister has just been murdered. Lord Liverpool and the Committee of Secrecy have a long reach and your wife was just caught with our enemy. You must understand that a whiff of treason is more dangerous than ever.

'Believe me, blue blood or not, the only thing that will keep your wife out of either an extremely humiliating public trial for treason or, more likely, a very unfortunate accident is for her to become indispensable. If Cressida was in enough trouble before Perceval was shot, in all honesty I now think she'll be luck to survive the next month.'

'Oh, spare me whatever devious sneaking bloody plot you have in mind,' Greville said; he wanted no part in Lascelles' intelligencing, and most particularly not if Lascelles had designs on involving his wife. 'Where is she?'

'Well.' Lascelles leaned back in his chair. He'd never been afraid of Greville.

Greville stared at him, his eyes narrowed. Lascelles would sooner cut his own throat than admit fault: he'd been like this since they were eight years old. 'She came back to England under your escort. You've lost her, haven't you?'

'Someone threw a grenade just as we were disembarking: it was a little chaotic. The *Hellion* lost a horse and sixteen crates of chambord. Your wife and her maid took the opportunity to lose themselves.'

'My God, if you've got even half a plan you'd better start talking,' Greville said.

Lascelles smiled, which had always meant trouble.

3

At Fife House, Cressida climbed out of the window, finding ledges and hand-holds with silk-slippered toes and scrabbling fingertips, praying for the embrace of London's streets, alleys and waterways. She fell the last four or five feet and landed on the wide paved walkway of Whitehall itself in a rolling motion, winded and tangled in the ruined satin skirts of her gown. She'd feel it later. There was still a crowd even at this small hour of the night, laid-off servants and rag-clad weavers with nothing left to lose, all followed by children with the sunken eyes and swollen bellies that signalled slow starvation.

Cressida got to her feet on a ragged exhalation, half expecting to hear the hue and cry for a house-breaker, but no one along the broad sweep of Whitehall seemed to notice or care that a woman in a satin gown had just tumbled from the first-floor window of Lord Liverpool's house. The mob seethed and swarmed down the wide street in a rising wave, away from Westminster Palace. Even a child could tell that the murder of a much-hated prime minister less than a mile away had already given birth to the sort of riot that would rage for days. Cressida dived in, elbowing past shouting women in filthy aprons and young bucks on the town struggling to hold on to their hats. Satin slippers were a bitch to run in, worse even than hobnailed boots.

At last, she reached the remnants of the Privy Gardens, where ornamental cherry trees in full blossom still encircled a moonlit oval of scythed grass. Sprinting for the cover of the trees, cold fear slicked down Cressida's back as one of the soldiers in pursuit called out her name, mocking, as if certain she could never get away. Damn, she hadn't lost them, not for a moment. With her draughtswoman's eye, Cressida recalled that the gardens ended in a red-brick wall covered in rose trellises. Again, not an option: instead, she tore across raked gravel and fallen cherry blossom, escaping through a latched gate into a quiet alleyway that backed onto the grim bulk of Scotland Yard. Darting past the chapel, running across the cobbles, Cressida sprinted down the alleyway; here, she breathed in the heavy green reek of the Thames.

Gathering up her skirts, Cressida ran towards the river. As she reached the Whitehall Steps that led down to the water, a curvaceous, dark-haired young girl of about seventeen stepped out from behind a heap of crates and barrels, respectably clad in clean pressed linen like the lady's maid she sometimes actually was.

'Mistress, come quickly – there's a boat!' Ines spoke in rapid Portuguese and Cressida followed her maid down the steps towards the river, casting a single look over her shoulder to confirm her suspicion: the three soldiers were now even closer.

Cressida grabbed Ines's arm, steadying her. A small skiff was indeed waiting, roped to an iron ring set into the bottom step. A lithe, weather-beaten riverman in the upper reaches of his forties climbed swiftly out as they approached and Cressida swallowed an astonished curse. Her father's groom wore the same old greasy jacket of boiled wool, a neckerchief of yellowed linen, and a watchful expression of exasperated patience. O'Neill had fled Dublin years before with Cressida's father, both of them lucky to escape the gallows in the ruins of the rebellion. Now, O'Neill was smoking a clay pipe that he tossed into the heaving Thames tide. Ines pressed both hands to her mouth in a silent scream. Cressida spun around to face a fourth soldier, smirking as he lounged in the shadowed wharf-edge. The soldier turned on her, quick as an eel, forcing her up against the warehouse, cold stone at her back.

'Might just have my fun with you before they stretch your neck, darling.'

O'Neill had always moved silently; he said the horses preferred it. He cut the soldier's throat from behind and lowered the corpse into the pooling tidewaters of the Thames with all the tenderness of a lover. There was a brief silence in which O'Neill wiped his hands on his breeches before handing Ines and then Cressida down into the boat with a blank expression that fooled no one. Cressida took one of the long oars, pushing them out into the Thames; she felt the pull of the tide and O'Neill took the oar from her without a word, now rowing hard.

'They'll shoot us!' Ines hissed, her gaze fixed on the gaggle of soldiers, who abruptly stopped running at the top of the steps with what would have been comical timing in any other circumstances.

'They won't,' Cressida said. Her mind raced: there was no other riverman within hailing distance, but the Thames teemed with skiffs and other small craft and it wouldn't be long before the soldiers managed to secure passage and pursue them, before or after they realised their comrade was now well on his way to an ignominious resting place on a Deptford Creek mudflat.

The back of Cressida's neck tingled but no one opened fire. Lascelles had quietly shipped her home from Spain under his own personal guard. Why? Facing Cressida and Ines, O'Neill gripped the oars with his sun-browned hands, steering the skiff with expert ease. For a moment she was eight years old again, O'Neill tossing her up into the saddle in the crumbling stable-yard at Rosmoney as he held the mare. *Gently does it now.* He wasn't smiling now.

'I'm only going to ask this once,' Cressida said, in the Irish she'd learned from O'Neill and the other servants, long ago. 'What in the devil's name are you doing here?'

He didn't grace that with a reply. In reality, there was only one person who could or would have ordered this.

Ines stared in thoughtful disgust at Cressida's gown as O'Neill worked the oars in a silence that spoke volumes. 'Look at that mud. It will never come out. I don't know why you had to ruin the best of the gowns before we've even been in England for five minutes. Milady.'

Cressida gave Ines a look that quelled her impertinence.

Her own thoughts would not quieten. It had been a long day and before that the crossing from the walled Atlantic city of Lisbon had not been pleasant under full guard. She and Lascelles had dined together every night on board the *Sophie*: it was the only time she was ever allowed to leave a locked cabin shared with Ines. Over supper and white burgundy their conversation had ranged with the familiarity of long friendship from the dark passion in Goya's paintings to how much Lascelles' young sister Georgiana loved sailing. They'd both been at war long enough that it felt natural never to touch on topics best left alone. Not once had Lascelles hinted at what would happen to her once they docked: he ought to have known she intended never to find out.

London flew past in darkness: wharves, torchlit palaces, medieval gardens leading down to the river. Even at this hour of the night, the waterway was crowded with skiffs and luggers and rivermen rowing gangs of workmen, clerks in cheap jackets and working girls in bonnets that had been fashionable two years before. Ines gave her a quick look from beneath thick dark lashes, but her fingers were twined hard together, white with pressure. Cressida was no liar, or never to Ines at least: there was no reassurance to give.

4

An hour later, outside a tall, cadaverous house deep in the slums of St Giles, Cressida watched as O'Neill approached a doorman with a broken nose and gave him a code-word. With O'Neill at her back and Ines sulkily climbing the torchlit stairs in front of her, Cressida went briskly up the stairway with her knife in one hand. Making short work of a long corridor lit only by a pair of guttering oil lamps on a side table, Cressida stepped across creaking floorboards. Disgraced Irish aristocrat, traitor, rebel and spy: the twelfth and last Earl of Rosmoney preferred to hear his visitors coming.

O'Neill gave word to the guard at the door and, with a directive to Ines in Portuguese, Cressida went into the room.

Pine sap and the faintest tang of orange-flower: the scent of Rosmoney's cologne transported her back to the rose garden at home, when he had by means of magic made a gold sovereign disappear before her eyes. Flames licked at a desultory heap of glowing coals behind the grate and weak moonlight lanced into a room through a gap between the shutters, revealing what she swiftly realised were framed paintings of all different shapes and sizes, wrapped in sack-cloth. She paused with the knife in her hand, listening to lowered voices. One was unknown: weak, but tutored and cultured. The other voice was low and musical, last heard in the drawing room at Rosmoney among the moth-eaten tapestries, still with a hint of the brogue he'd always affected.

'I'll do my best for you, of course, dear boy. But you know how these things are, the market being what it is.'

Cressida waited in a shaft of moonlight, conscious of her wild, tousled hair and the crumpled, mud-streaked satin skirts of her gown. A tall, lantern-jawed young buck wearing a tight jacket and high shirt points emerged at speed from behind a stack of paintings. Startled and blushing, he muttered something about being her humble servant and pushed past on his way to the door. A lissom aristocrat on the brink of his fifties stepped out into the moonlight, pocketing a roll of bank-notes tied with a thin strip of satin ribbon. Of middle height only, Rosmoney was still arrestingly handsome, with those long dark eyes and that twitch of a smile. The touch of grey in his dark coiffure snatched Cressida back through the years to her earliest childhood, when the fashion had still been for men to powder their hair.

'Poor boy,' Cressida's father remarked, as though he had simply left her at the breakfast table that morning and gone to ride out on the gallops. 'That was Duntisbourne's lad, you know – not a chance of squeezing a bent halfpenny out of his trustees, with some very unsavoury creditors at the door. But the Gainsborough is his to do with as he wishes. Far better to sell it in America where at least he'll be saved the embarrassment of some Nottingham mill-owner's wife trying to pretend his grandmother is a relation of hers.' Rosmoney halted, eying Cressida with a pained expression at her dishevelled state, not troubling to explain how he had gone from a would-be Irish rebel on the run to a series of dealings with the British consulate in Portugal, arriving now at art dealership. 'What a diamond you could have been, child. Let's have a huge drink.'

Without waiting for a response, Cressida's father turned his back on her and liberated a bottle of champagne from the bucket of ice standing on a dilapidated desk. He poured out two brimming glassfuls, treating Cressida to the negligent smile that had by all accounts done for her mother, otherwise a woman of good sense. Without taking her eyes from his, Cressida drank all of her champagne at once, savouring the rush, and held out her glass for more. Rosmoney filled it, raising his eyebrows as though she were a debutante who had gone too far at her first ball. Cressida dashed the contents of her glass in his face, savouring the sight of champagne dripping from her father's handsome, dissipated features as well as his brief expression of outraged astonishment that soon dissolved into laughter.

'You can stop the bloody act,' Cressida said, before he could speak. 'What in God's name are you doing on English soil? Surely it's too dangerous after Ireland, even now.'

Rosmoney shook the champagne from his hair and poured her another glass, sipping his own. 'Oh, tempers have cooled a little in fourteen years, and I'm here to raise funds, in fact. The most wonderful woman, you know – I never thought I would meet your mother's match, but my dear Mrs Winters holds a candle to Emilia. A very sensible woman, too.'

'And a rich one, I don't doubt. You're getting married?' Cressida stared at him. 'Papa, you were lucky to get out of Dublin alive in '98.'

Rosmoney made a dismissive gesture with his fingertips. 'The Cabinet has bigger fish to fry just now than to worry about an old rebel and a failed rising.'

'You turned spy for the British, didn't you?' Cressida said. 'A word here and a word there, and your aristocratic neck was saved, at a price. What a shame about all the others.' She didn't bother to keep the contempt out of her voice, having never forgotten the sight of so many less well-connected rebels swinging from the ramparts of Dublin Castle. 'What do you want?'

'Come now, shrewishness is inexcusable – I would have hoped my dear niece had taught you better. A well-brought-up girl ought to show an amiable face to the world.'

'*Shrewishness?*' Cressida repeated, incredulous. 'You swore blind you'd send for me as soon as you were settled in Lisbon. That was fourteen years ago and I had to endure the best part of ten of those with Annis. And then when I came to you myself, you denied me.'

'My existence was hardly the life for a child nor a young woman of any repute, and most particularly not a daughter of the FitzAlans.' He took on a wounded expression that made Cressida's palm itch with the unthinkable desire to slap him. 'It hasn't been a joyous existence, you know, living in the most appalling dingy rooms and passing on whatever gossip I could find to the Committee of Secrecy.' Rosmoney spoke with haughtiness that would have made her laugh in other circumstances. In any case he was lying: he had always been able to find the joy in even the darkest of moments. 'How do you think I felt all that time, hearing the most shocking reports of your marriage to that rackety boy of Crauford's? The less said about your conduct afterwards the better. I know Annis's company can be a little lowering at times – I can't think how my dear sister managed to rear such a penny-pinching, mealy-mouthed child – but it would have been far more suitable for you to have returned to your cousin, rather than running away to the Peninsula with a common soldier. I don't know why you couldn't just think of the name. I suppose the rift in the marriage was irreparable?'

'Quite beyond mending, sir, not that it's any concern of yours.' Cressida succumbed to a recollection of the Duke of Cleveland bending over to whisper in her ear, raising frothing skirts above her waist in her cousin Annis's private salon, his fingers lingering between her legs so that she writhed with pleasure even as an entire ballroom of people danced the mazurka just yards away. *My wicked little slut.* She recalled the expression of purest rage in Greville's dark eyes less than twenty memorable minutes later, too. Not long afterwards, knowing she was ruined, Cressida had crept out of Annis's respectable townhouse alone and still in the ballgown she'd chosen for what it revealed: let Greville flaunt his light-skirts all over London. No maid had come to undress her, though: she was already dead in that world, unmentionable. Hours later, in the taproom of a tavern on the Ratcliff Highway, two private soldiers and an unshaven apprentice backed her into the corner.

You look ripe and ready. We're gents, we'll take turns.

Pure fear, and then a stranger's voice bringing with it the sea mist and the gorse-scented air of home.

Lads, the girl's not willing, is she? Leave her alone.

Cressida knew she'd hear that voice again on her deathbed: Michael, who had abandoned his game of hazard to rescue a girl in a muddy cloak and a too-revealing gown of creased satin. He'd been so proud of his new uniform, the red and gold of the Connaught Rangers. He held out his hand to her in that taproom, where the air reeked of unwashed bodies and stale small-beer, showing her an honest smile without a hint of expectation or contempt. *You look like you could do with some help.*

They'd talked for hours at a table by the fire, speaking of white pudding and spiced goody in a bowl, and the particular scent of a peat-fire, and sunshine on the waters of Lough Carra, but never the people they'd known. Both of an age to remember the Rebellion, by tacit agreement it was a subject best left alone. If Michael guessed so soon that she was Lord Rosmoney's daughter, he never said. By nightfall, they were in agreement: they would travel on together. Michael's colonel was a good fellow, and in truth the regiment was in need of a few decent women on the strength to take care of the laundering. Michael was so newly joined up that who was to know he wasn't actually married?

In the end, she'd buried Michael herself, doing him that

honour, shovelling the last of the rubble across his ruined face in the aftermath of Talavera. He'd given her far more than protection, including his willing heart, and late-night dances around countless campfires, and his familiar touch at the end of a long day's march. But now Michael was dead, long gone, and she was here in St Giles with Rosmoney, who was watching her with impatient bemusement.

Cressida gathered her wits: she couldn't afford to get lost in the past. 'I don't even want to know what you're doing here, Papa, but since we both find ourselves in hostile territory, I suggest you stay out of my affairs, unless you want to pay for my maid and me to sail to New York – in the unlikely event that you're solvent enough to be of any use whatsoever.'

'Ingratitude doesn't become you,' Rosmoney said, dismissive. 'If it weren't for my efforts, you'd still be in the custody of Arthur Lascelles and on your way to some unsavoury gaol.'

Cressida fought to maintain a blank expression. It shouldn't have been a surprise that he knew so much, selling French secrets to the government as he had been for over a decade. 'I suppose you were responsible for that grenade when we were disembarking? What made you lift a finger to help me now?'

Rosmoney's smile was a little pained. 'Your escapades in Portugal and Spain were private, or at worst not known to anyone who matters. Without my intervention, this latest episode would have led to an unpleasant degree of publicity, and you're a FitzAlan.' He shrugged, as if no further explanation could be necessary. He was lying, or at the very least not telling the whole truth. Cressida swallowed rising fury: any such emotion was wasted on him.

'Actually, my dear,' her father went on, finishing the last of his champagne, 'I do have a scheme of sorts, which will all be to your benefit. All you have to do is trust me.'

5

'Listen, Greville. There's something else we need to discuss besides your wife.' In the Oxford Arms, Lascelles signalled for more porter and more gin.

'There really isn't,' Greville said, cursing his own irrationality. Why should he give a damn where Cressida was? Why should he care if her spymaster Lord Liverpool sent some hired blade to slip a knife between her ribs in some dark alley. Briefly, Greville closed his eyes and saw the winning hand he'd been holding when she burned his world to ash at her cousin's spring ball: two aces, a jack and a king. It was the silence he remembered, a kind of hush rolling through Annis Bute's card-room like a sea fog. It had sent him reaching for a weapon he didn't have, long before he'd learned the instincts of an army officer.

'It's a family matter, and it concerns your cousin,' Lascelles went on, inexorable.

'I haven't laid eyes on a single member of my family in

years, thank God.' For Christ's sake, was it not enough to have a dishonoured wife accused of treason?

Lascelles frowned, contemplating his port. 'James Nightingale needs to take greater care in the friends he chooses.'

Jamie. Greville watched flames flickering in the grate, recalling a studious youth with a tangle of dark blond hair made constantly untidy by his habit of raking his fingers through it as he translated Greek satires. Jamie Nightingale was the adopted son of Greville's dissolute Uncle Tristan, and his gift for incisive wit smoothed a path dogged by rumours that Lord Tristan Nightingale had actually been his natural father.

'What do you mean, Jamie needs to take more care in his friends?' Greville chose his words with the last of his patience. 'Tristan left him everything when he died: he's as rich as Croesus, but I wouldn't have had him tipped to get involved with fortune-hunters. He's not that green.' Nothing about this added up.

'I'm not talking about that kind of trouble,' Lascelles said. 'Last winter, Jamie and your brother Charles were part of a house party in Nottinghamshire, at Wyncham Court.'

'Listen, come to the point, Arthur. Jamie's affairs are nothing to do with me. If he accepts an invitation to some provincial house party, that's his business.'

'Wyncham Hall is four miles from Newstead Abbey,' Lascelles went on. The hairs on the back of Greville's neck rose up. He consoled himself with the knowledge that Lascelles was helplessly reliving the same unspeakable Newstead memories: Byron's housekeeper's niece, Meg, reclining on the dining room table wearing nothing but an arrangement of piped whipped cream and candied fruit around her quim; Byron arguing ferociously across the table with a newly married Cressida about the nature of morality and reality, even though all Greville could really recall was the fire in her fine dark eyes.

'Well?' Greville managed, at last.

Lascelles sighed. 'Last winter, George Byron regularly rode across from Newstead to join the young Wyncham party. And Byron thinks he's immortal, especially with all this attention about the poetry. I don't believe even he was prepared for how it would be received. It amounts to hysteria. Byron has been fêting Jamie – inviting him to suppers and those intellectual soirées of his.'

Greville cocked an eyebrow. 'And the rest, I take it.'

'Indeed. And people in my circle are starting to notice.'

'I bloody hope you've been careful since Vere Street,' Greville said, switching to Portuguese.

'Of course I've been careful.' Lascelles spoke in a low voice, as well he might – even in a language no one else in the tavern could likely understand. The scandal showed no sign of abating: six men convicted of sodomy in the wake of a raid on a molly-house, and two lads hanged. If the wrong people talked about Lascelles' private life then he stood to lose everything, perhaps even to face the gallows himself. 'Anyway, I didn't summon you to the Devil's Acre so that we could both indulge in an orgy of paranoia. I'm afraid Jamie's regard for Byron couldn't be more obvious, even if they do rage at one another. Jamie needs to hear a warning from someone he respects.'

'I'll talk to Jamie and tell him to steer a wide berth, for all the good it's likely to do. I'm little more than a stranger.'

Greville remembered with exhaustion exactly why he hadn't come on home leave in years and found his gaze drawn towards Thomas, who left the bar at a word from one of the pot-boys and went to the door, with a swift, tense glance over his shoulder at Greville and Lascelles.

Thomas came over holding the jug of porter, his face grim with concern. 'There's an individual to see you both in the top room, gents.'

Greville and Lascelles exchanged a glance: Thomas was a grizzled veteran of the American wars who had survived the first twenty years of his life enslaved on a plantation before taking the King's shilling. If Thomas was wary, Greville would have preferred to send a grenade into the top room first.

'Just mind out for the soft furnishings, all right?' Thomas said. 'Bess has enough to do on laundry day.'

With a nod of thanks to Thomas, Greville and Lascelles moved as one, Greville aware of Bessy's concerned gaze on him from across the taproom as she wiped down one battered pewter tankard after another. They went to the narrow door at the back of the taproom – Greville knew it led upstairs, to bedchambers with damp sheets and sad heaps of dust in dingy corners. Lascelles stood back to let him pass first; the stairs were dark, and he reached into his pocket, curling his fingers around the holster of his pistol.

'It's the third door on the right,' Lascelles said, behind him.

Greville counted the doors, the brass knob cool beneath his touch. He stepped into the lamp-lit bedchamber where the twelfth Earl of Rosmoney sat very much at his ease at a cracked marble-topped table drawn close to the fire; it was raining outside, and the woman standing at the window had opened it, leaning on the sill as she breathed in the scent of London air washed temporarily clean. She wore a gown of some pale stuff, impossible not to notice in this gloom, but then again, she'd always been impossible not to notice. Her hair was piled high atop her head, not loose down her back as, no matter how hard he tried, he could not stop recalling it, those long, tangled curls slipping between his fingers. Cressida turned to face him, expressionless as he felt the force of her hatred.

Cressida looked from her father to Greville and Lascelles and back again and let out a short burst of amazed laughter.

'Oh, for God's sake, no,' she said, speaking right across him to Lascelles. 'You can hang me outside Newgate before I'll have anything to do with bloody Devil.' She spat out his old nickname like a mouthful of pickled tripe alive with maggots.

Lascelles kept quiet.

'You don't mean that, child.' Rosmoney subjected Greville to a cursory inspection. 'A second son – you could have aimed higher, my dear.'

'I wish I could say it pleased me to make your acquaintance at last, my lord,' Greville said, forcing away a memory of how he used to hold Cressida at night when the worst of the dreams came. She would call for her father then, her voice cracking in the darkness.

'I'm charmed,' Rosmoney said, eyeing Greville with distaste. 'There's more of Sylvia about you than your father, which is something.' He turned to Lascelles, who concealed his anger well, but not from Greville. 'And now to business. It was a sorry affair this afternoon, Major Lascelles. But we were all foolish and inexperienced once, and I'm always disposed to help the young.'

Lascelles looked almost impressed. 'How much do you want for her, Rosmoney?'

Greville happened to glance at Cressida then; she wouldn't forgive him that, witnessing her swiftly concealed humiliation.

'Five hundred pounds should suffice,' Rosmoney went on. He turned to Greville. 'I hear you're something of a hot-head, Nightingale. Before you consider anything foolish, do bear in mind that I have a total of seventeen hungry, decommissioned soldiers surrounding this tavern. It would be a great pity if anyone were hurt.'

Greville walked out, smiling until he reached the street: there would be no witness to say that Lieutenant Colonel the Lord Greville Nightingale had left the Oxford Arms with a face like murder. He stepped to one side to avoid the thin young lad who lurched from the alleyway in a greasy shirt.

'Penny for a fuck, sir? You look like you need it.' The lad's gap-toothed professional smile died as he took in the expression on Greville's face. Turning tail, the boy ran lopsided back into the shelter of the alleyway. For a bare half moment, Greville toyed with the notion of taking the boy's advice and finding a woman. But when all was said and done, it was his cock that had got him into this mess in the first place, all those years ago: all roads led back to Cressida. They always did.

6

A week later

Lascelles second-best guest chamber must once have been a nursery: the window was barred. Cressida sat on the end of the bed, craving brandy. The past was not a place in which she cared to dwell, even with George Byron, and yet the present had little to recommend it. She shivered a little, the tell-tale prickling between her shoulder blades a sure sign that she was to be blessed with company at last, even before footfalls grew louder upon the staircase. Greville came in first and stood by the door with the light from the stairway casement window behind him, the set of his shoulders so breathtakingly familiar as he stepped forward out of the shadows. It was early and his gilded dark hair was a little damp from earthenware jug and basin, his face cast into shadow so that she could not read his expression.

'And so to what do I owe this pleasure?' Cressida said, looking past her husband to address Arthur Lascelles, who had come in after him, elegant and unruffled. Greville and

Lascelles shared the same ability to move quietly. Greville, she noticed, retired this trait on civilian territory, making his presence felt with a firm light tread. Lascelles did not, moving in complete silence, as though he were still tracking French troops across some deserted mountain pass.

'You look a ruin, Cress,' Lascelles said, with a perfunctory bow. 'Don't mind your husband: he's been demonstrating to polite society that Devil Nightingale is back in London – he's a little the worse for wear.'

Greville just stalked off to the window.

It cost Cressida something to ignore him, but she did, smiling at Lascelles. 'My maid hasn't been allowed to return to me, as you know very well, and I've worn the same gown since last week. Where is she?' Alone in a strange land, even Ines would be afraid.

'The chit is quite safe – she's been driving Gerard to distraction in the kitchen all week. She makes the most extraordinary custards and pastries, but has no notion of clearing up after herself.' Lascelles glanced at the clock above the mantelpiece, as if already wishing an unpleasant task to be over with. 'I don't know how in hell's name you thought you'd get away with escaping.'

'I managed nicely until I made the mistake of trusting Lord Rosmoney,' Cressida said.

'You made the mistake of hoping he was in possession of anything resembling a guiding principle or enough funds not to trade his own daughter like a heifer.'

'Shut up, Arthur.' Greville spoke from his place by the window; he flexed the fingers of one hand, responding as though she had touched him. He turned to address her then, Lascelles' presence be damned, all social nicety stripped away. 'How could you have done it, all this godforsaken time? Marching behind the *bloody* army with no protection—' Greville bit off the end of his sentence and turned back to the window, directing his disgust out at a nursemaid leading two starched, goffered children to the fenced garden, armed with a wooden hoop and a ball. That unspoken word was loudest of all: no protection, and no honour, either.

Of all the men to judge her. Sunlight streamed in past the open shutters. At Badajoz, he'd refused even to speak to her, but his lordship had clearly decided that now was the moment. She'd pictured this so many times, rehearsing it at odd moments, living through a reckoning with her estranged husband while climbing barefoot up an unforgiving hillside where the air was rich with the scent of wild juniper and thyme, or before drifting off into fitful sleep in some rain-soaked bivouac. In all those imagined scenes, Lord Greville Nightingale had been his usual louche and scornful self. Not once in all that time had she ever expected him to be angry.

She felt the force of his restrained emotion even across the room. Sunlight struck off his gilded epaulettes, picking out those dark curls bleached by the Spanish heat.

'Must we really do this now?' Lascelles said, leaning against the book-case with his arms folded.

'Anything could have happened to you, and it damn nearly did at Badajoz,' Greville went on, ignoring Lascelles completely and enunciating each word with a cold precision that sent a wild heat pooling in her belly. *No.*

Cressida chose her tone with great care. 'Is survival thus far something I should be ashamed of, my lord?'

Greville moved then with sudden, shocking speed, leaving the window to step closer with predatory ease – he kept his distance, though, the space between them a reminder of all they'd thrown away. 'You're the best judge of that; did you enjoy your war?' His eyes darkened. 'Was it a pleasant change from balls and rout parties, following the army with a man you had only just met, watching women and children die by the side of the road; did it make you really *feel* for the first time? I don't know what in hell's name you were thinking.'

Cressida spoke with deliberate, manufactured ennui; he'd never really known her at all. 'Oh yes, one feels changed, you know. As if one for the first time understands what really matters in terms of human experience. I shall have so much to talk about when I start going to parties again – people here don't really understand, do they? Living in their comfortable bubble.'

'No one you know will so much as look at you in the street if you get out of this house alive, and well you know it.'

Sitting apart from them both at the table, Lascelles raised one well-shaped brow. 'If we might turn to the matter in hand?'

Greville shrugged at that and walked over to the window again without looking at her this time. He was reading through a sheaf of papers now with complete absorption, as though making the best use of his time before sending some hapless private soldier to be flogged.

Lascelles glanced up at her then, tracing the tiled tabletop with the tip of one gloved finger. 'Listen, don't mind Nightingale.' His smile was gentle even as he moved in for the kill. 'We've been through this before, but you realise that on paper what you did is treason. A capital offence. All rather a mess, liaising, shall we say, for months with a French commandant.'

Pierre. He was so charming, so vividly alive in everything he did, from the way he savoured his coffee in the morning to his manner of ensuring her pleasure, that Cressida wouldn't have believed he was dead had she not seen what was left of his head. But he'd died at Badajoz like so many others.

At the window, Greville continued to leaf through his briefing with no more interest than if they were discussing the best way to jug a hare.

'Need we go over this again, Major Lascelles?' she said, calmly, using his title as a reminder of the professional distance that now yawned between them. 'And yes, as you're more than aware, I had been living under the protection of Commandant Pierre Moreau for several months when Badajoz fell to our own side, because you ordered it. Is it really treason when the information I provided at considerable risk allowed you to attack the city before Marshal Soult arrived with reinforcements?'

'You? Don't you mean us?' Lascelles asked, lightly.

Greville turned around to face them both then with something akin to murder in his eyes, which, despite Cressida's better judgement, her body responded to with sudden, violent arousal.

Lascelles glanced at her with his *I'll manage this* expression and Greville turned his attention back to his papers. 'Greville, a little while after Cressida's love died at Talavera, Cressida was captured with some of our other camp followers.' Lascelles met Cressida's eyes. She stared back. 'After some time, they made their way back to us. They all passed on as much information as they could: stores, morale, even supplies of ammunition, but being fluent in French, Cressida was able to be even more precise.'

Cressida recalled warm air against her naked skin, the jeers and laughter as she and the seven other women, aged between fifteen and sixty-three, were released to make their own way back to the English camp, albeit without a stitch of clothing.

A muscle twitched in Greville's jaw as he leafed through his papers.

'A while after that,' Lascelles said, carefully, 'Cressida was in a position to help us further. She returned to the French camp and fell into the protection of a French officer.'

Greville did look up then. 'Oh, this is all it needed.' The vicious humour in his voice was interwoven with that very apparent restrained anger, but it was genuine. He'd always been just as quick to laugh at his own absurdities as he would at anyone else's.

'So we've established to everyone's satisfaction including Lord Greville's that while it might have looked as though I were guilty of treason and consorting with the enemy, I'm in fact not. Can I suggest that you tell me what you actually want, Lascelles?' Cressida spoke with even calm: he'd be just as quick as any other man to accuse her of hysteria if she so much as raised her voice.

He shrugged. 'Any ordinary woman of the baggage train would have swung already. Not for consorting with a French officer but for getting caught, Cress. I have no use for incompetence.'

'Arthur, without Rosmoney's help, I wouldn't be here now.'

'You're a fool,' Lascelles said. 'For now, you're not a dead fool. I need your assistance, or more accurately the War Office and the Committee of Secrecy do.'

Greville leaned against the window frame, watching them both with renewed focus. 'You're in the Corps of Guides, Arthur. What are you doing, mixing yourself up with the War Office? Military intelligence is one thing, but you want a very long damn spoon if you're dining with Cressida's spymasters. Livepool and the Committee of Secrecy are ruthless.'

'Use your brains,' Cressida snapped. 'Your love affairs might be described as a series of bad decisions. Arthur's might take him to the gallows or the stocks.'

'Some of us need to make ourselves indispensable,' Lascelles said, dispassionate.

Cressida stared at him. 'Very well. What do you want me to do?'

7

Lascelles sighed and poured them each a glass of cognac, which Greville ignored. His head was pounding. 'Listen,' Lascelles said. 'The issue is, Cressida, you were compromised: you were caught with the French and on my watch. I can't let that go and you know it as well as I do. And if Greville hadn't found you when he did, you'd be buried in a pit somewhere outside Badajoz with every one else who died there. You've nothing more than the clothes on your back and nowhere to go.'

'Am I to thank you for the reminder?' Cressida's tone was effortlessly louche.

At the window, Greville leaned on the sill in his shirtsleeves, too angry to look at either of them.

She'd brought this on herself. All of it.

'Don't be facetious,' Lascelles said. 'In actual fact, you've got too much blue blood to find yourself on the gallows, but Greville is right: the Committee of Secrecy *is* utterly ruthless and sooner or later you'll find yourself with a knife between your ribs in some dark alley unless you make yourself indispensable like your father did. Fortunately for you, the prime minister was murdered a few days ago, and no one knows if that gunshot was the start of something bigger.'

'What the bloody hell are you playing at, Arthur?' Greville asked, turning around. He picked up the sheaf of papers and let them fall onto the table, speaking with slow, dangerous precision. 'It's pretty damn clear in my briefing: Luddites raiding the homes of mill-owners for weapons, and the whole of London rioting. What has Cressida got to do with murder, let alone revolution? How in God's name is that fortunate for her? Lord Perceval was shot in cold blood.'

Cressida accepted the brandy but didn't drink it, her dark eyes glittering as she watched Greville over the rim of her glass.

'I take it you've both heard about Byron's grand passion?' Lascelles went on, master of the art of non sequitur.

'Other than Caroline Lamb? He was giving her one hell of a flyer in Lady Liverpool's salon last time I saw him,' Cressida replied, with unthinking vulgarity.

Lascelles gave her a very cool look. 'What you may not know is that after Lord Perceval introduced the capital penalty for any weaver found guilty of destroying the machines, Byron spoke up in their defence in the House of Lords.'

Cressida smiled, her eyes alight with humour. 'Good boy, George.'

'He's the only peer ever to have done so,' Lascelles went on. 'You saw the state of everything before we brought you in: those riots are the least of it. Suspicion and completely hysterical gossip about the motive of Perceval's killer has been scorching through the entire country like wildfire. Heaven only knows the man had enough enemies.'

'What the bloody hell are you trying to suggest?' Greville demanded, finally losing the last of his patience. 'Spouting public sympathy with starving weavers doesn't indicate for a moment Byron would actually *do* something to achieve justice for them. He doesn't get out of bed before twelve.'

Cressida smiled again. 'George is far more careful than you give him credit for: he'll go so far with Caroline Lamb but not far enough to damage his own reputation, even if hers ends up as smoking rubble. And he's no rabble-rouser, either.'

'Keep up, the two of you: George Byron's actual personal stake in Perceval's murder doesn't have the slightest relevance to our current situation.' Lascelles spoke with cold precision. 'He's revered in a way that you'll certainly have never seen before; I haven't – *no one has*,' Lascelles went on. 'The prime minister was shot down in the House of Commons and the country's already on the brink of revolution: the last thing an enraged mob needs is a standard-bearer to gather behind, and especially not a figurehead like George Gordon Byron. It's mob rule the Cabinet fears now – luckily for you, Cressida.'

'I don't even want to know what you have in mind, but he was in our set of friends,' Greville said. 'He was one of us. Does that mean nothing to you?'

Lascelles shrugged. 'It means that he's a sight more likely to trust you with his revolutionary urges, even if the chances of him ever acting upon them are slim to none. Lord and Lady Greville Nightingale are to achieve a reconciliation at Lady Bute's house party this summer, where Lord Byron is to be a guest. There you will do what you can to investigate his true political leanings, Cressida; I don't care how. And if you get close enough to him to stir up a bit of distracting gossip, all to the good. Greville, you will ensure that your wife acts in the interests of His Majesty the King, and not against them. God only knows you were the sole person who ever came close to handling her.'

'What a ridiculous notion.' Greville spoke with the level self-possession that his men quailed at in Spain: hard and unforgiving soldiers, every last one. Lascelles stared back at him with another small shrug. 'If you want to know why Perceval was shot, why don't you just ask the man who did it? He's been cooling his heels in Newgate ever since.'

'Because they hanged him this morning.' Lascelles picked up a cloisonné snuff box from the mantelpiece and inhaled a dose of Macouba from the back of his hand.

Greville frowned, recalling what he'd read in that morning's newspaper, his interest piqued despite himself. 'Some trading dispute, wasn't it? Bellingham believed he was owed redress from Whitehall after being thrown into prison in Russia over something to do with export duties. How can he have been of sound mind in any way, shape or form? He ought to be in Bedlam now, not on his way to the dissection table.'

'Even you must see that someone had to hang, and quickly,' Lascelles said. 'The prime minister is dead: he was murdered at the heart of government. John Bellingham might be dead now too, and clearly was insane, but he also trained as a clerk. Here.' Lascelles laid a battered leather pocketbook on the table. 'Bellingham kept meticulous personal accounts. And a man with an unshakeable obsession like his might easily become the pawn of those wishing to cover their own tracks.' Lascelles opened the pocketbook with his gloved hands, and Greville took it, glancing at rows of neat figures penned by a man who had faced the gallows just hours ago. 'Bellingham was on the brink of bankruptcy when he came to London to petition for compensation in February. And yet he lived here in London for months, paying his rent, purchasing the niceties. Men with no means of support can't cough up to have their dressing-gowns laundered. Who paid his way?'

Cressida stood watching them both, her expression unreadable.

Greville extinguished a spurt of anger. It was the sheer incompetent stupidity of it all that he couldn't bear. 'Let me guess: Whitehall and the Committee of Secrecy now have every government spy trying to work out who was bankrolling a man now too dead to tell them anything. And if they can't find out who it really was, a nice juicy distracting scandal will do just as well.' He'd heard enough. 'Byron is insufferable but even he doesn't deserve to be dragged into this. I hate to say it but Cressida's right: he's far too lazy to be a real rabble-rouser, and even pretending that he would or starting rumours that amount to the same thing is bloody immoral. My wife will be having nothing to do with it.'

Cressida turned on him then, dark eyes alight with

mockery. 'So commanding, Greville. Whoever would think that we used to fantasise about the emancipation of womankind, all that time ago? Although perhaps I was the one doing the fantasising, and you were saying whatever you thought would beat the quickest path up my skirts.'

'It didn't take long,' Greville said: she had been liquid with desire at his touch.

Cressida chose not to dignify that with a response, even though she could not disguise the faint betraying flush across her cheekbones. Those skirts had been of exceptionally fine muslin that crumpled to nothing.

'I won't work with Nightingale, Lascelles,' she said. 'I'll bring you George Byron's head on a plate if I must, but I'll do this my way or not at all.'

Lascelles shrugged, with a glimmer of the Arthur who had waltzed with her in laughing splendour at Carlton House. 'Apart from the fact I don't trust you, without Greville to lend you countenance, you won't gain entry into the right circles and your life depends on it. And before you say you won't fail, you failed at Badajoz: you were caught at the wrong place, at the wrong time, with the wrong people, even if most of them were dead. You won't get out of the country with your maid if you fail me in this, Cressida. You won't even live out the summer: the Committee of Secrecy has a very long reach and Lord Liverpool can and will authorise your removal unless you make yourself visibly indispensable. Poison, a knife – I won't be able to stop them: come, you know better than anyone how it is.'

Cressida watched him across the room. 'Try me, Arthur,'

she said. 'Or else do attempt to see if you can manage this affair without my help.' She smiled. 'I'm sure you'll find someone else with the requisite skills and experience.'

'I'm sure Arthur knows dozens of women who are just as equally at home in a drawing room as they are on the battlefield,' Greville said, and turned to address Lascelles in fluent Portuguese. 'You truly are the limit of what a man can reasonably endure. If you were a woman, or I were the right sort of man, I really would take you home this minute and give you something else to think about other than dealing death and ruin.'

'Lucky Arthur,' Cressida said, in the same tongue, and Greville just about managed to quell his irritation. Of course she'd been just as quick to learn the language as they had: how the hell else had she survived in the baggage train?

Lascelles got up with a barely perceptible smile. 'Greville, take a horse from your brother's stables and gallop off all that spleen. Don't fail me,' he said. 'Either of you.'

8

The coachman's boy opened the carriage door with a smile of suppressed scorn. He arranged the step so that Cressida and Ines could alight outside Bute House, the Mayfair home of Cressida's former and extremely reluctant guardian, her cousin Annis, Countess of Bute. With a jolt of familiarity, Cressida breathed in the scent of honeysuckle drifting from the iron railings surrounding the garden in the middle of the square, mingling with the more noisome aroma of London at the end of a hot spring.

'My lady.' The coachman's lad took her gloved hand, helping her down onto the wide flagstones. She didn't miss the sarcasm laced through his voice at the sight of Ines travelling in the same carriage. With the scanty coins at her disposal, arranging another hackney for her maid was out of reach. It wasn't high society she must fool or die trying, but the staff.

On the doorstep, Annis's butler Twisden swallowed like a landed fish. 'Lady Bute is not at home, ma'am.'

Cressida smiled in such a way that his eyes bulged a little. 'Come now, Twisden. She will be at home to me. Be a darling and tell her that I await her pleasure.'

'Of course, milady.' Twisden bowed, and she remembered how he'd once made a grape appear from behind her left ear when she was a young girl: the untouchable Irish traitor's child no one wanted, too English in Ireland, too Irish here. And everywhere she went, too much a Rosmoney.

Annis and Bute had redecorated again and the wall-hangings in the hallway were new: pale green watered silk. It was Bute who had the eye for refurbishment, unlike his plain, practical wife. The newest portraits were by Rowlandson and framed in elaborate gilt, all children with dimpled arms and glossy ringlets. The Bute girls had reached the pretty age, which suited Cressida's purposes nicely. With daughters to be fired off within the next few years, Lady Bute was vulnerable to persuasion.

It was odd how the smell of the place hadn't changed: the marble-tiled hallway was still rich with lily of the valley and nicotiana arranged in pewter vases with curling acid-green ferns. This was the scent of late spring, all the blooms gathered by Annis's lower footmen in the flower market at Covent Garden. Soon there would be no need for flowers and the Butes would join that great annual exodus of the *haut ton* and flee London, leaving most of their servants to weather out the stink of high summer. When the Butes went, Cressida would go with them whether they liked it or not.

Cressida followed Twisden upstairs, pinning on a smile as he opened a pair of gilded double doors into the morning salon. To Twisden's credit, there was not a quiver in his voice, even when her name was met with silence. Every last one of Annis's chintz-upholstered chairs was occupied by a woman from the first circles: everyone who was anyone was here. Christ, had she aged as much as they all had?

Annis alone was unchanged, elegant as a Vigée Le Brun and fresh-faced in green linen adorned with a wide band of crisp ruffles at the hem, her grey-streaked curls arranged à la Grecque. Her eyes were hard, like chips of golden-green peridot, her shrewd gaze calculating the full cost of Cressida's outfit in under half a minute, down to the nearest sixpence. There was an audible gasp from somewhere near the window. Cressida's skin prickled as Twisden closed the double doors; one of the large windows was slightly ajar, but there was now no way out other than through a servants' door set into the blue-painted wainscoting.

It would have helped had Annis not been entertaining Greville's mother. The Dowager Marchioness of Crauford sat by the window. Cressida saw why Sylvia still wore mourning so many years after the death of Greville's father: the black velvet set off her colouring to an advantage, even if the lustre of those golden curls owed less to nature than the skill of her apothecary.

Lady Crauford alone was not staring at Cressida; instead, she studied the polished fingernails of her right hand, wearing a smile of grim amusement. Cressida's gaze flickered around the room. Even Annis's rival Sally Jersey was here, leading light of society, all watered silk and trailing coral beads.

A handful of young people congregated in the

window-seat, but they would all have been drilled against staring, the girls' behaviour especially governed with parade-ground rigour. Cressida didn't immediately know any of them: likely they had all been in the schoolroom when she'd left. This was a dangerous age and stage of life, when a tender reputation might wither on the vine just by being in the same room as Cressida. And yet Twisden had been given orders to let her in.

Standing among the girls like a deerhound among kittens, a tall, louche young man leaned on the window frame, looking out at the square, his long legs encased in well-cut black kerseymere and his honey-fair hair dishevelled. He had a very comely arse like all the Nightingale men, even that prosy fossil Crauford. He turned around, and Cressida wasn't at all surprised to recognise Jamie Nightingale. At just shy of twenty, Jamie was breathtaking. Tall and lean, with brilliant dark eyes, he was the image of Greville's uncle Tristan, his long-dead adopted father. Surely no one was still bothering to deny that he was a Nightingale bastard?

Jamie grinned at her in recognition. Sylvia was never reliable in the sickroom, and Cressida had once nursed Jamie through a particularly nasty bout of scarlet fever with the aid of a lurid novel entitled *Necromancer of the Black Forest*, some highly colourful stories of her own, and more ginger wine than was strictly advisable.

Trouble, complete and utter trouble, Cressida thought, idly considering that it took one to know one.

'My dearest girl.' Annis broke the silence at last, raising a languid finger at one of her footmen to signal for more tea things. 'Goodness. How wonderful that you're here.'

She was livid: her voice always became quieter and more musical the angrier she got. Jamie would have to wait. Cressida ignored a queer rushing noise in her head.

'And how awful of me to have intruded.' Cressida smiled, noticing vivid details from the corner of her eye: a spray of freesias in a bronze pot on the side table, the collection of Sèvres china bowls in a row on the mantelpiece of green marble. The air thickened; it was like trying to breathe turtle soup.

Annis smiled. 'Nonsense; if you'd come to London without visiting me after all these years, I should have been very cross indeed. Won't you sit down? Most of my friends are familiar faces, but perhaps I might make some others known to you? Mary Sidgwick you know, of course.'

Mary Sidgwick got to her feet with an expression of frozen scorn, ringlets held immobile with quince-seed gum. Cressida recognised her now: they'd debuted in the same year. Marriage obviously agreed with Mary like a bad oyster and who could blame her. She got up, curtseyed to the room and went out, leaving another ringing silence behind her. Jamie frowned a little, but the girls watched in undisguised horror. *Reputation, reputation, reputation.* Well, here she was, a living example of what happened when you lost it. God, it was airless in here. Cressida's gaze shifted towards the open sash window. Would she ever walk into a room again without bloodlessly assessing every possible way out of it?

Annis turned to the girls Jamie Nightingale was busy ignoring, bidding them to the music room with an expression of smiling amiability that brooked no argument.

Jamie yawned. 'Come on, we're under orders.'

Whispering and giggling, taught from the cradle never to entertain a serious thought in their heads, the girls got up and departed with him, a flurry of flounces, dimpled arms and impractical satin slippers, leaving behind yet another silence. Sylvia smiled as she watched Jamie escort them out with all that easy grace, in just the same way that she had always smiled at Greville's faults. Sylvia assessed Cressida with a swift nod of approval: the gossips had always said the only common ground they shared was an enviable eye for a gown and a fatal ability to look past the shortcomings of Lady Crauford's second oldest son.

'Well, Mary has the sense of a recalcitrant child,' Sylvia said, with a social smile. 'There could be nothing more likely to stir up gossip, which is the last thing we need now you've decided to grace us with your presence, madam.' The expression in her eyes was unforgiving; it was said that her fondness for Greville had been the ruin of him, as she made excuses for her wickedest and most favourite child, time after time.

Annis smiled again, passing Cressida a cup of tea with thin-lipped venom. 'Mary Sidgwick is indeed a foolish woman – she'll miss out on all your news. You must tell us all about your time in the Levant. How exciting to travel.'

Cressida sipped her tea, silently cursing her. Why couldn't Annis have told everyone she'd gone to ground somewhere easier to lie about? Thanks to Napoleon's efforts in Portugal and Spain, the entire Levant teemed with rich young Englishmen from Damascus to Aleppo who could easily give the lie to any story.

'I'm afraid I swore I'd never become a travel bore,' she said. 'No doubt you have no more desire to look at my sketchbook than I wish to catch up with years of criminal conversation.'

'I'll grant you that.' Lady Crauford raised both eyebrows, settling back into her chair as if to watch the opera.

Sally Jersey laughed, watching them all from the Queen Anne chair in the corner. 'We ought to be grateful you plan to spare us the sketchbooks, at least.'

'Indeed, we have enough of that sort of thing from the wretched poet,' Sylvia said, with a level gaze at Annis.

Sally smiled. 'It's much worse than sketchbooks with Lord Byron,' she said. 'You've condemned yourself to an entire summer of poetry recitals, Annis. But I grant you it's a stunning victory, all the same. Everyone's spitting pins that you've snared him for Drochcala.'

'The Byrons are not a good family, and he looks the sort to upset the housemaids, if you ask me,' Sylvia said. 'He's not showing much circumspection with his affairs. This carry-on with Caro Lamb is a little too obvious, to put it mildly. But I can see that it will at least put an end to all that distressing gossip about you and Bute not having a feather to fly with, Annis. Honestly, people can be so crass.'

Annis sipped her tea, ignoring the barb. 'Oh, indeed, and poor Caro will be sorry for it before long. I would usually have asked her to Drochcala, but one simply can't – not with the way she's behaving – a married woman! But when is it ever the man who really suffers when an affair's too public?'

For a moment, they all stared unguardedly at Cressida, even Annis.

'Yes, well,' Sylvia said, 'such is the way of the world, and Caroline Lamb is a little fool to forget it, as is every other woman who allows passion to get the better of her. Men cannot help their appetites, but we of the fair sex know we must have more sense than they do. I wish you all the very best of luck with George Byron, my dear.'

Cressida smiled at her estranged mother-in-law. 'Oh, never fear, ma'am. My cousin is more than capable of managing a fashionable poet. I must say, I'm rather looking forward to seeing Lord Byron at Drochcala.'

Annis showed no sign of being outflanked, drinking her tea without so much as a sideways glance, as though there were nothing extraordinary in a disgraced cousin joining her house party.

Cressida turned to her. 'It's quite exciting, isn't it, Annis? We might even find ourselves immortalised in verse! I don't doubt George will be waxing lyrical. Loch Iffrin is impossibly romantic in summer. I for one shan't let a rude poet spoil my enjoyment of Scotland, and if any of you think Annis will allow him to ruin it for anyone else, I daresay you're wrong. My cousin is far too experienced a hostess for that.'

Cressida smiled into another shattering silence, watching sunlight play across the blue-and-white Delft tiles surrounding the fireplace. She'd deal with the aftermath later. She always did: she would not, however, deal with Lord Greville Nightingale. Lady Crauford and Sally Jersey exchanged a single slow and pregnant glance. Annis stirred her tea, not betraying by word or gesture that a disgraced, unwanted cousin had just fabricated an invitation to the house party of the Season.

9

At Bute House, Cressida was shown to her old bedchamber, following Annis's disapproving housekeeper up wide stairs redolent of beeswax and the scent of boiled trout emanating from a servants' door left open. A tall, austere woman with a weather-beaten face, Roberts hadn't altered in years, still favouring a hostile attitude and gowns of heavy serge made up high to her neck. When she'd gone, leaving both Ines and Cressida with a wide-eyed chambermaid, Ines sent for hot water and Cressida stepped out of her travel-stained clothes in a room papered with jarringly familiar hand-painted twisting vines and palm fronds. Now, she sat before the old rosewood Queen Anne dressing table, staring at her own reflection in the mirror as Ines pinned and arranged her chestnut-brown curls into a fashionable artless tumble.

London. It was really as if her life in this world had happened to someone else; readying herself for balls and opera breakfasts in this very room; a gracious smile from

Queen Charlotte in an overheated palace chamber; a pair of green silk dancing slippers with gold satin roses cast aside on the bedchamber floor.

'You're tired, milady,' Ines said, sharply, pinning the last ringlet into position in a coronet of curls atop Cressida's head. 'And this sort of place is exactly where you'll give in to the exhaustion, if anywhere. It's not like being on the march, is it, to say the least?'

'I can't afford to make any mistakes, so don't worry your head about that,' Cressida said. Here at Bute House, both versions of herself converged into one, sharing the same characteristic of fatal overreach. She pictured Annis's cold smile, which no longer had the power to frighten her: *One day, young lady, you'll go too far and then we'll see what comes to the likes of you.*

Less than half an hour later, Cressida paused at the bottom of the staircase, steeling herself as she stepped out onto the floor of black-and-white tiled marble. She'd bargained for the evening gown of peacock-blue silk in a Madrid back alley and Ines had adjusted it to devastating effect, creating a clinging sheath of a silhouette. She was going to need all the help she could get. After the scene in the drawing room earlier, there'd been no guarantee that the Butes wouldn't throw her out into the street via the servants' door.

Aware that she was being watched, Cressida stopped where she stood, turning to look over her shoulder to face Roberts in one of her interminable dark gowns like some sort of rent-a-penny angel of death. Moments passed before Roberts finally curtseyed. Cressida ignored the frisson of alarm that swept in a burning sensation down her arms, right down to her fingertips. In Spain or Portugal, a jolt of animal instinct like this would have been her signal to pick up her skirts and run, or at least to draw a knife. Here, she could do neither. Instead, she just winked over her bare shoulder, knowing such vulgarity would annoy the woman. They'd always had the measure of one another anyway. No amount of false contrition or assumed shame would change Roberts's opinion of a saucy, forward miss.

Annis's two footmen were too well trained to allow a roving eye to wander, but at least she could be sure of the effect of the peacock-blue gown, sensing their awareness of her breasts rising from ruched silk. The footmen had thrown open the doors, the drawing room now sparkling before her, all shadow and soft candlelight.

'*Milady!* I've announced you. Please to go in?' The footman addressed her in a desperate undertone, risking a summons from Twisden by speaking to her.

Cressida murmured her thanks, tossing him a smile as she walked into the room. One never knew who one might need and when, after all. And good heavens, she must get a hold on herself: Ines was right. She found Annis and Bute also in evening dress and sharing the club fender. An elaborate arrangement of dried flowers garlanded the fireplace, and the warm air was heavy with the scent of orange oil and fine candlewax. Bute's grey head was bent close to Annis's coiffure as they conversed in low voices, only looking up as she was announced.

Annis's mouth was set in a bloodless line, and Bute's appreciative smile was not predatory but that of the aesthete, and therefore useless. Cressida was one of the few who understood the true nature of her cousin's marriage: a long friendship, and a largely unspoken understanding of Annis's discreet relations with her head gardener and Bute's relationship with Hemmings, his unmarried steward at their Oxfordshire estate, Seekings Court. For years, Seekings had been mismanaged and bled dry, first by Bute's libertine father, and then by Bute himself, who always had a scheme for either agricultural or architectural improvement guaranteed to be ahead of its time, adding to a litany of expensive failures.

Bute got up and kissed Cressida's outstretched hand, tall, cadaverous and deceptively gentle as ever.

'My dear girl,' Bute said and shook his head. 'One hardly knows where to begin.' He glanced down at Annis. 'Come, my love: you might as well unbend a little. The situation being as it is, we must act. Your cousin is here: everyone knows she's here.'

'Yes, I know I'm putting you both to a great deal of trouble, and I'm sorry for it,' Cressida said, accepting a glass of champagne. A swift glance at the table confirmed it was laid only for two. Whatever Annis's plans for her, they didn't include dining.

Annis took a brief sip from her own glass, and Cressida wondered if she knew that Rosmoney was back in England. 'When were you ever sorry for anything, Cressida?' Annis let out a swift exhalation, looking up at her from her seat by the fire.

'Rarely, I will admit.' Cressida's gaze was drawn to the emeralds and diamonds at her cousin's throat: was it just the angle of the candlelight, or had those emeralds lost their lustre? Cressida would have comfortably bet they were paste. 'How are the children?'

'Already staying with Louisa,' Annis said. 'You can be very sure that I'm not bringing them to Scotland with you there into the bargain. If Hetty were any closer to her first Season, you wouldn't still be in this house, mark my words.'

Cressida didn't volunteer an answer to that.

'Yes,' Bute said, perspiring a little. 'My sister's happy enough to entertain Hetty and Charlotte, so let's not concern ourselves with problems that don't exist. We must deal with the situation as it is, not the worst case.'

'Which it very nearly is,' Annis went on, casting her gaze over Cressida. 'At least you haven't lost your eye for a gown. Shall we get to the point? Davies will sulk about the soufflés if they sink, and I can't have my cook in a brown study with twenty-five to dine here tomorrow.'

'As you wish.' Cressida raised her glass. With soufflés soon to be brought up from the kitchen, Annis obviously planned to despatch her within minutes. If the Butes were so badly on the rocks that Sylvia risked mentioning it in public, Annis would be doing everything she could to maintain appearances: to do otherwise was fatal.

Annis smiled. 'Now that half of London knows you're joining our party at Drochcala, people will talk. They'll want to know why you're here. Why you came back. I need a story, and a convincing one.'

'Come now, my dear,' Bute said. 'Cressida is only human. To be exiled is to be cut off from all one knows. It must be miserably uncomfortable. Is that not reason enough to return home?'

Annis let out an unladylike snort. 'Don't put words into her mouth. Has she ever cared for what other people think? Loneliness is just the price one pays for that sort of selfishness, unfortunately – much as I'm sorry for it. I'm afraid that if you want money, you won't get a penny from me. Thanks to Rosmoney, I must have spent hundreds of pounds on silks and satins for you.'

'My love—' Bute began.

Annis ignored him. 'Not to mention the cost of your come-out, only to have it all thrown back in my face when you were caught half naked with the Duke of Cleveland in this very house, like some sort of common trull.' She spoke with that easy musicality that would once have sent Cressida running for the attics, but her eyes blazed with angry dislike. 'How dared you humiliate me in such a way, Cressida? And how dare you come here now, insinuating yourself into an invitation to Drochcala? You can at least do me the courtesy of telling me why.'

'I've travelled alone for years in circumstances I won't bore you with,' Cressida said. 'I want what's due to me. I left in disgrace, yes, while neither my husband nor the other creature who are equal in fault share any of the blame.' *The most successful lie is a bedfellow to the truth.* She allowed long-suppressed fury to bloom. 'Tell me, Annis, if Lord Greville Nightingale or the Duke of Cleveland walked into your front parlour one morning, would anyone even remark upon it?'

Annis's expression changed to one of alarm as Cressida looked up from her glass of champagne. 'I'm tired of living like a recluse when all the while my equally guilty husband

and lover are still welcomed everywhere they go. I don't care about Cleveland, but I do want revenge on Nightingale. By the end of the summer, every drawing room will be hot with gossip about me and Lord Byron, and there will be nothing Nightingale can do about it but wear the cuckold's horns again.'

Annis glanced at Bute who was staring open-mouthed. She made an obvious decision that he was going to be of no use to her whatsoever, turning back to Cressida. 'Women don't get revenge for their husbands' indiscretions. We're not allowed it. Not publicly in the way you chose, not unless we wish to court ruin.'

'But I've never been more serious about anything in my life,' Cressida said, sweetly, even as a thick sweat soaked into the fine linen fabric of the chemise she'd stolen from a washing line in Porto. 'And the fact is, Annis, now that I'm here, you need me under control.'

Bute set down his glass. 'Annis, Hetty debuts in three years. Either we get this wrong and it follows her everywhere, or you can make Cressida's return a success. She's well born and still well dressed, and she was always fashionable. She hasn't lost her figure or any teeth, thank God. Look at her: it's not as if you don't have a fighting chance. George Byron has the power to have her fêted across London: he's the only man on earth with a chance of bringing her back into style.'

Annis took a sip of her own champagne, never taking her eyes off Cressida as she drank it. 'Very well. Come to Drochcala and I'll sponsor your return into society, with George Byron's help whether he likes it or not. But take my word for it, Cressida. We'll do this my way, or not at all.' Her expression altered then: there was an element of uncertainty, even of well-disguised alarm. 'I take it you've heard nothing from your father? If we're extremely strategic I can make you fashionable again, even if you'd never receive an invitation from some of the more conservative hostesses. But Rosmoney would be a bridge too far.'

Lord Bute grimaced, as though he'd just stepped into an open sewer. 'Heaven forbid.'

Cressida smiled, already waiting for the day when she never again had to lay eyes on the Butes. 'Don't worry, Annis. If I see Lord Rosmoney before I go to hell, where I'm perfectly sure I won't be able to avoid him, it will be too soon.'

10

Half a mile away, Greville crossed Berkeley Square at an impatient pace. The wind was in an unusual quarter, and so this evening Mayfair reeked of the same effluvia as the slums to the east: chimney-smoke and the rich green stink of London's many rivers. Greville heard the crowd that had gathered outside his family's seat in London before he actually saw it: a mellifluous babble of feminine voices carried on the breeze. Having cut across the garden in the middle of the square, Greville let himself out of the wrought iron gate, stepping back onto the wide, well-swept street: at least thirty assorted young women clad in a variety of inexpensive muslins had gathered on the walkway outside Crauford House. Most of them were accompanied by maidservants: respectable if not fashionable.

'Oh, for the love of God,' Greville said, quietly, walking up to the front steps; the little crowd scattered at his approach.

As he passed, a girl with wax cherries fastened to her

bonnet whispered to her companion. 'Is that him? Doesn't he look ferocious and so brooding?'

Greville didn't wait to hear the reply, and thank God the front door opened before the knocker had even struck. Crauford's footman was almost as tall as Greville himself, redolent of carbolic soap, his well-scrubbed brown face expressionless as a hen's egg. Greville didn't miss the exact sward-green shade of his eyes, though, or the faint crater left by some form of pox on the side of his nose. Nor did Greville miss the swift head-to-toe appraisal that he himself received; one could hardly blame the man. As a footman, he was trained to spot interlopers from a mile off; he exuded ambition and doubtless had half an eye on Crauford's butler's job. Greville knew very well that he couldn't have looked much more disreputable if he'd tried.

The interlude lasted no more than a moment, with Greville aware of the hum of voices drifting downstairs from his mother's salon. 'I'm here to see Lady Crauford. The Dowager Lady Crauford.'

The footman didn't smile, of course, stepping back to allow Greville into the house. 'I regret to say her ladyship is not at home, but do come this way, my lord.'

Greville stepped into the hall, instantly surrounded by the familiar and half-forgotten: a sun-bleached Turkey rug, peonies bursting from a blue-and-white Delftware vase, dark oil paintings in heavily gilded frames.

'I see you've studied this lot,' he said, with a terse nod at the family portraits lining the stairwell, which included his own. 'What's your name, and what is happening outside?'

'My name is Somers, your honour. And yes, your lordship's

likeness is very exact, if I may be permitted to say so. If I might also say, your lordship is the image of the Dowager Marchioness of Crauford: a strikingly clear resemblance, my lord, so that I should have immediately comprehended you are one of the family. The females have come to see Lord Byron, my lord. They are quite impossible to dissuade from their object; the more we cleared them away, the more they returned. It is, if I may be permitted to remark, quite an extraordinary thing to observe in respectably bred women.' Somers swept up the stairs with such grace of movement that he seemed almost to be propelled by wheels up a ramp imperceptible to the human eye. 'I perceive that your honour has only very recently arrived from Spain. Might I arrange hot water? Your baggage?'

'You can see to it all apart from the hot water, thank you.' Greville had no intention of remaining in his brother's house long enough to put up with the consequences of offending the Craufords with his travel-stained state.

'And your manservant, sir?' Somers said, stepping smoothly onto the landing. 'Will I have Mistress Houghton arrange for his accommodation?'

'Thank you, no. I'm not staying here, and my batman is dead.' Greville was now only half listening to the hum of voices drifting down the corridor from the salon. He'd already written to Jackson's people; the letter would likely reach the sleepy Northamptonshire village tomorrow. There was no justice when a man could survive Badajoz and succumb to a rotting wound a few days later.

'Very good, sir.' Somers dispensed a benevolent smile at a maidservant hurrying along the corridor bearing a pile of folded, bloodstained linen, her face grey and immobile with shock. Somers didn't so much as flinch.

'Where did you serve?' Greville asked.

'I was last in at Walcheren, sir.'

'An unpleasant business. I take it you were invalided out?'

'Indeed, sir. I was fortunate enough to recover from the Walcheren fever, but sadly my lungs are not what they were. I retired from the military life and returned to service, your honour.'

By this time, Greville and Somers had arrived at the double doors. Crauford must have been practising economies again, for there were no footmen stationed outside the salon and it was left to Somers to toss his name into the hubbub as though it were a grenade.

'Lieutenant Colonel Lord Greville d'Eresby Nightingale.'

The shocked silence was palpable; the room heaved with massed humanity reeking of pomade, sweat, and coal-smoke from the grate. Even after years in Spain, it was all so jarringly humdrum, despite the crowd and the chattering excitement. Greville's brother the Marquess of Crauford stood hemmed into a corner by a gathering of earnest-looking women, looking much like a peevish shadow of their father, and also much like a man who regretted not being at his club. His wife, Marianne, who had engineered all this, was ensconced on a chaise longue beneath the window in bile-yellow dupion silk, her expression of triumph fading into one of dismay at the sight of Greville, who didn't really blame her for returning his dislike, all things considered.

'Why, Greville! What a wonderful surprise!' Marianne

was still as fragile and insincere as ever, with those blonde curls swept up like a seventeen-year-old debutante's.

Hard pushed to spit out the niceties, Greville bowed in the direction of his brother and sister-in-law and went to the sofa where his half-sister Kitty held court.

'Oh, do go away, darlings – I need to talk to my disgracefully rude brother.' Kitty, Lady Alasdair watched her audience scatter with an air of tolerant boredom and Greville kissed her outstretched hand. Ten years Greville's senior, Kitty was married to a kindly but distant Scottish laird who shared her passion for word-games of fiendish complexity. He was an offshoot of the more famous Fraser family; she was a child of her father's first marriage in the last years of the old century. Kitty's mother had been the daughter of a Mughal noblewoman and the fourth son of an English viscount. Brought to England as a six-year-old when her widowed father unexpectedly succeeded to the title, Kitty herself was slender and immaculate in white muslin, with long-lashed dark eyes and her heavy black hair swept up into a crown of braids. She gave Greville a single, appraising look, as well as her hand to kiss, and then instantly sliced through all his defences.

'Heavens, Greville, someone is in trouble – what has happened to you?'

'Nothing at all.' Greville smiled at her, releasing her hand; she was the first person in London he'd actually been glad to see.

'You liar,' Kitty said, unmoved. 'But who am I to force confidences?'

'I know you'd never do so. What the devil are you playing

at, though, Kit, going along with this idiotic charade? It's not like you to court fashion. Where's my mother?'

'Mama? She's been out exchanging shots across the bows with Annis Fane.' Kitty dealt him a wry smile: her fond relationship with his mother had always flown in the faces of those who secretly hoped the elder Lady Crauford might make her stepdaughter's life a misery. 'And as if all this Byron nonsense is anything to do with me. Come on, Greville, do you suppose me to have altered that much?'

'You haven't altered at all,' Greville said, truthfully, smiling at her and unable to help himself. 'Although I fully expect your offspring not to know me.'

Kitty rolled her eyes. 'Not with Johnny's obsession – he's been counting down the days until his father can be persuaded to buy him a commission and he's been in alt ever since we found out you were coming home. Anyway, our dear sister-in-law is being insufferable about Byron, as you can imagine. It's pretty unbearable to see Marianne have the satisfaction of snaring him for an evening when most people would sell their own dead grandmother to the resurrection men just to have him in the house. But look at the man, isn't it fascinating? He was such an awkward boy, too, but you'd never believe it now, would you?'

Greville stretched out his long legs, crossing one ankle over the other. The morning room was crowded, the air thick with the scent of overheated bodies and stale breath; their brother's wife had deliberately selected this smaller, more intimate chamber over the drawing room which would have easily swallowed the seventy or so members of the haut ton. Even so, a young man stood alone by one of the long book-cases, absorbed in examining the spines, dark hair curling over his pale forehead.

'No one will talk to him, is that your point?' Greville accepted a glass of champagne from a footman he didn't recognise.

'Marianne's fatal error.' Kitty spoke with a wicked light in her eyes that didn't disguise a thread of tension in her voice. 'They're all too fashionable. As if Brummell and Princess Esterházy would lower themselves to public hero-worship like those extraordinary girls outside. I haven't seen anything like it since you were first on the town, and even so it's far more intensive than the attention you and Cressida got—' She broke off at the expression on his face, with a small, brisk shake of her head. 'Oh, don't. What would you prefer, that we never mentioned you and Cressida in the same breath? It was the rest of us who had to live with the aftermath of your opera dancer and her duke, and I don't see why I should protect your feelings now.'

'I'll try to maintain a better command of my features, I promise.'

'You should. I always have to. Anyway, Byron is far more interesting than you, and he's scorching across the haut ton like a comet. They're all fascinated by him, and they've obviously all read *Childe Harold* – or pretended to – but everyone here is far too self-conscious to lower themselves to actually speak to the poor boy. You knew him, though, didn't you?' Kitty's gaze was just as penetrating as it had ever been; she'd always been difficult to lie to. Either she really knew nothing of Lascelles' concerns about Byron and Jamie, or had chosen to play those cards close to her chest.

'Byron was far more a friend of Arthur Lascelles – they were in the same circle at Cambridge.' Greville wondered idly if the traumatised maidservant had made it to the laundry room with her pile of bloodied clothing, and if his sister was even aware of the melodrama unfolding elsewhere in the house.

'Hmm.' Kitty picked up a madeleine from one of the absurdly small gilded china plates that had belonged to their paternal grandmother, never taking her eyes off Greville as she demolished it down to the last bite. He waited until she'd dabbed at her mouth with a damask napkin. 'Look at Crauford: poor thing. He's obviously wishing the whole crowd of us to the devil. I don't know why he and Marianne insist on parties when neither of them really enjoy the experience. They'd both rather be at Summercourt annoying Phelps in the garden. Although, to be honest, Jamie hasn't been helping.'

'Oh?' Greville said, as discouraging as possible.

'He's got into Radical politics. You may guess how that was received.' Kitty glanced at their brother. Crauford stood in the corner still, eyeing Byron as if he were an unexploded grenade, unique in his ability to make a jacket tailored by Schulz look as if it had been run over by a coach and horses.

'Kitty, Jamie's been spouting the Rights of Man over the breakfast table since he was about fourteen. Maybe one day the force of his conviction will induce him to actually do something other than just talking about it, like actually study for his bar examinations.'

'Obviously, but the prime minister's just been killed. You must have heard the rumours, that it was all part of a Radical plot,' Kitty said; she looked genuinely worried. 'Jamie took Chas to see Thomas Spence and Robert Wedderburn give a talk somewhere in Limehouse. Crauford was furious: Jamie might as well have indoctrinated Chas into Satanism. You won't have heard,' Kitty went on with a particular inflection in her voice he recognised only too well from his childhood, 'but Chas is a little out of sorts. He won't be at the Vennings' drum later, poor thing, which is such a pity.'

'Out of sorts?' Greville said. Their scapegrace younger brother had always been predictable if nothing else. 'Stale drunk, more like.'

Then Kitty mouthed at him: *He's been shot.*

Greville closed his eyes, very briefly. *Christ.* 'Perhaps I'll look in on him.'

'I would if I were you.' Kitty spoke with a creditable assumption of carelessness. She gave him a flinty smile. 'I bet you wish you were still in Spain, don't you?'

Greville left her on the chaise longue, in awe of his sister's nerve as well as her ability to speak without drawing breath. Kitty was right: if she absented herself, the younger Lady Crauford's guests would comment.

Greville had barely reached the bookshelves before he had to pass Byron, who was still examining a shelf of calf-bound Greek philosophy with a glass of champagne in one hand, as if the sweating throng of people were nothing more than smoke from a badly laid fire. He looked up as Greville approached, all tempered aggression and well-cut plain dark jacket and breeches. Byron lifted his gaze to meet Greville's own and raised his glass in a silent salute, as if they were the only two men of flesh and blood in the room.

Even as a boy, he'd possessed the rare gift of bestowing the whole of his attention on a single person, making it all too easy to believe that you were the only one in the world for him. Greville returned the salute but couldn't ignore a cold sensation of unease. What was it Kitty had said of George Gordon, Lord Byron? *He scorches across the haut ton like a comet.* When all was said and done, what was a comet but a star that left destruction where it fell?

11

Greville left the salon and loped along the corridor at a brisk pace, not stopping until he reached a servants' door set into the wainscoting. Waiting briefly to allow a harried-looking footman to emerge, he ran up three flights of narrow stairs lit only by plain windows set at intervals into the whitewashed walls. Stepping out at last into family quarters on the third floor, Greville found himself in familiar territory. A wide corridor carpeted in old-fashioned buckram led to the nursery and schoolroom still inhabited by his youngest siblings. A warm golden light shone around the schoolroom door; he heard muffled hysteria, and what sounded very like a large piece of furniture being moved apace across waxed floorboards. He smiled briefly, but this was no time to reacquaint himself with children who would scarcely remember his face.

Bloody Chas, in every possible sense of the word. Greville's long stride took him quickly away from the children's quarters at the back of the third floor to the second-best family bedchambers overlooking the square. Above the wainscoting, the walls here were still hung with once-bright flowered silk, a pattern of blowsy roses liberally spattered with faded ink beside the linen-press door. He still remembered his father watching him from across the desk in his library: a thoughtful, intelligent man whose bewildered disappointment was more painful to endure than any physical punishment.

Greville, we must use the reason and judgement God gave us. What has happened to yours?

Sometimes it was a relief the old man was dead. Greville strode with unerring instinct towards his former bedchamber, favoured in his youth because of a window providing easy egress to the stable mews. At this hour of the day, one might reasonably expect to hear his young sisters and cousin calling to one another as they dressed for a rout party, or Chas and Jamie arguing over some finer point of backgammon, even as he remembered with a jolt that years had passed. Estella and Charis were married and gone, and Jane avoided routs wherever possible, according to Kitty's worried correspondence. Likely those boys had long since swapped backgammon in the schoolroom for hazard at Watier's.

Greville knew this kind of thick, hushed silence and he increased his pace. Finally reaching his old bedchamber, he came upon the same maidservant he'd seen bearing armfuls of bloodied linen through the formal quarters of the house.

The maid froze as he approached and dropped into a curtsey; the faded linen apron pinned to the front of her gown was streaked with dark blood, too. Her throat fluttered as she swallowed hard.

'Milord, Mr Somers said I should not allow anyone in.' She spoke with the steady nerve Greville favoured in young recruits, but here she was sweeping grates and emptying chamber-pots for his family. Was there any wonder, really, that some craved revolution just as much as others feared it?

'Never mind, Susan.' Greville never forgot a face, even if she had just been a twelve-year-old scullery maid the last time he'd seen her. Dropping into another curtsey, she stepped out of the way, her shoulders sagging a little with relief.

Greville walked into chaos: the air was thick with fresh sweat and the dirty reek of a butcher's shop or a battlefield; he registered familiar faded wall-hangings, the same old battered velvet bed-curtains. A bloodstained fine lawn shirt lay discarded on the rug. Somers had taken off his jacket, and stood bent over the four-poster with his sleeves rolled up. A tall, rangy young man with untidy fair hair stood at the other side of the bed, staring down at the occupant with undisguised irritation, arms folded across his chest.

'Oh, for Christ's sake.' Jamie spoke with bored distaste. 'Just cut off his breeches, Somers. If you don't want to do it, I suppose I must— *Christ.*' He broke off, staring across the room at Greville.

'Bloody nonsense.' The bed's occupant spoke up in a breathless rush. 'It's a scratch, nothing more.'

'Shut up, Chas,' Jamie said, never taking his eyes off Greville. 'Shit.'

'I'll be the judge of that, shall I?' Greville spoke into an immense silence, with a nod at Somers. 'Thank you. I suppose we have you to thank for the fact that the whole household has not been set about its ears?'

Somers cleared his throat. 'It seemed undesirable, my lord. Lord Charles has sustained an injury, I'm afraid.'

Jamie's face was a picture of uncharacteristic uncertainty and overwhelming guilt. 'Greville—'

'Keep it to yourself for now, why don't you?' Greville braced himself for the inevitable confession later and reached the bedside where he found his younger brother white-faced, great pearls of sweat standing on his forehead as dark blood seeped from a wound on his thigh and into a pile of folded linen placed beneath his leg; Chas was fair like Jamie, but he shared the handsome, patrician features of Crauford and their father. Now, his hair was dank with sweat. Vivid red spots stained Chas's cheekbones, his lips white with the effort of pressing them together. 'Hurts like the very devil, doesn't it?' Greville went on, sounding a lot more casual than he felt. Chas had been shot in the leg, the ball resting too near the femoral artery for either Somers or Greville himself to attempt the extraction alone. Greville was fairly certain that Somers would have had the thing out by now if he'd thought it worth the risk.

'*Grev.* What are you doing here?' Chas spoke in an explosive burst of false enthusiasm before falling into the wide-eyed silence of a man enduring considerable pain.

'Furlough, not that you need allow it to concern you.' Greville rested a hand on his brother's hot forehead and turned to Somers, filing away for later the certainty that if Chas lived, he was going to spin him a tale worthy of a gothic novel. 'We need Smythe, I think, don't you?' Which was his way of saying he couldn't get the ball out without likely killing his own brother in a spray of arterial blood any more than Somers could.

'The girl can be relied upon,' Somers said. 'I believe Dr Smythe's home is not more than a quarter-hour away.'

Greville's gaze rested on Jamie. 'Go with her,' he said. 'We can't risk her not being taken seriously by Smythe's staff. Be quick. As soon as you get back, you and I are going down to dine.'

'Going down to what?' Jamie demanded, incredulous. Chas was still bleeding into the folded pile of sheets even as he lapsed deeper into fever, turning his hot head from side to side on the creased pillow.

Greville smiled, with a patient glance at the brass carriage clock on the mantelpiece. 'Crauford and Marianne have gathered the most fashionable people in the entire haut ton in the blue salon downstairs, including the most famous man in England. They all know you and I are at home. It's going to look a little odd if we eschew supper, isn't it? Or would you prefer news of this interesting scenario to spread right across Mayfair before morning?'

Greville didn't miss the flash of shielded defiance in Jamie's expression.

12

Half an hour later, Greville took Kitty's elbow and walked her into the candlelit dining room to face the Craufords' idea of a light repast; in the time he'd been upstairs, Kitty's demeanour had altered, tension now thrumming through her slender form.

'I see you're still master of the art of dressing to dine in under ten minutes,' she said, with asperity. 'What on earth have you done to Jamie? *What's going on?*'

Ignoring Jamie's mutinous presence at the far end of the dining room, Greville shrugged as he steered Kitty towards a seat furthest from the fire; anyone sitting near it would be sweating before the soup was even despatched. 'It only took me five minutes to dress this evening, as a matter of fact. Dr Smythe is with Charles now, or soon will be. I don't suppose you have the smallest notion of why or how he managed to get himself shot in the thigh on a Thursday night?'

Kitty's eyes widened as they approached the long,

damask-covered table, but she held her nerve. 'I wonder you don't worry about being overheard. And all I know is they came in through the kitchen, and of course then Mrs Green went off into hysterics. I've no idea how it happened. What did he tell you?'

'Nothing, of course.' Greville cast a look down the table. Jamie had already taken his seat beside the slender and fragile Annabella Milbanke, who was the daughter of one of his mother's oldest friends. Greville had been to many a schoolroom dance with Annabella, who was gifted at mathematics and devoutly religious. Now, she looked furious and overcome to have Byron on her other side, the poor bloody lamb. Byron spoke across her to address Jamie, leaning on the table, using his fork to make a point. 'Jamie ought to remember his manners,' Greville said. 'He's no better than Byron: they're both treating Annabella like a piece of furniture.'

'Jamie ought to remember a particle of common sense—' Kitty broke off, turning with prescient instinct to face Lady Melbourne, who, despite her rheumatism, approached them both like a ship under full sail, tall and statuesque in beaded silk, even as she leaned on a jet-inlaid stick.

Kitty pinched Greville's elbow. 'If she cuts me, I'll never forgive you, Grev.'

Instead, Lady Melbourne smiled and nodded at them both, before turning away to speak to Crauford, who was leading her into supper; Kitty visibly sagged with relief.

'It seems your scandalous presence is to be tolerated, then.' Kitty turned back to Greville with a humourless smile. 'Never mind Chas, you're fortunate that my reputation survives you, brother dear, otherwise you'd stand in need of Dr Smythe's services yourself.'

'Forgive me,' Greville said. 'So where Lady Melbourne leads, everyone else still follows?'

'For leadership of the ton, it's neck and neck between her, Sally Jersey and Annis Bute.' Kitty placed her empty glass on the table with suppressed anger. 'I hope you know what you're doing. Why did you not consult with Mama at least before coming home? With you turning up here I almost feel sorry for Marianne, which is saying something.'

'I did consult with my mother,' he said, holding out his sister's seat, 'and you know quite well what a strategist she is. Where is she, in fact?'

Kitty frowned. 'I don't know, in all honesty.'

Greville closed his eyes. *Oh, shit.*

'Mama not being here is another oddity about this evening,' Kitty went on, with sotto voce understatement. 'We all expected her, and then at about four o'clock she sent Jamie home to say she might be delayed and we weren't to wait for her. She sent another note for Marianne saying she'd be so obliged if an extra place might be laid at table.'

'What a termagant she is.' Greville cast a swift glance down the table at his satin-clad sister-in-law Marianne, who paid no heed to the two empty Queen Anne dining chairs that yawned like the gaps left by diseased teeth. 'At any rate, my mother knows I'm in town, and I wouldn't be surprised if she'd summoned the Melbournes here tonight to lend me countenance. Listen, Chas seems to think the shooting was a case of mistaken identity. Do you believe him?'

'I could believe anything of this spring.' Kitty sat back

in her chair, allowing a footman to fill her glass with champagne. 'I don't know what you hear from Spain, but London feels like a powder-keg ready to blow at any minute. Our dear brother Crauford is always telling anyone who will listen that the man who shot poor Lord Perceval had his own private vendetta, but he was the prime minister. And even I hear of unrest and unhappiness everywhere from the Lake District to London. One can sense it, too – the way the poor people beg, and stare and call out to one. Can you not, Greville?' Kitty shook her head, fretting with the damascened ring that had hung around her neck on a delicate gold chain for as long as Greville could remember, slipping the ring on and off her thumb, before finally setting down her fork. 'Things have changed. I can't rid myself of a hag-ridden sensation, as if we've all woken up in a nightmare.'

Greville smiled at her. 'You used to light candles for me at the hearth when I had nightmares.' There was more to say, only Lord Melbourne had turned to them both, seated at Kitty's other side.

Melbourne smiled at Kitty as if to a child of below par intelligence, even as his gaze rested on her décolletage.

'What an exotic ring you have there, my dear. I believe it is a Mughal custom for ladies to wear such ornaments upon their thumbs? There's something so compelling about oriental beauty.'

'I'm sure you think so,' Greville said, amiably.

Lord Melbourne swallowed hard: there was something damned reptilian about the man.

Kitty pinched Greville's hand beneath the table. He

knew quite well that the ring was all she had left of her grandmother, save stories and poems. With weary expertise, she directed Lord Melbourne into a conversation about imported silk, before ruthlessly despatching him to the attentions of the lady sitting at his other side, one of Marianne's particular friends.

'Greville, you must stop looking at people in such a murderous fashion,' Kitty said. 'Anyway, I'll stop being so maudlin. I think you could safely read nothing at all into what's happened to Chas. If the prime minister can be killed in cold blood by some merchant with an obsessive grudge, goodness only knows what could happen to any one of us by some foolish accident. Everything feels so febrile—' She broke off, her attention called away by Lord Melbourne once more, who drew her into an off-colour conversation about the merits of sea-bathing that sent a frisson of rage down Greville's spine. But Kitty was no debutante and more than experienced enough to laughingly redirect lascivious table-talk. Greville allowed his gaze to wander down the long table, resting at last on Jamie and Byron, a fair head and a dark head close together, Annabella Milbanke still angrily blushing between them. She had every right: both Jamie and the poet were ignoring her in a manner likely to attract vicious comment.

Byron leaned closer with a hungry look, speaking to Jamie in a low voice. And then, as if sensing an undercurrent in the room, he smiled at Jamie and turned away from him, reaching out with one fingertip to brush one of Annabella's shining ringlets away from her forehead. Her blush deepened, spreading down her pale throat; she was liquefied and Byron observed it with unconcealed hunger, which at least explained why he hadn't tired of Marianne's party and left before supper – an insult he was more than capable of. The man was exhausting. Greville didn't miss the briefest flash of chagrin in Jamie's expression, suppressed as he drained his wine glass. Jamie gave him a quick, wolfish smile, and Greville looked away, crushing the urge to haul his young cousin unceremoniously out of the room. To Jamie's left, Lady Melbourne had turned to watch, her lips parted. Marianne, too, sat still as Byron whispered in Annabella's ear so that her blush deepened even further, fork raised halfway to her mouth, her eyes darkening. They were like moths drawn to a candle-flame, every last one.

At that moment, the double doors swung open, and Greville's brother's butler, Eames, stepped into the room, with a sense of alarm that Greville could not help but taste on the air like the sort of bad miasma bringing sickness into London with the rolling Thames mist. A quick glance confirmed Jamie and also Byron had noticed it, both shifting infinitesimally in their seats. With the exception of Jamie, they'd served on the battlefield or had got close enough to smell it. Greville had a knife on him but wished it was a pistol. He quietly digested the fact that Jamie had honed his instinct for self-preservation somewhere other than the theatre of war, and most likely in the molly-houses of Vere Street.

'The Dowager Lady Crauford,' Eames said. 'And Lady Greville Nightingale.'

Greville's mother walked into the dining room,

fascinating in midnight-blue satin trimmed with black velvet and black lace gloves up past her elbows, arm in arm with her daughter-in-law. Cressida was draped in peacock-blue, auburn curls arranged to fall over one pale shoulder. She looked straight at him across the room, with that dark, direct gaze he had never forgotten, despite his best efforts. At Greville's side Kitty sucked in a ragged breath, snatching at his hand beneath the table. Greville gave his sister's fingers a brief squeeze and signalled to the footman to fill his glass once more, knowing full well all eyes were on him.

'Well goodness, I'm sorry to be late,' Sylvia said, addressing the entire room with all the confiding charm that had smoothed over her quiet little scandals for more than thirty Seasons. 'Cressy and I have just made the most enormous exhibition of ourselves – would you believe the barouche threw a wheel on Pall Mall, of all places? We had an audience of social mushrooms, grubby little boys, and a dandy with shirt points so high he couldn't see to assist us.' Pausing for breath, she turned to the footman and took a glass of champagne from the tray. 'I've never been nearer to a state of complete hysterical collapse.'

'Lady Crauford does herself a disservice, as usual.' Cressida spoke into the fragile silence as if the Duke of Cleveland had never been interrupted pleasuring her in a quiet corner at a ball. Cressida smiled at the twenty-six members of high society waiting for her to fall again. 'My mama-in-law was redoubtable,' Cressida went on. 'We had an incompetent wheelwright and I thought she was going to kick him out of the way and mend it herself.'

'He was drunk, dear,' Sylvia said. 'We must sit – I'm so

sorry, Marianne! You're waiting for the second remove to come in, aren't you? Don't worry, Cressida and I won't keep you all waiting while we gobble fried oysters. Let's go straight on to the goose and all the rest of it and Mrs Green's chocolate pie, which is gorgeous, although I ought not to say so.'

Only then did Sylvia allow her gaze to fix on Greville. Even she had the grace to look alarmed. Cressida faced them all with a cool self-possession that he'd soon shake. Jamie shot Greville a look of concern along with a flicker of another emotion that he couldn't quite identify. Byron glanced from Greville to Cressida and back again, and rolled his eyes. To the devil with them all. Greville turned now to his wife: escorted by a footman, she crossed the room towards her seat at the table with her usual mannish stride, the silk skirts of her gown clinging about her waist and hips, dear God.

Greville addressed the table with the edge of dissolution that they'd all be expecting. 'I propose a toast to Cressida, who has honoured us all by returning from her travels and coming home to England.' He raised his glass to her, enjoying the brief flare of indignation in her eyes. 'You chose a fine time to return to these shores, my lady, but how glad we all are that you did.'

13

An hour later, in the drawing room at Crauford House, Cressida let herself out of a side door set into the painted wainscoting. In her mind's eye, all she could see was Greville's kindling, sardonic expression as he'd raised his glass to her before all of those people, and Sylvia's irresistible smile – the very image of her son's. God only knew how she'd got through supper but she had, talking commonplaces to the men seated to her right and left, one a second son in the Cabinet Office who didn't have the breeding to conceal the worried glances he kept casting towards his wife, and the other a civil old man sitting to her left who had either forgotten what she'd done or was too aged to care, having been a young man in wilder times than these.

She had endured the goose, the poached cod cheeks and boiled lamb studded with sweet jellies; she had endured retiring with a flock of women to drink orgeat for the first time in nearly half a decade. She had submitted as Sylvia paraded her from one group of purse-lipped dowagers to another, pouring forth a stream of light inconsequential chatter about anything, from the new soloist at the Royal Opera House, who was thought to be dreadful, to the unflattering cut of sleeves this spring. On the other hand, a little judicious prompting about current affairs had later provided Cressida with the information that several ladies of the ton were wicked enough to feel a flutter of relief at the assassination of the prime minister. After all, Lord Perceval's relentless pursuit of slave-traders and his hard-headed dealings with America had led to a collapse in trade certain to cause all sorts of inconvenience. An expertly led conversation even revealed that the Duchess of Argyle suspected Luddites, Radicals and frame-breakers of having a hand in Perceval's death, and that the Bellingham fellow had been hanged far too quickly to prove it, more was the pity.

Kitty, however, had met Cressida's gaze from across the room and then looked away, so that she felt a plummeting sensation in her belly as if in the half moment after the hangman released the trapdoor. Long ago, she and Kitty sat up all night playing hazard, talking of books, laughing until it hurt or railing against injustice, laying out their plans for a better world. Now, Kitty couldn't even bring herself to look at her. *What else did you expect, you bloody fool?*

What did any of it matter if the whole charade got her closer to Drochcala? Once she'd delivered Lascelles his precious gossip about Byron, she and Ines would be free to take Byron's money, if she charmed it from him after all. Cressida didn't much care if the Committee of Secrecy sent a man with a garrotting wire after her one night, but she did care about leaving Ines unprotected: the girl had no one else. No, she'd obey Lascelles one last time, make herself indispensable, and then leave this small, grey benighted island behind for good. Now stepping into the neglected music room where the Nightingale girls used to practise their scales, Cressida leaned on the door with her eyes closed, still gripping the brass knob, cold to the touch beneath her fingertips.

'Running away already?' Byron leaned on the cherrywood pianoforte, watching her across the room.

'I could say the same for you.' Cressida swept past him, making for the window. He'd promised to help: promised her money. She could ask for it now and be gone from here by morning, out of Greville Nightingale's life for ever. Cressida shut her eyes and thought of Ines looking up at her in the ruins of a shelled nunnery, long ago, so trusting. *What are we going to do next?*

We. There was never meant to be a 'we'.

Pushing up the sash window, she drank in the cold twilit air, with the faint London taste of coal-smoke and the distant green tang of the Thames.

Without discussion, she and Byron sat side by side on the chaise longue, his thigh warm against her own. Only a fool would be flattered.

'You know me,' he said. 'I can't stand after-dinner chat once the women have gone.'

She smiled at him. 'What, finally leaving you all with the opportunity to discuss topics beyond our intellectual capacity?'

'The chance would be a fine thing in a room of Englishmen with the intellectual heft of chopped ham and completely unjustified self-confidence.'

'Jamie Nightingale included?' Cressida said.

'Don't look at me like that.' Byron cast her an uncharacteristically stern look. 'Jamie's a liability. I'm not even going to ask why you're here.'

Side by side once more, they leaned into one another, his presence still a comfort.

Cressida's hand closed around the handle of the dagger sheathed at her ankle before she was even fully aware that the door had opened. At her side, Byron lifted his head from her shoulder and sat watchful as she got to her feet with the blade out, polished steel catching the last of the light. Greville came in holding a pewter branch of candles, bringing with him the honeyed warmth of beeswax and the faint scent that was all his own, chamomile laundry soap, rosemary shaving water and something else that she had never been quite able to articulate. All the feline intensity he'd possessed as Devil Nightingale had crystallised into something far more dangerous. His gaze travelled between her and Byron, and he smiled in such a way a chilly thread of awareness slid down Cressida's spine, igniting a pulse of spreading heat between her legs that would soak through her silk chemise. He smiled, in fact, as if he knew all about that.

Get up. 'What can I do for you, Greville?'

'Might I have five minutes of your time?' Greville spoke

to her as if Byron wasn't even in the room. Byron got up and walked out without a backward glance at either of them and closed the door behind him, candle-flames shivering in the breeze. Cressida knew she must tread carefully to get the most out of him. George Byron hadn't changed: he would only be happy to indulge himself in a little obsession if he felt some competition but not so much that he risked rejection. She ignored the small voice at the back of her mind: *What have you become?*

'I suppose you've come to gloat.' Cressida revelled in the brief flare of desire in Greville's eyes. 'But as a matter of fact, I didn't need your mother's help earlier this evening and I don't need yours now. I've already secured my invitation to Drochcala. Go home to Summercourt and enjoy your furlough, and I'll deal with George Byron for Lascelles without your interference.'

Greville's gaze travelled to the knife and then away from it, so dismissive, before looking up at her. He exuded reined-in distracted tension like a man bringing a message from the battlefield. 'I've come to ask for your help, much as it pains me to do it.'

Cressida let out an airless laugh. 'What?'

'Lascelles told me you assisted the surgeons in the peninsula.' He was close to her now, no more than a handspan away. Greville briefly closed his eyes in her presence, those gold-touched lashes so dark against his sun-bronzed skin. 'Cressida, please.'

It was the first time in so very many years that she'd heard her given name upon his lips. Greville moved in one stride to the servants' door beside the piano; Cressida crushed indecision and followed him up the narrow whitewashed stairwell, going to the aid of a man who had betrayed her in so many different ways.

Having set down the pewter candle-branch on the windowsill, he went up the plain stairs of oiled oak at a swift pace, lighting their way with just one taper, his long, well-shaped legs clad in close-cut breeches of dark kerseymere. Upon reaching a narrow landing, he stood back to let her pass. She was aware of his gaze upon her as she gathered up her skirts, taking the next flight of stairs at a run, sensing they were nearing the shabbier bedrooms on the upper floors where the younger Craufords slept in starched linen sheets and had their fires kindled each morning by exhausted twelve-year-old maidservants.

He went ahead of her again before they reached his old bedchamber, a room that by rights she ought never to have set foot in. Even as a clueless girl of nineteen, she should really have understood that to leave her in such a permanent state of despoiled need, Lord Greville Nightingale must have indulged in a considerable amount of practice. She recalled how he'd laughed with gratification, looking down at her in his canopied bed, so adept with the touch of his fingertips and lips that she had never known such a shocking combination of pleasure and shame. She remembered the rise and fall of his naked chest, the darned linen pillowcase. *You'd do well to bite something*, he'd said, bringing her to merciless release with the touch of his fingertips. She had: his shoulder, and hard.

Their eyes met as they reached the door and she recalled the salty taste of his damp skin.

'Ready?' Greville asked, as if they were about to climb a siege tower together. 'I doubt very much it will shock you, but my brother has been shot.'

He opened the door into his old bedchamber, where so many things were screamingly wrong that she had to steady herself. There was too much blood, for a start. By the window, a middle-aged society doctor still dressed for dinner stood arguing in a repressed, furious whisper with a tall footman. Chas was in the bed, motionless with pain – Cressida had seen many of them like this on the battlefield. Boys in field hospitals often went very still, tutored never to betray their pain by either privation or sadistic boarding schools, and then they died.

'The gentleman insists there's nothing for it but to have the leg off entirely, sir,' the footman said. 'With the ball lodged so close to the femoral artery he says there's no other option. I explained about cauterising, we've all seen the surgeons do it on the field, but he says it's not possible. Sir.'

'Thank you, Somers.' Greville turned to the doctor, who to his credit had come out in the middle of dinner, with a napkin still tucked into the front of his waistcoat. 'You may leave us now, if you can do nothing.'

'No, don't let him leave, not yet,' Cressida said, and they all turned to look at her: the serving-girl, the doctor, even Chas on the bed, turning his head from side to side as the fever mounted. If the wound didn't kill him, the fever would. 'We'll need all the hands we can get, as long as he can keep his mouth shut and not interfere.' She crossed the room to the bed, Greville at her side. They had cut off

Chas's breeches, and only a darned linen sheet covered him. 'May I?' she said.

Chas managed to smile through the agony. 'Who am I to say no, ma'am?'

Did he recognise her or not? There was little time to wonder. She lifted the sheet and, with iron self-control, refused to let the dismay show in her face as she removed the thick wadding of bloodied cloth. The ball had gone in close to Chas's hip joint. She'd seen this before, tearing bandages for the surgeons, lending a hand when they called for it. If they didn't get the ball out, Chas really would be lucky to only lose his leg. If they tried to get the ball out and failed, he'd bleed to death in minutes. Which at the very least would be quick.

The doctor loomed behind her, stinking of smoked trout and champagne, breathing down her neck as he spoke to Greville. 'This is no place for hedge-witch potions and hysteria, my lord.'

'Does she look hysterical?' Greville said, and she heard the grim smile in his voice.

Cressida smoothed down the silk skirts of her evening gown. 'Someone get this thing off me and I'll tell you what to do. *Quickly.* I'm damned if I'll sacrifice my second-best gown for a Nightingale.'

The servant girl was the first to understand, her deft fingers dealing with the fastening at the back of Cressida's bodice. The doctor looked away, but for a moment Greville caught her gaze, an unfathomable expression in his dark eyes as she stepped out of a puddle of peacock-blue silk and stripped off her long gloves.

'I beg that you will forgive me if I take my leave.' The doctor sounded as if he were about to choke.

'The devil you will go anywhere,' Greville said, emotionless. 'We might need you yet. Susan, assist my lady.'

The girl stepped forward, grey with shock but still functioning. Cressida waved away the girl's own proffered apron, which would barely have covered her petticoat-skirts, and between them they pinned a hastily folded sheet to the front of her stays, securing it around her waist with a strip torn from one edge. There was already warm water set by the fire, so Cressida scrubbed her hands, working up a lather with the yellowed rock of lavender soap by the wash basin. Behind her back, she overheard the doctor's querulous demand to know what in heaven's name she was doing.

'Have you ever wondered why babies delivered by laundrywomen die less often than babies delivered by your unwashed self?' Cressida said, not looking at him but at the damage as Chas sucked in a long, shuddering breath, pearls of sweat all over his forehead. The skin around the bleeding entry wound was black with gunpowder, already beginning to bruise. He was a brave lad as well as a pretty one, and it would be a shame if he died. It generally was, when they did.

Greville turned to Smythe with a pleasant smile that made the man stop gaping and take two swift steps backwards. 'I don't give a flying damn about propriety. Follow every last instruction that she gives.'

Smythe opened his mouth and then closed it again, wisely.

14

An hour later saw Greville in Jamie's bedchamber, splashing cold water from the basin onto his face, his bloodied shirt discarded on the waxed floorboards. The water swirled with hypnotic red as he took the fine linen shirt that Somers handed to him.

'How is he now?' Greville asked, rolling up the sleeves. Cufflinks could wait; he couldn't get the smell of burning flesh out of his nostrils. If Chas lived, it would be the cauterisation that saved his life: Smythe had gone to pieces, more used to prescribing remedies for bored society matrons than dealing with gunshot wounds. Cressida had talked him through the cauterisation step by step, and Greville could only hope that no one ever found out she'd learned the method on a battlefield.

'Still alive, and he managed to pass water, sir, which was clear with no blood or ill humours in it. The laudanum has taken effect, which is a mercy.' Somers picked up the shirt as though it were a discarded stocking. 'Susan is assisting her ladyship in Lord Charles's dressing room, but the girl's in a bad way. Young Mr Nightingale has gone to the library.'

Greville thanked him and left, still rolling up the sleeves of his shirt as he walked into the oak-panelled library to find Jamie standing beside the leather-topped desk that overlooked the square, leaning on the tall window frame with his back to the door. A heap of calf-bound Greek satires and Radical pamphlets lay on the desk, the topmost still open. Jamie stood still, absorbed in staring out at the lamp-lit square below, so unaware of his presence that Greville fought a rising wave of exasperation: God help him in any London street after dark.

'You are not downstairs with the poet?' he said, keeping his tone light.

Jamie turned then, arms still folded. 'No. Apparently not.' Greville didn't miss the flare of emotion in his eyes. Jamie sighed, looking suddenly younger than he was, pale with tension. 'Will Chas be all right? Trust him to kick up a dust.'

'It depends on the fever,' Greville said, ruthless. 'How did it come about?'

Jamie shrugged, his expression blank. 'He says he was robbed. It could happen to anyone at the moment.'

'How unfortunate.' Greville went to the sideboard and poured them each a glass of brandy from the cut-glass decanter. 'I felt for the Milbanke girl, having the misfortune to sit between you and George Byron this evening. You and he drew rather a lot of attention even as you talked across her.'

'*He* draws attention, you mean,' Jamie said, accepting the brandy. 'No one's really that interested in me, thank Christ.

Am I about to receive a homily about manners and propriety from you, of all people?' He smiled, all fierce intelligence and the patience of the young towards their elders. He had the self-preservation if not the innate respect not to mention Cressida.

Greville raised his glass in a silent toast to King and country. God help him if he were to start lecturing greenhorns. 'No, I'll leave the moralising to my dear brother Crauford.'

Jamie shrugged. 'He doesn't need much encouragement.'

'Consider it instead a warning from an expert in the field,' Greville said, watching his cousin drink; Jamie's eyes shone with the briefest glimpse of dissipation. So, he was that brand of Nightingale after all. 'Byron has unusual charisma, does he not? I've known him for years and that's always been the case. But you know how society works: what goes up must come down. Reputations rise and then are destroyed. Take it from me, once that's happened, there's nothing the ton loves more than gathering like so many spectators at a hanging. Make sure you do remain a spectator, rather than the sport. Jigging at the end of that particular rope is no way to live.'

Jamie watched him, eyes narrowed. 'A lecture, then. I thought better of you, of all people. You're just as bad as the rest of them.' He set down his glass with angry deliberation and Greville stepped back to let him walk past, watching as he closed the door.

He found Cressida in Chas's dressing room, holding a huge measure of brandy.

'Poor Susan. She was too overset to pin up the back of

my gown,' Cressida drawled, raising her glass to him as she adopted that cold, careless persona once more.

Greville poured the last of the brandy into the other glass and drank it like water.

'Come here,' Greville said; he had wondered for days what would happen when he reached the end of his rope.

Cressida got up, never taking her eyes from him. She crossed the silent room half undressed, her gown gathered in handfuls; he heard only the whisper of heavy folds of silk and told himself to get a damned grip.

'Turn around,' Greville said. A single chestnut curl clung to the back of her neck, trailing over one naked shoulder, her skin dusted with pale gold freckles. With a workmanlike shrug, she pulled up the bodice, sliding her strong, slender arms into the short, pearl-studded sleeves of her gown, leaving the back of her bodice open, even as he inhaled her warm scent.

'It's a maid's task,' she said, without turning her head to look at him. 'And you're no such thing.'

'Whether I like it or not, my family is now in debt to you. No one else could have done what you did for Chas tonight. Not just your insistence on the cauterisation but your nursing of him. I beg that you will allow me to be your servant for this moment.'

'Very well,' Cressida said, her shoulders rising and falling almost imperceptibly with every breath. How often he had lain awake, wondering if she did in fact still breathe. He'd helped many a girl back into her gown, but this was Cressida and for now there was nothing but blue silk and the fresh linen of her shift beneath his fingertips. When it was done she let out a sigh, and he allowed his thumb to brush the bare skin at the nape of her neck. She responded, turning to him, eyes dark in her white face. They both reached for each other in the same moment, his hands in her hair, then running down her back as she responded to his touch, pulling him towards her with primal urgency. He looked down at her, running his hands over her backside: Cressida had always been beyond the common, but, if anything, the appalling way she'd lived had lent a lean, watchful air to her beauty. He ducked to kiss her, to make her his once more, and her hands cupped the back of his head, her fingers in his hair, and at the familiar taste of her something within him unravelled.

'I do actually want you just as much as I hate you,' she said, speaking softly into his ear.

'Is that so?' Greville measured out each word and ran his hands down her back again with slow deliberation, relishing the warmth of her lithe form as she pushed herself against him in response. He spread his long fingers across her rear with proprietorial ease, teasing through layers of disordered silk and fine linen until she writhed, liquescent. She let out a controlled gasp and when he took her mouth again she bit his lip. He'd waited so long to inhale her scent, which was the same as it always had been: only Cressida could spend years in the train of an army and return with a supply of the costliest attar of roses. He pushed her back against the panelled wall, holding both hands above her head with just one of his own, kissing her again as he should have done in the ruins of Badajoz. He abandoned her mouth and brushed his lips instead against the white skin of her neck.

She brought down her hands, cradling his face as she kissed him in return.

'You truly are the worst of men,' she said.

'Do you think I don't know it?' Greville dealt with the fall of his breeches and Cressida's skirts in short order. Lifting her, holding her against the wall, he made her his own once more, and she him, with her legs wrapped around his waist and her arms loose around his neck, so that he held her and took her with all of his strength and will, and holy God she had better not remember the way he allowed his forehead to rest for a moment in the warm, smooth hollow of her clavicle.

Sometime later, they sat side by side on the floor, still in disarray and a little breathless, both leaning against the heavy chest of carved oak where Chas's valet kept his spare riding breeches.

Cressida turned her head away. 'That was an unforced error.' Her voice was hard, even though she was still flushed. 'It's too late for this to make any difference, Greville. You do know that, don't you? Only a fool allows a man to betray her more than once.'

Banked-down anger rose up: how dared she question his actions? 'I served you no worse a turn than any other husband of our station.'

So they had finally arrived at this: an opera dancer with frightened eyes whose name he couldn't remember, and a thoughtless decision to go to Vauxhall Gardens with a party of unmarried friends and an entourage of paid girls.

Cressida faced him again then, her eyes hot with scorn and a flicker of naked hurt that cut him to the quick. 'Didn't you think I'd care? I've never known humiliation like it: everywhere I went, to be in receipt of pitying glances and ill-meant advice about how it was not worth trying to hold Devil Nightingale.'

'You were reared to turn a blind eye, and to conduct your own affairs with discretion. You did neither,' Greville snapped. It was just the order of things: the way lives like theirs had been lived for centuries. Hang the fact that she'd precisely echoed the soft, insistent voice that had plagued his rare moments of reflection over all the years since, arguing that perhaps Cressida had not been the only one at fault, embarking on an affair with the Duke of Cleveland which could not have been more public. Perhaps he'd angered and humiliated a young girl who'd already known the sort of abandonment he could never hope to understand, provoking her beyond what she could bear. He remembered the bitterest of the accusations she had thrown at him before frozen silence had descended on the marriage: *Never mind how you humiliate me, what of those girls? You may as well have pushed each one into the gutter yourself.*

Cressida didn't know it, but he'd stuck to bored society matrons ever since: women of his own class.

'More fool me for ever believing that you were out of the ordinary,' Cressida said, now in control once more and staring straight ahead. 'Why are you even in England, Greville?'

Greville wanted to shake her, but never once had he allowed a woman or girl to witness the more volcanic extremes of a temper he'd been brought up to consider a fault.

'Because you're my wife and you bear my name, and I'd as lief you didn't drag it through the mud again.' Greville steadied himself. 'And I don't care what Arthur Lascelles says, but you will not do so at Drochcala, with Byron's help or without it.'

She gifted him a mocking smile. 'So even after all these years you still regard me as your property. Are you sure it's not just too shaming to think of your own wife swiving George Byron, and for everyone to know about it?'

Silently, Greville counted to five, before turning to her with the insolent smile that had fetched her from right across a ballroom, years before. 'He can have you over the billiard table at Drochcala before the whole household for all I care, but I've sisters still in the schoolroom and I won't allow you to ruin their chances with another one of your scandals. By the way, I take my hat off to Annis for that fairytale she spun about where exactly you've been. Travelling with only servants throughout the Levant is eccentric, but reasonably unexceptionable. If you toe the line, some of the not-so-high sticklers might even forget the past and receive you again. So let's just pray that no one except Lascelles and a very select few in the Cabinet know where you really have been. And if everyone else finds out you whored your way across Portugal and Spain in the company of half the British army, I'd imagine you'll become more of a liability than an asset. It's a risk, isn't it? Disobey me if you please. Just don't imagine it will be without consequence.'

Somehow, they were now on their feet, and standing just inches apart again. Her mute anger scorched the air between them, as did his own not inconsiderable fury. A smile teased Cressida's lips. 'If I see you at Drochcala, Nightingale, be very aware that I regard you as an obstacle. I leave it to you to consider whether that's wise.'

Part Two

But while the exalted offender can find means to baffle the law, new capital punishments must be devised, new snares of death must be spread for the wretched mechanic, who is famished into guilt. These men were willing to dig, but the spade was in other hands; they were not ashamed to beg, but there was none to relieve them: their own means of subsistence were cut off, all other employments pre-occupied, and their excesses, however to be deplored and condemned, can hardly be subject of surprise.

Lord Byron's speech to the House of Lords in defence of the frame-breakers, February 1812

15

In the far north of Scotland, at the furthest edge of Sutherland, a wild coastline of granite cliffs and lonely windswept pebbled beaches turned away from the Atlantic and the Isle of Lewis towards Thurso, the Pentland Firth, and the Orkneys. Here, at the head of a quiet, almost forgotten sea-loch, the great house of Drochcala sat against a heathered flank of hillside, watching out over the glittering expanse of the loch-head. An island rose up in the middle of Loch Iffrin: black granite streaked with limpets, topped with a forest of beech trees and verdant heather uncurling in the warmth of summer. Once inhabited by a hermit, Eilean nam Fiadh was now home only to the red deer who had given it a name. A little to the east, the cottages of Droch Cala village hurried downhill in pursuit of the house, like so many chicks following a moorhen, all grey granite, whitewashed walls and slate tiles. Behind the house and the village, fast white streams hurtled down the slopes where, as a little girl, Cressida had jumped from bank to bank, her Irish governess never far behind, pink with exertion but indefatigable.

'The Butes keep a traditional house here, do they not?' Ines drew back heavy velvet curtains, revealing the silvery spread of Loch Iffrin beyond the birch trees. She could always be relied on to spy out the lie of the land. 'They won't be expecting you to go down to breakfast. If I had the chance to stay in bed until all hours drinking spiced chocolate and eating white bread, I would.'

'I don't doubt it.' Cressida got out of bed, restless with the need to act. It had been three days and there was still no sign or word from Byron. She pushed away a memory of Crauford House, Greville taking her up against the wall with the sheer brute force of his strength, skirts and petticoats around her waist in disorder. He'd sent her over the edge with ruthless expertise – all except for that one moment when he'd allowed his forehead to rest upon her shoulder like an exhausted child.

Disobey me if you please, he'd said. *Just don't imagine it will be without consequence.*

What in hell's name did he propose she did instead? The question was unanswerable, snatching away the prospect of sleep every night since.

And yet there was no sign of him, either. Greville had directed every move of this game since the moment he'd saved her from a mob in Badajoz, her dizzying, angry relief at the sight of him immediately extinguished by his cold, high-handed behaviour, turning her over to Lascelles in the ruins of a shelled church with barely a word. In truth, Cressida relished the prospect of flouting Lord Greville Nightingale's clearly expressed instruction, but doing so would be a lot less enjoyable without forcing him to witness it.

Cressida allowed Ines to dress her in silence.

'Be careful,' Ines said, a muscle in her jaw twitching. 'I don't like this place; I don't like the feel of it at all.'

Downstairs, Cressida paused outside the dining room door of carved oak, long enough to hear subdued female voices: Annis and Kitty. She froze. Ines was right: the Butes did keep a traditional house, and it was unusual if not unsettling to discover married women at the breakfast table.

'Annis, let's speak plainly for once,' Kitty whispered with an edge of banked-down fury in her voice. Cressida rolled her eyes: how many times had she warned Kitty in their misspent youth that a whisper carried far further than a low voice? 'Twenty years or more you have called Sylvia a friend,' Kitty went on. 'This will break her, and you know it as well as I do.'

'If Sylvia really cared, she'd be here herself,' Annis replied. 'But as usual, she's using you as her obedient little messenger girl. In her eyes you're next up from the better class of servant, tidying up the Nightingale family messes, including those made by herself.'

Trust Annis to sow discord between Kitty and Sylvia, whatever this was about. Kitty had endured barb after malicious barb about her late mother's people, despite the fact that her maternal grandmother had been far more ennobled in Mughal society than most of the whey-faced second-rate baronets' wives who liked to whisper behind their hands about what a fortunate thing it was that Kitty's skin tone was so light. No one dared blow such poison darts in Sylvia's presence.

'What on earth are you talking about?' Kitty hissed, too wise to take Annis's bait. 'Of course Sylvia cares. This will ruin the Nightingales if it gets out and most of all it will ruin *her*. Sylvia's conceited at times but even she's not arrogant enough to believe she'll get away with this. Jamie—'

Kitty broke off at the sound of approaching footfalls, and Annis's grim-faced housekeeper, Roberts, rounded the corner clad in her usual black bombazine gown, but now with the addition of a tartan sash. Cressida saw at a glance that the tartan wasn't related to Roberts's own clan. Annis had no understanding of such matters: she probably just liked the combination of colours. Roberts was carrying a heavily laden tray of silver dishes with clattering lids, and she looked Cressida up and down as she opened the door. Cressida surprised herself with a flicker of pity. Not that long ago, Drochcala had its own butler and housekeeper. Now, Roberts had been shipped up from London to bear the burdens of both. As a lady's maid, the work was beneath her – a humiliation that Annis wouldn't have stopped to consider for a moment.

In the dining room, Kitty and Annis presented a united front of determined charm, spooning greengage jam onto fresh tattie scones as they discussed what might happen in the next canto of *Childe Harold*. Cressida would have cheerfully laid a bet that Annis hadn't actually read a single word of Byron's poetry and couldn't give a damn about when the third canto would be published, let alone what it contained. She accepted hot coffee from Roberts, glancing at the muddle of unfolded letters by Annis's plate.

'Not bad news, I hope?'

'Of course not – it's going to be the most gorgeous summer,' Kitty said, stumbling into non sequitur. 'The thrift is out all over the hillside. Did you see? Like a cloak of palest pink.'

Annis smiled. 'Well, it's rather a shame about Mary Sidgwick.'

Roberts failed to hide a smile, obviously priding herself on still having the ear of her mistress, even if she was also reduced to waiting at table like a fourteen-year-old girl trusted with the crockery for the first time.

Kitty ploughed on: 'I'm never sure if I prefer the thrift or the Michaelmas daisies.'

Cressida sipped her coffee, looking at Annis. 'Oh?'

Annis spooned more jam onto her plate, cool and unruffled in a morning gown of pale ivory. 'She's written to say that she's not coming, darling. Her eldest stepdaughter is out next year, and I'm afraid you were a bridge too far, even with Byron to make you irresistible.'

'Oh, hell, I'm sorry. I knew it would be hard, but I didn't even fear it would be this bad, not after so long – it was naive of me at best, stupid at worst,' Cressida said, glancing down to stir honey into her coffee, glad that Greville wasn't here to see straight through her.

'It's a shame about Mary, but I've heard from four different people that you're Lord Byron's muse, Cressida,' Kitty said, quickly.

Annis let out a bright burst of laughter. 'We've nothing

to fear in that case – I know you find poetry a dead bore, Cressida, but you'll be the envy of every woman in the ton.'

Neither Kitty nor Annis mentioned the fact that George Byron was now three days late.

Annis turned to Kitty with a smile. 'Your cousin Jamie's quite thick with Byron at the moment, I hear. Jamie's such a revoltingly beautiful young man, isn't he? Has anyone had a word in Crauford's ear? I'm certain a hint would be enough.'

Kitty briefly shut her eyes. 'Honestly, I hope not. Crauford has no knack or capacity for dealing with young people. Believe me, Greville is best placed to manage Jamie, so I can only thank goodness he's on furlough.'

Annis smiled at Cressida. 'Maybe Jamie is the reason why he's not here yet? But you mustn't be downcast: I'm sure you can still hold Greville if you only lift a finger. Once he's dealt with any family scandals, of course. Every man has his priorities.'

Cressida yawned. *You awful bitch*, she thought, idly. 'I'm longing for a walk. I hope you won't find me rude if I set out after breakfast. I never was any good at doing the pretty indoors, and I'm no better after my travels.'

Kitty looked as if she were about to say something – did she want to come? – but Annis spoke over her. 'Do you know,' Annis said, 'as soon as Jamie Nightingale walked into my salon, my first thought was how gorgeous he is. And then I was struck by the oddest sensation of familiarity. Obviously, I knew him as a child. But since he and Chas went off to school and then Jamie went to Cambridge, they're both strangers to me. As a grown man, I feel sure I've seen Jamie somewhere before. How foolish of me.'

Kitty set down her spoon too quickly, with a discordant clatter of silver against china.

'Oh, come on, Annis,' said Cressida. 'Everyone knows Jamie was Tristan Nightingale's natural son. Why stir the pot? We can talk about this like adults, as long as we're discreet. And it's hardly news. People have been gossiping about Jamie's parentage since the day Tristan adopted him.'

'I'm sure. Only, the last time I saw Jamie,' Annis went on, 'it wasn't just Tristan Nightingale I thought of. I suppose the real mother was some chambermaid? Perhaps I saw the poor girl once.'

Kitty pressed her lips together so hard they went white. 'Must we do this?' she asked.

'Of course not,' Cressida said. 'It's pretty crass. I'm sorry, Kitty.' She turned the conversation towards domestic matters, drawing Annis out on a grievance about a lazy laundry-maid who hadn't bothered to wash the tablecloths.

'I daresay she felt contriving to dry them in last week's rain was a task beneath her notice. It's almost impossible to get good staff at the moment.'

Kitty excused herself and Cressida drank her coffee. She let Annis run on, biting into a tattie scone sweet with golden greengage jam, stitching together what she knew. First, the urgency in Kitty's tone, breaking off as she had spoken her young cousin's name, *Jamie*, when neither Kitty nor Annis knew she had overheard. Second, Jamie himself, whom Cressida had found in the passageway outside his cousin's room on the night Chas was shot, leaning on the wall with his eyes shut, disconsolate.

What on earth is wrong? she'd asked him. *I know it looks bad and an injury like that is an awful thing to witness for the first time, but chances are he'll recover.*

Jamie had turned his head to look at her then, his eyes dark with pain. *If he doesn't, the fault's mine.*

The pause hadn't lasted long. *What do you mean?* She still hated herself for that, just a little bit, coaxing Jamie of all people into a confidence, just because one never knew what might be useful and when.

It's my fault Chas was shot. Jamie had spoken with youthful bravado, daring her to contradict. *They thought Chas was me.*

She didn't have to do this, to stay here. She didn't have to involve herself in any such mess. Cressida fought the need to leave the breakfast table and go up to her room to fetch Ines immediately. Hang Lascelles and his dirty money, and hang his warning about the promise of a traitor's death when one was too aristocratic for the gallows: a knife in her back or strong, supple hands around her throat on a dark night. She and Ines would find a way because they must: old shawls for backpacks, the hobnailed boots. A week or so's march and they'd be in Lochinver, then on a boat to the Americas, or Russia, anywhere but here.

16

Cressida left Annis and Lord Bute on the south lawn, clad in newly tailored country clothes, interrogating their monosyllabic head gardener about the seedlings Bute had sent up by the mail coach. It was a hard climb for the first half hour, but she'd faced worse terrain many times over. She left the plantation behind and followed the heather-fringed stream in a winding path with a pleasurable heat in her thighs as her muscles worked; please God, clarity of thought would come with the long view of the sea-loch and the North Atlantic. Lascelles was hundreds of miles away, and there was no sign of Byron or Greville. It really was possible: she and Ines could leave with the scanty collection of coinage still in their possession and heaven only knew they ought to.

She rounded a bend and the skirts of her linen gown caught on the heather as she spotted a lone figure on the path ahead. June sunshine warmed the back of her neck, still a treat after the quiet gloom of Lascelles' second-best guest-chamber, with that door bolted from the outside. Squinting into the sunlight, Cressida shielded her eyes with one hand and recognised even at this distance the familiar figure of the Butes' young but extremely able estate manager. Oliver Tait had met Cressida, the Butes and Kitty Alasdair off the schooner, organising the vast heap of baggage on the dockside at Fraserburgh and stowing it in the Drochcala landau and the baggage cart with good-humoured competence. He was just as easy on the eye as ever, with smooth brown skin, curling black hair, and a reticent but sincere smile. He'd grown into his bulk, now filling out a well-cut jacket of plain green kerseymere to admirable effect.

Oliver was several hundred yards ahead of her now: he'd left the path, skilfully navigating tussocks of grass and heather not far from the ruined bothy where Lord Bute sometimes hosted stalking lunches. Rosmoney had only ever come to Drochcala for the stalking, silencing the drawing room with his politics: a free Ireland or death. In the end, of course, her father's known views had ended in neither. Rosmoney hadn't joined his fellow rebels, hanged on the ramparts of Dublin Castle as the British army swept from farmstead to village, dealing retribution. Cressida could almost see her father making his way catlike down the hill towards her, lean and roguish in ancient twill, the rifle cocked and leaning against his shoulder.

Think of the name, my dear.

It would be foolish to recall the way Greville had looked at Rosmoney in that gloomy bedchamber at the Oxford Arms, as if he would still kill for her.

Sensing a presence behind her before she even heard footfalls, Cressida turned to find Kitty labouring up the rocky hillside, pink in the face beneath a chip-straw bonnet, tied under her chin. Cressida turned back to the path, walking on. What did they have to say to one another, anyway?

They thought Chas was me.

The secret Jamie had shared with her at Crauford House was a revelation any woman of kindness or good sense would divulge to his people. She had neither and it was more than time to sever her ties with that family for good. Cressida recalled Greville looking down at her in Chas's dressing room with that scalding expression. She'd had her share of lovers, both in pleasure and in desperation; it was truly ridiculous that none had been his match.

'Cressida, wait!' Kitty's voice rang out, a fraction less self-assured than usual.

Walk away, Cressida told herself, furious. *Ignore her and walk up the hill.* Instead, she waited, looking down at the glittering surface of Loch Iffrin, just visible beyond the canopy of birch trees below. Kitty caught up, taking off her bonnet and fanning her scarlet face, and for what felt like a long time they stood side by side: the time for polite conversation was over.

Cressida gazed out across the loch, with a profound realisation that pretending to return to the bosom of the Nightingale family was almost as complicated as actually doing so. 'Chas was in a bad way when we left. Have you heard anything from your mother?'

'Well, his fever broke. I'd scarcely have come, otherwise,'

Kitty said. She looked uncharacteristically tired and unkempt and had left the house in her morning gown of sprigged muslin. 'You know what Mama is like. She's equal to almost anything else but always goes to pieces in a sickroom, and will do nothing but make dire pronouncements. I hate to think of how it would have turned out if Greville hadn't been in England. Can you imagine leaving Crauford and Marianne to manage Chas and Jamie in that sort of mess?' Kitty visibly shuddered. 'If it hadn't been for Susan, I wouldn't have come at all.' She shook her head a little as she spoke: a small motion that would have been easy to miss.

'Susan has a steady head on her shoulders,' Cressida said. 'You've shaken off your husband and the children for a few weeks, at least.'

Kitty looked pinched and pale now that her flush had faded, with a wild light in her eyes. Always a terrible liar, she hated being forced into an untruth. 'I shouldn't say it, but how nice to have some time away from them all.'

'I'm sure. I could never bear domesticity.' Kitty was transparent: if not mopping Chas's brow and supporting Sylvia's spirits, she'd much rather have been at Straloch for the summer with her husband and their four children. Which begged a question: why was she here?

'You certainly didn't give home and hearth much of a chance,' Kitty said. Cressida ignored that, turning to glance back up the hill at Oliver, always a fast, efficient walker. It was odd he hadn't passed them yet. He stood by a stand of wind-battered pine trees, looking fixedly out across the loch, and Cressida felt a trickling, chilly awareness of danger. 'I wish Greville would show his face, or at least that I'd get a letter from Mama,' Kitty went on. 'I can't help worrying that Chas has taken a turn for the worse, and that's why he's not here. He was expected only days after us.'

'I'm afraid none of this is my affair, and I'm the last person you should be confiding in,' Cressida said.

'It *is* your affair,' Kitty snapped. 'You and Greville are still married.' She let out a mirthless laugh. 'You're a Nightingale of Crauford, like it or not. And I'm afraid we can't just be – you mustn't just forget us at your own convenience.' Her voice cracked with emotion. 'Listen, our father was the only person who could ever really manage Greville. I'm not blind to how truly badly he behaved, in every possible way, especially towards you, racketing around with those girls when you were first married, never even troubled by the prospect of discretion. *And* how mortifying it must have been when everyone found out about you and Cleveland at Annis's ball. But for you to have just walked away from the rest of us, Cressida – how could you? I viewed you as a sister. Mama accepted you as her own. She blamed herself for what happened and when you disappeared.'

'A *sister*?' White-hot rage flashed through Cressida. 'That's the first and only really disingenuous thing I've ever heard you say, Kitty Alasdair. You were very quick to dispel Annis's gossip about Jamie's parentage this morning, if I'm such a trusted sister.'

'Oh, stop trying to push me away by being an absolute hell cat,' Kitty shot back. 'Why don't you just listen for once? The scandal with you and Greville would have blown over if you'd let my stepmother handle it.'

Cressida stared at her, momentarily silenced. She relived the aftermath in a rush of intruding memories: sunshine on her back as she left Bute House in the early hours of the morning with only a bundle of clothing and a few shillings in pin money; the smiling young Irish soldier in a tavern on the Ratcliff Highway who had only just joined up; looking down to find the black pebble in her hand when the lots were drawn on the dockside at Plymouth – *Mistress O'Malley is to go*; the camaraderie and the stink of the troop ship; months later, facing a servant on the doorstep of the consulate in Lisbon, who had regarded her with roving eyes even as he lied to her face, under orders. *There is no one by the name of Lord Rosmoney here.*

'Don't look at me like that – you look as if you've seen the dead!' Kitty said. 'Annis may have turned you out of doors, although she always denied that, but I don't know why on earth you fled. Greville and you might even have been happy had you only allowed us the chance to bang your heads together. You probably wouldn't ever have been accepted by the highest sticklers, but when were either of you interested in their set? You were the only one who ever brought him contentment, if only he'd had the wit to admit that to himself at the time. Why did you have to make everything ten times worse by running away?'

'And how was I supposed to know of this startling personal generosity?' Cressida demanded. 'Most people in your shoes or Sylvia's would have washed their hands of me altogether. How on earth was I to know that you intended anything other than that?'

Kitty stared, her dark eyes alight with emotion. 'We

wrote to you on the night you were found with Cleveland, Cressida. Mama and me. I put the letters into Annis's own hands myself. Mama and I both begged you to go to Crauford House even if you couldn't face Greville.'

They stared at each other for a moment, Cressida unable to shake a sickening shifting sensation, as if the ground were moving beneath her feet. She didn't have time for the Nightingales: not here and not now. On her deathbed, she'd relive that night in Annis's ballroom, friend after friend turning their backs upon her. The following morning, she'd sat in her old bed clutching the sheets to her chest, wishing for a letter. And yet there *had* been a letter. Two of them, in fact. Annis had just opted not to give them to her. For a moment, Cressida was intensely aware of the scent of pine sap on the air. Then she turned and walked away up the hill, leaving Kitty to pick her way back down the stony path to the house alone. The sooner she and Ines left Drochcala, the better. Let Lascelles do his worst; let the Committee of Secrecy do their worst. They'd have to catch her first.

Cressida climbed the steep hillside so fast that all she knew was the heat in her thighs and calves and the sweat in her hair, forcing herself to smile when she met Oliver on the path. He stepped back to let her pass first where the path narrowed, and she caught the sharp, herbal scent of his shaving water.

'This is a fair hill, but you make short work of it.' Oliver spoke with forced civility: she'd have to get used to formality from him. They'd been on first-name terms in the days when his father was steward here, playing marbles in the laundry yard.

She smiled, still surprised at how much such familiarity hurt after so many years as a stranger to almost everyone she met. 'I walked a lot in the Levant, when it was a great deal hotter than this. One gets used to it.'

Cressida glimpsed movement at the edge of her vision and with a Herculean effort managed not to draw her knife. Side by side, she and Oliver stood watching as an adder slid away into the heather.

'Always better to let a small evil pass by unchallenged?' Cressida said, lightly.

'It's only that they're more afraid of us than we are of them. What's the point in taking a life for no reason?' Oliver did smile then as he had in their childhood: the frank, open smile in which it was hard not to see the ghost of Annis's father, who had brought Oliver's mother, Ann, to Scotland from Jamaica, long ago.

Reaching a cleft in the heather-fringed granite hillside rearing up on either side of them, they were rewarded with the vista ahead, a dramatic plunge of heathered fell tumbling down towards the loch far below. Eilean nam Fiadh rose up from the middle of the loch, where against all odds vivid green woodland had taken hold above granite flanks streaked with heather. A cutter emerged into view at speed, tacking into the wind, sails hauled in with expert precision as the boat turned.

'Oh, for heaven's sake,' Oliver said, letting his guard fall with disarming speed.

'Are they preventives?' Cressida said; the cutter was under sail now, but even from here she spotted space enough for eight oarsmen, which made ownership of such a vessel a hanging matter for anyone save the customs and excise men.

Oliver nodded, curt. 'Your eyesight's just as sharp as it ever was. That's Fraser MacGuigan and his boys – they've been all over the coast this summer and to be frank we could do without the disruption this evening. It's merry hell below stairs as I'm sure you can imagine, with Mrs Scudamore never knowing how many we'll have to dine from one evening to the next.' He turned to smile at her again, the unwary flash of anger now subdued: she could hardly blame him for it. 'I beg your pardon. There's been a great deal of free-trading this year, ever since the ban on distilling. The authorities in England don't like unrest in Scotland and they like it even less now, as you can imagine. Lord Perceval's death hasn't helped, to put it mildly. They're concerned about insurrection here just as they are about it happening everywhere else, and I suppose they're afraid the free and fair consumption of whisky will set Highland blood to an unhealthy boil. I must go back down to the house – I'd be a fool to leave his lordship to deal with Fraser MacGuigan.'

'Or Lady Bute, God forbid. Surely MacGuigan doesn't bother you all at Drochcala?'

Oliver was silent for a moment as they headed downhill, falling into an easy, practised stride on the narrow, rock-littered path. 'I'm afraid the Butes aid and abet free-traders whenever they get the opportunity: heaven forbid they should pay a penny of taxation to restock their own cellars.' He frowned. 'It's hardly as if they can't afford the duty, but instead they just legitimise the criminality. It wouldn't have happened in my father's day, but MacGuigan will want to search the outbuildings for any evidence of distilling or free-trading.'

'What an awful mess it all is.'

'The assassination of the prime minister?' Oliver spoke with a lilt of the sardonic humour she remembered from their youth. 'You're not wrong. MacGuigan's wife is nearly at her confinement, too, so he'll be in an even worse temper than usual. Please tell me about the Levant instead!'

They reached the second gate, and he held it open for her as they descended from the bare hillside into the plantation surrounding the white limewashed bulk of the house. Cressida smiled at Oliver over her shoulder and spun him an effortless lie about a man selling pomegranates from a basket in the ancient city of Petra. If only she really had lived such a life.

17

Cressida and Oliver reached the house, coming down the steep path to the gate leading into a dank, mossy courtyard criss-crossed with empty washing lines, and Cressida laid a hand on Oliver's arm, sensing his swift inhalation at her touch. Please heaven she'd never need to use that weapon against him, of all people.

'Shall I come in?' she asked. 'I'm very happy to. I always used to have the trick of soothing Mrs Scudamore's nerves.'

Oliver's smile was now a little tight. 'You could certainly cosset her out of a fury – after you'd had your ears boxed for shaving slices off the sugar loaf with my pocket knife, as I recall.'

It was as much of an invitation as she was going to get; Oliver had already opened a door shedding peeling green paint, his well-sculpted jaw set firm. Raised voices travelled along the stone-flagged corridor from the kitchens within. He stepped aside to let her go first, and Cressida steeled herself for the body-blow of familiarity when she stepped inside the vast warm room. There was a new range with the same copper pans hanging above it, the same scrubbed table still home to a bowl of costly lemons. A thin grey shadow of the Mrs Scudamore from Cressida's schoolroom years faced down the chief excise-man, MacGuigan, and two of his lads, one of whom had got a bootful coming ashore and was now dripping onto Mrs Scudamore's well-swept flagstone floor.

'Say that again, Fraser MacGuigan,' Mrs Scudamore invited, still just as fearsome as she had ever been, even if age and work had taken their toll. 'You might want to explain to Mr Tait and her ladyship here what you just saw fit to say to me.' Her eyes narrowed as she moved in for the kill. 'What was it again about the laundry room?'

MacGuigan was tall, with pale, sunburnt skin, prematurely thinning hair, a sour expression, and very much the air of a man at the end of his tether. He turned to Oliver, with the briefest of nods in Cressida's direction. Like a bloody fool, she'd spent so long anticipating her reception in the ton that Fraser MacGuigan's very ordinary embarrassment at the sight of her ignited a cold flash of anger.

'Well, Fraser?' Oliver said. 'You can speak in front of Lady Greville: we all know one another. What can we do for you and your men? Lord and Lady Bute have guests still to come. If you don't mind, we're all busy.'

'I've no doubt of that,' MacGuigan said, his gaze sliding from the new range to the little door that led to the scullery and the laundry room. 'We've had reports of whisky run up the loch-head in recent weeks, that's all, and someone making it in these parts.'

'Are you really suggesting that Drochcala has anything to do with such foolishness?' Oliver sounded dangerously harassed, not like Greville, who would have just sounded dangerous, but she must put that sort of damn fool thought to the back of her mind.

'He says there's talk of using the big laundry copper here to make whisky mash.' Mrs Scudamore glared at MacGuigan, who only shrugged.

'I'm sure you'll agree, mistress, that we've all got no choice but to do our jobs, and this is mine. If there's talk, I must follow up the enquiries. And no one else in these parts has a vessel large enough for distilling, legal or otherwise.'

'Mr MacGuigan,' Cressida said, all sweetness. 'May I ask what you and your men likely failed to notice as you tramped across the yard before making a mess in the corridor out there?'

She remembered him from a boy – a serious lad who had been sent up the loch every morning to get his learning from the curate at Sangobeg.

'I don't catch your ladyship's meaning,' MacGuigan said, averting his gaze from her own.

Cressida leaned against the whitewashed wall, folding her arms. 'No, very likely you wouldn't, although I've no doubt that Mrs MacGuigan would.' MacGuigan flinched at the sound of his wife's name on her lips, but he could go to hell. 'It's simple, Fraser. There isn't a single shift or sheet set to dry on the lines, and if you'll care to come with us to the laundry room you'll see why.'

Cressida swept past them all, exchanging the briefest flickering glance with Mrs Scudamore, who maintained a card-player's control over her features: according to Ines, that miserable crow of a woman Roberts had lost an entire thirty pence to Mrs Scudamore at gin rummy. MacGuigan said nothing and gave no indication that he was about to take advice let alone orders from a woman, but he followed all the same; Cressida was well aware of the heat of his gaze upon her from behind. Let him look: he couldn't touch.

A young scullery maid emerged from the laundry room just as they reached it, face flushed, linen cap askew as she dropped into a curtsey when she saw Cressida. With hair that particular shade of flame-red and those peat-dark eyes, she was almost certain to be a Tait. She went to Oliver's side, and he let one protective hand rest upon her narrow shoulder. A cousin, perhaps: Oliver's mother had only presented Mr Tait senior with one child before her death. He'd never married again, and had been far from the type to get bastards.

'Well, and what is the state of affairs in the laundry room?' Cressida asked the child. 'Is it really the case that my cousin has a houseful of guests and we can't wash *anything*?'

The girl flushed, not quite managing to hide a flash of irritation at such interference into her mistress's affairs. 'The copper's still not fit to be used, ma'am.' She explained as if to a very young child: 'Mr MacGuigan, that means we can't boil the water to wash, let alone make whisky mash. The lid cracked sheer in two and so it needs riveting. Sir.'

Cressida stepped aside to let MacGuigan pass. The laundry room was piled high to the narrow windows with heaps of yellowed, dirty linen. Even silks, satins and woollens vomited forth from lidded baskets to a degree that would have engendered blood-deep panic in any woman, from the youngest scullery maid right up to her mistress.

MacGuigan frowned. 'Very well.' Ignoring Cressida, he turned to Mrs Scudamore, who stood with her arms folded. 'I'll be staying out of your hair for now then, mistress, Mr Tait. For now, mind you. I'm not a complete fool.'

Mrs Scudamore curtseyed, and Oliver substituted a curt nod for a bow.

'I should think so too, Fraser,' Cressida said. 'Honestly, I know you're only doing your duty, but have some common sense at least.'

It was Ines, a little later, who gave voice to the creeping sense of disquiet that Cressida could no longer ignore. Cressida lay on her bed in the quiet time before dressing to dine, gazing out of the window at the shifting surface of Loch Iffrin, trying and failing to fit together the logic of what she had seen and heard. Sitting in the low chair beneath the window, Ines looked up from the stocking she was darning with tiny, featherlight stitches.

'I don't even know if it's free-trading that they should all be fretting about. This is a lonely coast and there's a war. I would bet on my life that they're smuggling more than black-market whisky and brandy: it will surely be information or worse.'

Cressida stared up at the embroidered bed canopy, uneasy: Ines was more likely to be right than not.

18

In the Loch Iffrin Tavern, three hours south of Drochcala, Lord Greville Nightingale leaned with his elbows on the polished bar, signalling for the bored but pretty girl behind the bar to pour him another whisky. She kept looking at him, but he wasn't minded to flirt. The whisky burned a track down his throat, which was just as well, considering the regrettable interviews in London with first his pompous ass of a brother, Crauford, and then their mother in her dressing room. He had revenged himself on Crauford by poaching Somers, who was relieved to serve a military man again. The latter had been far worse: Sylvia, still in her evening gown with a net shawl draped across her shoulders, looking up at him as she waited for her maid to come in.

You must deal with her before she ruins us all.

Cressida, for her part, had disobeyed him: of course she had. Never mind the fact she'd saved Chas's skin less than a week past, Greville felt the cold shiver in his belly that usually only came before a battle or some other killing. It was a sensation he enjoyed, especially when his opponent was a worthy one, which by God she was.

'Another whisky, if you please.' Greville shoved his greasy glass back across the bar. The redhead stopped smiling at the look on his face, her eyes darkening with fear.

Greville watched the girl's gaze flicker towards the door as she handed him the dose. A battered and ancient stag-horn hung above the lintel; Greville felt an odd sense of being hunted himself. There was something wrong in all this. He didn't watch the door swing open but he was very aware of the knife strapped to the inside of his hessian. There was a low rumble of voices outside and Greville got up and walked to the window. Pale sunlight glinted off the water outside, but the inn was a good way down a sandy lane from the little quay, and from this vantage point he couldn't see who was coming.

The girl's nerves at his presence told their own story: unless for the first time instinct was about to fail him, the Loch Iffrin Tavern was due to receive a company of free-traders. Information, after all, was just as highly prized on the black market as salt or brandy with no tariff.

There was an incoming racket of hobnailed boots on the yard-stones outside and a low rumble of Gaelic. When the door opened and the smugglers came in, Greville felt a cold touch at the back of his neck. He remained at the window, ready to draw the knife if he had to. He sensed the group of men assess and dismiss both him and Somers, who had come in through the far door. Greville watched sidelong and identified their broad-shouldered young leader, tallying not only the pale brown skin, immaculate linen and unfashionable cocked hat, but also the irritable watchfulness of a man who had more than enough on his plate, as if this free-trading mission were an extra task dealt out to him by a thoughtless employer. He looked up, glancing at Greville with a flash of recognition before turning away to speak to his men. That couldn't be possible: for a start, Greville had never been to this part of Scotland before. He didn't forget faces, either.

Byron followed them in, bareheaded to reveal dishevelled dark hair with a muffler thrown artlessly about his neck. The inn-girl stared, wiping the same tot-jug over again. You had to hand it to the man: he had the same effect on women wherever he went. Those charms would soon dim if Greville punched his teeth through the back of his throat.

Bloody fool, Greville told himself. *What century do you think this is?*

'There's hot water ready for you, my lord,' Somers said, with no more than a flickering glance at the newcomers behind which Greville sensed meticulous observation. 'Interesting company, if I might make so bold. Will you come and shave, your honour?'

'In a moment,' Greville said, girding his loins to dine at Drochcala in just a few short hours, at the same table as his lawful wife. Somers looked as if he was doing his level best not to laugh. He turned around to face the gathering again – red-faced, weather-beaten men flushed with the cold and the sea air, jackets of oiled wool steaming as pine logs smouldered in the great hearth. Save Byron himself, busy playing at smugglers, only one was familiar. He leaned on the bar in a long black greatcoat that might have once been another colour beneath years of grease and soot. Greville had last laid eyes on Lord Rosmoney's groom in the Devil's Acre, in that damp, stuffy bedchamber at the Oxford Arms.

John O'Neill glanced fleetingly across the tavern at Greville, not bothering to conceal an expression of extreme dislike. Did anyone else here know they were in the company of a man who had once blown up the English garrison in Dublin?

Byron himself paid no heed to O'Neill: he was far more intent on their young leader, who was quietly dispensing a series of instructions in Gaelic. Greville and Somers retreated to the window, acting on the same instinct; Somers had the sense to keep his mouth shut, watching as Byron and his free-trading friends gathered at the bar. The poet was far more at his ease here among lawbreaking Scots than he'd been in the Craufords' drawing room, so bound up in his own adventure that he hadn't yet acknowledged Greville. If it hadn't been for the lame foot, Greville wouldn't have put it past him to join the army.

'His lordship went out to tour the battlefields of Spain in 1809, as I understand.' Somers spoke in a well-practised low voice that would not carry, as if he'd just read Greville's mind.

'Tour but not fight,' Greville replied, curt; he hadn't been at headquarters when Byron visited. Like everyone else, he'd heard about it afterwards. He wasn't about to take Somers into his confidence, but in truth he reserved a particular depth of loathing for civilians drawn to battlefields when they had no business there.

Somers kept his mouth shut, not the sort to stand on

his dignity. Instead, he kept one eye on Byron and his companions. Greville flexed the fingers of his right hand and cast a quick glance at the girl behind the bar; she'd been looking at him in a certain way, she'd likely be willing. It would be wiser to quench this thirst before he encountered his wife. The girl smiled at him, and Greville briefly shut his eyes to imagine kissing her neck, her pulse gathering speed at his touch as he made short work of her skirts.

'Sir,' Somers said, quietly.

Byron had chosen to notice them at last, then: Greville looked up, irritable.

Byron smiled, granting the rare gift of his full attention, so paralysing to those who were not immune. 'Nightingale? I suppose I shouldn't be surprised to see you here. You're weathering out the summer with Annis Bute as well, I take it? What have you done to deserve that, Grev?' Byron spoke with the drawl he always used when holding one at a distance; after London, Greville wouldn't have put it past the man to cut him.

'Where my wife commands, I obey,' Greville said, enjoying the concealed flash of alarm in the poet's eyes as he spoke.

'Oh, please,' Byron said. 'You've never been anything less than a mastering fool, which as I've tried to tell you before is one of the many, many reasons you managed to mislay her for years.'

'Fuck off, George. I take it Caroline Lamb has rendered literally everywhere else too hot for you to bear, my dear?'

'God love her, but Caro does nothing by halves and one can't offend the proprieties,' Byron said, yawning. 'I've no desire to end in the shoes you were in, with nowhere to go but the Continent. Caro has no understanding of subtlety.'

'She's a pain in the bloody arse and always has been,' Greville said. As a child, he'd been thrashed no fewer than five times as a direct result of Lady Caroline's escapades. Briefly, he closed his eyes and thought of Jamie standing by the window in the library, all youthful clueless arrogance, either not knowing or not caring just how easily Byron might ruin them both with his favour. Three years ago, Greville had been standing in the same place when Crauford told him never to consider either Summercourt or Crauford House his home again. *You of all people*, Jamie had said.

Greville turned away from the window to find that Byron was now watching him with a flicker of something unreadable in his expression. He left women making fools of themselves to get just one glimpse of his face, and yet what would remain of the man once Cressida had finished with him?

Part Three

Eris, Goddess of Chaos, Strife and Discord

19

Cressida leaned on the wall outside the drawing room at Drochcala, closing her eyes as she listened to the jovial hum of voices and the clatter of Annis's lead-glass champagne coupes. Mrs Scudamore would still be spitting fire about the puddles of seawater Fraser MacGuigan and his men had left all over her clean flagstones; all the servants looked unusually harassed, and there was no footman to announce her. Cressida tasted salt upon her lips; she could leave, she and Ines could light a fire and bivouac in the wild places, among the heather and fog. In reality, she'd always be more at home out there.

The low hum of conversation stopped as she opened the door.

'*Good heavens.*' Lord Bute's familiar voice rang out into a thick silence, and Cressida only just had time to register Annis and Kitty on the chaise longue nearest the grate, Kitty immaculate in bronze lace. Annis was composed enough in a gown of pale grey silk, her coral beads bright in the firelight, but Kitty held onto her glass of champagne with both hands as though it were a life-raft. There was still no sign of Byron.

Bute rose arthritically from his armchair by the fire. His jacket was cut with an impeccable taste most people would have noticed before his increasing infirmity. 'My dear girl, you do look a jewel.' He took her outstretched hand in his own, kissing it.

'Thank you, I'm sorry to be late down. I was so indecisive about my gown, I've put my woman quite out of charity with me.'

'Well, you'll permit me to say your woman has done a fine job regardless,' Bute went on, waving one blue-veined hand in the direction of a fair-haired gentleman who stood examining the case of calf-bound miniature books. A little out of the way of the chandelier, he was half concealed by shadow.

Bute's well-trained smile didn't falter even for a moment as he turned to this new arrival. 'His Grace the Duke of Cleveland – Lady Greville Nightingale. You may be acquainted already, of course – our dear Cressida has been travelling in the Levant for so many years.'

Cressida caught her breath, turning with composure towards the man who had ruined her. If Bute hadn't just announced his name, she might have mistaken Cleveland for Arthur Lascelles as he was now: lean and muscular rather than the lissom creature Arthur had been in their first Season. As brothers, they were cut from the same cloth: unmistakable, and very expensive.

'Oh, come on, Bute, let's not beat around the bush,'

Cleveland said. 'Everyone knows Lady Greville and I are already acquainted.' Cleveland was angry, furiously angry. No one else had noticed, smiling and chatting in the candlelight: they didn't know him well enough. Had he shared her ignorance about Annis's guest list?

'My dear boy, you must forgive my poor memory.' Bute spoke with quelling good manners and Cleveland could do nothing but raise his glass in a lazy toast. Sitting by the fire with Annis, Kitty watched with her glass of champagne halfway to her lips. Making an obvious effort to collect herself, she answered Bute's enquiries about her youngest boy's career at Eton with a grateful smile.

'Delighted to see you, Cleveland.' Cressida faced him with the frank smile that had served her everywhere from a campfire in a Portuguese downpour to the Queen's drawing room. Annis must be relishing every minute of this.

'You're not,' Cleveland said softly, just as irresistibly badly behaved as ever. 'Not that I blame you.'

In Cressida's experience, most men of the highest nobility had grey teeth and a complete lack of charm, but Dominic Lascelles was that rare creature: next to a prince in rank, yet more handsome and appallingly charismatic than a half-pay officer. A man of medium height only, he was lean still and dressed with subdued good taste in a superbly cut jacket of charcoal superfine. His honey-gold hair was cropped close, his eyes the peat-water dark of the north – unusual, for a man of his fair colouring.

In the drawing room at Drochcala, Cressida allowed the Duke of Cleveland to raise her hand to his lips and then lead her a little apart from the rest. His own hands were beautiful – well shaped and strong, with a musician's sensitivity, as she recalled only too clearly. There was no pianoforte at Drochcala, and Cleveland needed to play as other men must eat. So why in hell's name was he here, rather than playing his own part as lord and master over his acres south of the border?

He smiled, looking bored, which in Cleveland was always lethal. He spoke in a low voice that only she could hear. 'If you think about it, you were quite fortunate that those footmen didn't interrupt us five minutes later, all those years ago, because otherwise I'd have been giving you the swiving you thoroughly deserved over your cousin's chaise longue, and then it would have been your delectable naked arse presented to those footmen, instead of only your magnificent tits.' He smiled then, revealing wolfishly sharp canine teeth.

Cressida returned his gaze with level calm, refusing to give him satisfaction. 'Goodness, I never expected you of all people to become one of those lewd old roués that girls are taught to avoid at parties, Dominic. Why aren't you settled yet with a nice complaisant duchess?'

'Still dagger-tongued, then,' Cleveland said, idly.

'Was a summer at Drochcala really your best offer? Why aren't you at Kielder: surely you haven't exhausted the Cleveland coffers?'

Cleveland's eyes hardened, emotionless. 'Do you really think I would, damn you?' Cleveland had always been serious about his land, if nothing else.

'No need to come the schoolmaster with me. It's just that

I don't see why you even came here if you haven't mortgaged your estates.'

'Come on, Cressida, stop asking shrewish questions. To confound the gossips, we must be on the most easy terms with one another – almost cousinly, one might say. Annis knows what she's doing.' Cleveland raised his glass to her again; she longed to smack the smile off his face.

'Please. Anyone would think you were actually sorry that I suffered all the consequences for our indiscretions whereas you got off like a lucky little pickpocket fast enough to outrun the law.'

Cleveland smiled again. 'I didn't escape consequence: I just knew from the start of our liaison that I'd be vanishingly unlikely to experience it. Whereas you can't say the same for yourself, can you?' He shrugged. 'You're no fool. You understood the risks. Here you are back in society once more – at Annis Bute's house party, no less. Was it really all so bad?'

Cressida ignored a series of rapid-fire memories: dodging grapeshot to raid the pockets of dead French infantrymen, cutting off a dead man's fingers to get at his rings, squatting in the mud at the side of the road to deliver the child of a Spanish woman in a slither of blood and birth-fluid, holding the damp solid bundle as the new mother forced herself to her feet because if she stopped marching, she'd die. Luckily for Cleveland, Annis's youngest footman, Tam MacCannell, chose that moment to appear at Cressida's shoulder with his gilt tray and she selected one of the ice-cold glasses, bubbles drifting within the straw-gold champagne. Cressida remembered him as a sturdy little boy turning somersaults in the laundry yard outside, invariably cheerful. Now, Tam wore a pinched expression, with dark circles beneath his eyes. All at once the atmosphere at Drochcala felt overwhelmingly malignant, and Cressida left Cleveland standing at the fireplace, just as he had once left her. There was, after all, nothing more to say. The room was too hot, airless like a sun-scorched bivouac in Spain. She had to get outside before the worst of the memories caught up. The champagne was cool and dry against her lips. *Breathe: just breathe.*

Her voice rang out like a bell: 'I think there'll be a fine display of St Elmo's fire over the loch tonight.' She stepped out of the drawing room and into the warm gloom of the lamp-lit corridor: *breathe.* The hallway faced west and evening summer light cast long shadows across a rough-hewn stone floor. Instinct forced her to turn as she reached the foyer and Annis emerged out of the shadows. It was so quiet, the faint susurration of Annis's silk gown all she could hear. Annis brought with her a refined signature scent, wisteria on a warm day in May.

'I hope you enjoyed that little scenario with Cleveland,' Cressida said. Annis took a quick step backwards. In the Peninsula Cressida would have taught her cousin better manners by now, but the rules were different here. 'I was squirming like a worm on a fish-hook. You must have looked forward to it for years.'

Annis leaned mannishly on the doorframe, folding her slender arms. 'Who on earth would say you didn't deserve it? If you want to return to society, you need to get this encounter with Cleveland over and done with. You know as I well as I do that you'd have argued me out of it. Listen, Cleveland and Lascelles's sister is soon to be out, and I know Cleveland means to bring her to their aunt in London for the Little Season. She's a shy girl, and it's thought best for her not to be overwhelmed in the spring. If you behave yourself now, by November your reputation might recover enough for people to accept you during the Little Season, too. Would you prefer this meeting had taken place then, under much greater scrutiny? Do you want this revenge of yours on Greville or not? Yes, a house party with Cleveland now might be unpleasant for you and, yes, it might be a little mortifying, but we won't go into all the spadework I had to do to restore the reputation of my own household after you absconded from it with everyone knowing you'd graced Cleveland's bed.'

'It was more usually his desk, to be honest – I used to think he was saving his bed for whichever poor soul becomes his wife,' Cressida said, recalling the movement of Cleveland's lean torso as he pushed gilded muslin skirts up to her waist in the candlelit library, and the taste of his best port upon her lips which, at nineteen, she had insisted on wanting. She remembered, too, how she used to hold on to the edge of the desk as Cleveland kissed further and further up her exposed bare thigh, wishing that she might open her eyes to look down upon Greville's dark curls.

Annis stepped forward and slapped her face, a burst of bright pain that was still so inconsequential that Cressida could have laughed, dimly aware of Tam stepping back into the shadows with his tray, his lips parted in shock. 'This isn't a game.' Annis spoke in a savage undertone. 'This is our lives.'

'I'm sorry, Annis.' Cressida fought the urge to press one hand to her burning cheek. 'Cleveland knew damn well he should never have taken advantage of my situation and I was a fool to let him. It's so interesting talking to Kitty after all this time: I'm surprised you allowed that to happen. What did you do with the letters that she and Sylvia wrote to me after I was caught with Cleveland? You must really have hated me. You could have just let the Nightingales manage the entire mess for you. Did you hope I'd be so ruined we'd never lay eyes on one another again? I'm so sorry to disappoint.'

'How dare you?' Annis spoke with precise enunciation. Two bright spots of colour appeared on her cheeks. 'I've always acted in your best interests, Cressida.'

Cressida smiled. 'Have you, though?'

'Take care with that sort of accusation,' Annis said, sweet as honey. 'We know so much about each other, after all.'

Cressida executed a measured curtsey before turning her back on her cousin, walking out into the vestibule, where she breathed in the suffocating wet-dog scent of boiling langoustine shells emanating from the kitchen. She'd be sorry for goading Annis before she was much older, but it was too late now. By God she must control herself by the time they all sat at table for the bouillabaisse and creamed spinach tart. She leaned against the wall, closing her eyes.

What hold had Annis got over Dominic Lascelles, Duke of Cleveland?

20

'Cressida?' Kitty Alasdair's no-nonsense tone was unmistakable. Cressida turned to find her sister-in-law standing in the hallway. She felt hunted in one moment and foolish relief the next. The row with Annis must have been audible from the drawing room, and probably the blow, too. Kitty raised both eyebrows as if to warn Cressida she could not escape the reckoning that was due between them for much longer. *Christ.*

Kitty's gaze flickered away from hers, and Cressida turned to face Roberts, who stood watching with her high-coloured face devoid of expression.

'Can I help, ma'am?' Roberts said to Kitty, talking past Cressida. 'Is something amiss?'

'Nothing at all,' Cressida said. 'Lady Alasdair and I are going outside to look at the St Elmo's fire.'

'I doubt you'll see any this evening, ma'am,' Roberts said, equal parts deference and hostility.

'We'll take our chances.' Cressida smiled, waiting for her to open the door.

Outside, they walked in silence to the edge of the lawn, pea-gravel crunching beneath their feet, the surface of the loch shining through a gap in the plantation.

In the cooler air Cressida's cheek stung where Annis had struck her.

'Goodness, isn't it beautiful here?' Kitty said, smiling out at the water with no sign that she must have at least heard raised voices. 'It's like another world.'

So, they were doing yet more commonplaces. 'A fairy realm, yes. That's what I always used to think when we came over from Ireland when I was a little girl. Roberts still hates me, as you can see.' Cressida tugged the gold-threaded Kashmiri wrap closer around her shoulders.

'Who can blame her?' Kitty folded satin-gloved arms across her chest. 'If a servant behaved as you did, she'd be dead on the streets or on the gallows for theft within a few months. Roberts is from a local family, is she not?'

'Yes. They came from a different part of the Highlands – quite far inland. Annis petitioned Bute to move them here to make a more honest and useful living – her words, not mine. Roberts usually spreads cheer and delight in town instead, but Annis is cutting corners in the servants' hall and so here she is.'

'Bright women with little education and even less occupation are the very devil,' Kitty said, and Cressida felt the warm flare of the old companionship between them, which Kitty then ruined by asking where Cressida had left her common sense. 'I wish you had just come to Mama the moment you set foot on English soil,' Kitty said, staring angrily out across the loch.

'How much of a monster do you actually think me?' Cressida demanded, distracted by a cold trickle of awareness: were they being watched?

'I wish you would finally understand that some of us actually care what happens to you, Cressida,' Kitty said. 'Annis doesn't have your best interests at heart and, if you ask me, she never did. When you were a girl it was so obvious to everyone how deeply she resented every penny she deigned to spend on your behalf. And very few people know of this, but Bute wasn't Annis's first choice.'

'What has that to do with anything?' Cressida said, irritably glancing over her shoulder, back towards the house, unable to shake the instinct that they were both under observation; the last thing she wanted to do was dwell on Annis's romantic affairs.

Kitty flushed. 'Quite a lot, I've always thought. When you were just a child and still in Ireland, Annis came quite close to marrying Crauford. You never knew that, did you? Crauford was young – not much older than Jamie and Chas are now. Mama especially didn't quite like the match, and so our father advised Crauford to look elsewhere before two dances developed into an understanding between them. Annis was never overjoyed at having you on her hands as I'm sure you knew only too well, but when you married into our family, you succeeded where she'd failed—' Kitty broke off. 'Cressida, after this house party is over, I sincerely hope you'll come with me to Summercourt as Mama's guest.'

'A necrotic limb is always best removed lest it kill the rest. Hush.' Placing one hand on Kitty's slender arm, Cressida turned to the plantation just as the crack of a snapped twig rang out, followed by a muffled sob.

Cressida moved first. She held up a hand for silence and Kitty advanced behind, holding her skirts out of the damp grass. Another sob rang out as they neared the stand of Scots pine, and Cressida dropped into a squat by a fuchsia bush that had gone wild, bursting forth from the bracken with spray after spray of plump pink-streaked flowers. The bush shuddered. Kitty would have to wait.

'Come out.' Cressida spoke in a tone that left no room for argument. The girl emerged from the tangle of fuchsia and fresh green bracken on her hands and knees, clad in a sturdy worsted gown with a hand-knitted shawl around her shoulders, her face tear-stained.

'Who does this child belong to?' Kitty demanded, turning to cast an accusatory glance back over her shoulder at the house.

'I've no idea. I'm fairly sure she's a Tait, though.' Cressida turned to the girl, who flushed scarlet. 'Come now: what's your name and what are you doing out here at this hour? You work in the house, don't you?'

The girl dipped another curtsey, showing Cressida a bold look from behind her tangle of red hair. 'My name is Lilias Tait, ma'am. I'm sorry, I hid when I heard you coming.' She glanced at the grass at their feet. 'I do work in the big house but I don't lodge there – I go away home each night to help my grandmother. She's old, and she can't do for herself. Only tonight, I didn't go. I couldn't.'

'Well, we'll tell no tales,' Cressida said, her gaze travelling irresistibly out across the glittering surface of the loch, away towards the open ocean. 'Why are you still here? Will your grandmother not be worrying for you?'

'Yes, but I didn't go because I was afraid.'

'Because you had to walk all the way home by yourself?' Kitty demanded, with a sharp glance at Cressida. 'Where do you live?'

Lilias turned to the loch, tugging the home-knitted shawl tighter around her shoulders. 'In one of the wee houses on the loch-side, milady. In fairness, I walk home every night along the path, but I—' She broke off: it was an admirable performance all round.

'Go on,' Kitty said, with the same brisk gentleness she would have employed had the girl scalded herself in the laundry room. 'What happened to frighten you? Anyone can see you're not one to startle at some silly trifle.'

Lilias swallowed, glancing down at her boots, unconsciously fidgeting with the skirts of her gown: a liar's move. 'I know it's only stories, milady,' she said, facing Kitty now with a wide-eyed stare. 'But they do say there's a presence on that path after dark. I don't believe in such unchristian stories, only the night before last when I went home I was sure there was someone else on the path with me. Except every time I turned back to look over my shoulder there was no one there.'

'I don't believe in ghosts either, but how unpleasant all the same,' Kitty said, darting another quick glance at Cressida. 'Must you really go alone?'

Lilias bowed her head, but not before Cressida glimpsed

the flash of suppressed scorn in her eyes. 'I could never put Tam or Stuart to the bother, thank you, milady, and I'd catch it if I tried. There is no one at the house this evening who doesn't have their work cut out. But you ladies should go back up to the house. It's hardly safe out here tonight.'

Kitty frowned. 'Someone must accompany you home, Lilias – if there is some footpad or desperate person in the area, it's no safer for you than it is for us.'

Lilias was now engaged in shoving at the pebbles with one booted foot in between maintaining a watch down the loch. If she was really afraid of someone on the path, why was her attention fixed out on the water? Following Lilias's gaze, Cressida spotted the long, low line of MacGuigan's cutter, a faint blur on the horizon: he was still cruising up and down the loch-head, then. She'd lay a monkey that Lilias herself had made the same observation.

'Milady?' Lilias Tait said to Cressida, still doing her best to pretend she wasn't watching MacGuigan's cutter, which was now sliding south across the loch, away from the narrows that led out towards the North Atlantic and the Pentland Firth. 'What shall I do?'

'Just be quiet, if you can bear it.' Cressida turned to Kitty, switching to French.

'The girl's right, you should just go back to the house – you're of no use here.'

'You can be as vile as you please, but you and I will still have a proper conversation about your future, Cressida, whether you like it or not,' Kitty retorted in the perfectly accented French she'd learned from the Parisian governess Sylvia had insisted upon for all her girls.

'Listen,' Cressida said to Kitty, switching back to English, not bothering to disguise her irritation. 'I'll walk the child home: I knew her grandmother when I was a girl and the path is easy to follow.' This was greeted with stunned silence by Lilias and Kitty alike. A single tern took off from the far side of the loch, rising up, wingbeat after wingbeat, a white reflection on the beaten silver water.

Kitty found her voice first, but not before reverting to French again. 'Don't be absurd, Cressida. How can you possibly? Listen, we're both angry but you and I must speak—'

Cressida smiled. 'I'm a married woman, Kitty – hardly a debutante straight out of the schoolroom. It won't be dark for hours. And you must admit that Annis won't be able to send anyone.'

Their eyes met as she spoke Annis's name.

'You can't.' Kitty opened her mouth, then closed it again as she realised who she was speaking to. 'What if it really isn't safe?'

'I'm hardly planning to cross Covent Garden in the middle of the night.' Cressida replied sweetly, quite sure that Lilias had been lying about her fears, and that as the mother of young children still in the nursery Kitty knew that too. She'd be damned if the girl hadn't meant to keep them away from the path and away from the loch altogether, which only made an early evening walk along it a more attractive proposition. 'Come along, Miss Tait,' she said, speaking now in English. 'If I remember your grandmother, she won't be delighted at your tardiness.'

*

Cressida gave orders for Lilias to walk ahead of her along the path that skirted the western reaches of Loch Iffrin. The child picked her way over tussocks and ridges of mud thick with pine needles, moving with deft speed in fourth-hand hobnailed boots, her long red hair loose and uncovered in such a way that would have marked her price in the Peninsula, even at twelve summers old. On their left-hand side, a tangle of bracken, saplings and scrub gave way to a sheer, granite drop down to the water: the tide was fairly high already. Across the water, the seaweed-clad lower slopes of Eilean nam Fiadh were almost completely concealed by swirling dark water as the tide pooled. To the right, young beech and pine trees reached for the summer sky of the far north.

Lilias turned, her freckled face a little flushed with the walk. Her gaze shifted, wary. 'You need not come any further with me, ma'am. I shouldn't have put you to this much trouble in the first place. I'll go the rest of the way home myself.'

Cressida smiled cheerfully. 'The devil you will, my dear. So when exactly are we to experience this spectre? Here, or a little further up the path?'

'I don't know that we will, ma'am,' Lilias said, with a flare of sly scorn. 'Doubtless it was just a pack-trader I heard hiding in the bushes the last time I came this way – like as not the man was drunk. I – I wish you'd just let me go on alone. I'll be skelped for putting your ladyship to all this trouble.'

'If you've any sense in that head, you'd fear a pack-trader

far more than any phantom. Coming upon a man alone and without protection is by far the most dangerous thing that might happen to you or me, so let's hear no more of this melodrama about ghosts,' Cressida said, not unkindly. 'The next time some tuppence ha'penny free-trader orders you to stir up gossip about phantoms among the fools above stairs, do make a better fist of it, especially with Mr MacGuigan scenting blood as he is doing. You'll all need to make very sure that no intrepid guest travels this path at night, won't you? What is it, whisky or salt?'

Lilias's mouth fell open and she reached convulsively for her apron, twisting the faded linen in her fingers, obviously a childhood habit she hadn't quite let go of. 'Ma'am—'

'Don't stand there and lie to my head,' Cressida said, pleasantly. 'I couldn't give a flying damn if my cousin's entire household is otherwise employed with some sort of bloody predictable free-trading scam. It might be salt, I suppose, but let's face it, it's probably whisky, considering they've banned distilling again completely this year. I don't care. Who is this spectre?'

Lilias shrugged, looking sideways at Cressida. 'They call him the Gentleman, but I don't know who he is. None of us do. And, mistress, truth be told I think my cousin Oliver and everyone else here are fools to have anything to do with him. It's not to do with whisky, I'm sure. Why would they caulk all the barrels with pitch if they were only free-trading that? They never do, usually. How can they trust this Gentleman anyway? Whoever he is, he's like to be English, with a name like that.' Lilias bit off the end of her sentence, but her chin was set firm.

'You think it's foolishness, having anything to do with this person?' Cressida probed. 'But because you're a lass, and only twelve, no one ever listens to you?'

'Thirteen, mistress.' Lilias pushed at the gravel with the toe of her boot. 'And I think it's like to lead to the gallows, myself.'

'More so than common or garden free-trading?' Cressida asked. 'I suppose you're right. But if you're going to get caught up in this sort of mess whether you like it or not, you'd better become a sight better at lying, do you understand? Shall we go on? Your grandmother will indeed be wondering where you are, and I'd as lief get back to the house to join everyone for supper, if that suits your convenience?'

Lilias opened her mouth and then closed it again. 'Yes, ma'am.'

21

The cutter slid south towards the loch-head at a good lick and a damp sea breeze sliced across Greville's left cheekbone as he sat in the thwarts with George Byron, who was leaning back against the shrouds with the breeze tearing the dark hair away from his forehead. Somers sat some distance off, whey-faced as he repeated the Lord's prayer between bouts of vomiting.

Greville spoke idly over his shoulder to one of the seamen tightening the sails; the man looked to be in his forties, with faded reddish hair. He had the pinch-faced look of someone who endured regular bouts of hunger. 'You're making good time,' Greville told him. 'But is it not quicker to take the lobsters overland? It seems a fair risk to sail up around the Pentland Firth, even at this time of year.'

The seaman cleated off his line. 'Aye, sir, it is, but overland it would take weeks, which is fine for wool but too long for rock-lobsters, sir, and the waters here are rich with them this year, whereas it's slim pickings on the east coast. They fetch a better price at Fraserburgh, too.' He treated Greville to a disingenuous smile. 'It's not far to Drochcala now, sir. That's the village you can see there.'

He turned away to answer the call of the shorter seaman, who had a clay pipe clamped between yellowed teeth, leaving Greville alone with Byron once more.

'I wonder what they're actually doing here,' Byron said, apparently untroubled by the prospect of finding himself at the bottom of the loch if they were overheard. 'It's probably free-traded whisky, isn't it? And if anyone asks why a trading-vessel bound for Fraserburgh and then Archangel is sailing the wrong way down Loch Iffrin, delivering us to Drochcala offers the perfect convenient excuse, does it not?'

'Only *you* could manage to fall in with free-traders on the way to a house party, George,' Greville said. 'But I wish you would shut up, unless you want a knife between your ribs.'

Byron grinned at him. 'You realise I'm meant to fête your wife all summer and bring her back into society? I might have her as well, you know. I've always fancied the prospect.' Byron glanced down at his beautiful long white fingers. He had the hands of a true aristocrat, idle as hell. 'It must be like taming a wild horse. Careful handling at all times but worth the effort.'

'Much you'd know about that,' Greville said. He'd chop those hands off, then his cock.

Did Byron even suspect how Lascelles and Cressida in her turn both meant to use him, or rather his fame? God, Greville hated lying, even as he wearily constructed a tale as close to the truth as he dared risk.

'I have little enough desire to endure a house party with my wife, but the Cheltenham tragedy between us has gone on long enough. It simmered nicely while I was out in Spain, but now she's come home and I can't risk letting scandal-broth boil up in the face of my family. The boys will weather it, but the sort of talk Cressida's return is bound to generate will hurt my sisters unless she and I put up a united front. Not that this is any of your affair. Haven't you enough scandals, dealing with Caroline Lamb?'

Stay away from my wife. The unspoken words hung between them.

Byron watched him. 'For God's sake, Grev, just arrange a formal separation if you want to silence the gossips. Why put yourselves through this charade? It's absolutely bloody and I still don't understand what you're playing at.'

'There's nothing to understand and if you think a high society divorce would silence anyone, you're a greater sapskull than I took you for.' Greville fixed his gaze on the bracken-cloaked fellside rearing up from the dark waters of the loch. What sort of dissembling shit had he become, anyway? This kind of manipulative carry-on was exactly what Greville had always liked least in Lascelles and in Cressida herself. Dishing up such fairytales right in the face of a man who had endured the same schoolroom dancing lessons revolted him. The fact was, Lascelles and Cressida were two of a kind. If Greville had anything resembling a choice, he would have told Arthur Lascelles where to shove all these lies. Instead, there had been no choice, not just because of Jamie, but because of his own decisions and that extremely civil court martial. Instead of sunlight moving across the loch, all he could see was that rubble-strewn street in Badajoz, where dark blood had splattered across the cobblestones, and he couldn't hear the people shouting at him to stop. The fact he would do it again in a heartbeat was no consolation.

'Although perhaps I have it all wrong,' Byron went on, not looking at Greville but out across the water. Theirs was the only boat on the loch that night, and the quiet and sense of solitude was overwhelming. 'Perhaps in truth you don't actually want to be separated from Cressida?'

'Shut up, George.' Greville passed him the hip flask, stretching out the fingers of his right hand, even as he felt a ghost of an impact, driving that fist over and over again into the face of the guardsman who had dared lay hands on his wife in the streets of a Spanish town.

22

Cressida left Lilias with her grandmother in the slate-roofed bothy and closed the door behind her, leaning on the painted wood for a moment with her eyes shut. The elderly Mistress Tait had been stewing herbs for the Drochcala stillroom. Immersed in fragrant clouds of steam, she was embarrassingly pleased to lay her eyes on Lady Cressida once more. She didn't believe a single word of all that nasty gossip no matter what anyone said. Lord help the poor woman if she ever heard the worst of it.

Cressida reached the spot where she'd stopped to take Lilias to task earlier, suppressing anger as she eyed the tumble of fresh green ferns and lichen-covered rock. Any preventive officer worth his salt would have seen through Lilias's inept little ghost-tale just as easily as Cressida herself had done. No doubt the reprisals for giving away such incriminating information would be as swift as they were brutal.

Cressida hitched up the damp and filthy skirts of her

gown and stepped off the path – the incline was steep and sudden, and she had to climb to reach the exact position Lilias Tait hadn't been able to help herself looking at: a cleft left by the tumble of rocks, mostly concealed by bracken and beech saplings. Climbing higher, Cressida adjusted her skirts with an irritable sweep. The flagstones downstairs at Drochcala were always freezing, so she wore jean boots instead of satin evening slippers. Even so, her feet were now sodden, her heels rubbed raw. She reached into the cleft with one hand, her fingers brushing against cold metal. Clinging onto the tough grass, she peered at a faint bronze gleam. So here was the lid of the laundry copper, and the very good reason why Annis had ordered the table to be laid with her second-best linen.

Big houses like Drochcala had substantial laundry rooms and large coppers for boiling linens. A laundry copper was good for heating whisky mash, too. They'd probably steeped the barley in it first and laid it out across the wide, flagstoned floor to sprout. That must have been several weeks ago now, but with MacGuigan suspicious enough to search the house, all evidence had vanished. The lid of the laundry copper had gone, too: even the most suspicious preventive couldn't accuse Drochcala of making whisky mash now. Cressida left the copper lid hidden, stepping backwards onto the path. Lilias Tait had lied to Fraser MacGuigan, telling him to his head that the copper had gone away to be mended because it couldn't be done at Drochcala. Instinct told Cressida that the Butes knew about the practice of distilling duty-free whisky on their estate. Very little escaped Annis where the potential for a profit was concerned, and especially not with dangerous secrets to hold over others into the bargain. *I know so much about you, after all.* Annis had smiled when she said that. To hell with it: she was here to get what she needed from Byron, no more and no less, not to meddle in what was best left alone.

Less than half an hour later, Cressida had almost reached the furthest extent of the gardens when the plantation of birch trees concealing the loch from the path thinned out, revealing glinting stretches of water. She heard faint splashing and a male voice, quickly silenced. At this time of the evening, anyone with lobster pots in the loch might well be out to haul in their catch and then to move the pots to a fresh trapping ground, but in that case why the need for hushed voices?

Go back to the house. Instead, Cressida stood and watched the tide pooling beyond the beech trees. Something was definitely wrong. A familiar chill prickled all the way down her arms and across the backs of her hands, then down each fingertip. Stepping off the path, slipping a little on the damp leaf mould in her jean boots, she held on to one of the silver birch trees, now with a much better view of the loch. As usual, gulls hunted along the fringes of the water, graceful shapes tossed in the air like so many children's paper cut-outs, pale against the dark green backdrop of the wooded hillside rearing up from the pebbled shore. There was no sign at all of MacGuigan's cutter.

In her mind's eye, Cressida retraced her steps. The loch-side path split only a few yards before it wound past the Taits' waterside home if you were approaching from Drochcala and the loch-head. Cressida hadn't taken the other path for years – it veered off through the trees at a sharp left, a stony trail down to a deep cleft where Drochcala often kept a small wooden dinghy. Out on the water, the inlet was concealed by outcrops of rock and trees unless you sailed directly alongside.

Staring out across the loch, listening to the lowered voices of men in hiding, Cressida's past and present merged. She breathed in the orange-flower warmth of Rosmoney's cologne, expensively floral and just as redolent of the old century as his Jacobite rebel politics. She felt his presence beside her, even as the years fell away and she was a child once more. When the tide was too low to moor further up the loch near the house, Rosmoney would put in here instead and carry her upon his shoulders along the bracken-lined path back to the house, slate rooftops just visible beyond and between the spreading dark green canopy of Scots pine.

Do the smugglers come this way after dark, Papa?

They use this very mooring, but you need have no fear of them whilst I am here. She recalled the timbre of his voice with painful intensity. Like her, in Ireland Rosmoney was not Irish enough, and in England, too Irish by far. When they were alone together he retained the lilt learned from his nurses and from the people at home. The old, cold fear seeped through her at his absence. In truth, that secret, hidden part of her had been terrified ever since the moment Rosmoney had walked out of that dark room in a Dublin tavern with a careless smile over his shoulder as he left her.

I'll come back for you, a linbh. My child.

Get a bloody hold on yourself. Cressida forced away the

memory, gripping the tree trunk as she gazed out across the loch, listening to the men in hiding at the running mooring. It was a fine place of concealment for anyone lying in wait on the water. Who were they hiding from?

Crouching in damp undergrowth, Cressida watched the loch from her vantage point near the cliff-side path, inhaling the sulphuric reek of seaweed exposed by the retreating tide far below. And then, even as she watched, a small yacht cleared the narrows, tacking across the approach to the loch-head. Cressida's thighs ached and she shifted her position with practised care. Her gown was in a hell of a state, but Ines was perfectly capable of kindling a fire on the lawn and scrubbing a gown in an old cook-pot with her own supply of Marseille soap, even if she would spit pins about it.

Cressida watched as the yacht tacked, making a neat turn in the water as she caught a glimpse of starched white. A man in his shirtsleeves stood up at the bow, holding on to the shrouds; several others sat in the stern.

As the yacht sailed on, Cressida caught a clearer glimpse of the three figures who sat next to each other on the port side. She knew the casual set of one man's broad shoulders immediately, the graceful, arrogant tilt of his chin as he turned his attention to the mainsail, even though he wasn't sailing the boat himself. Cressida looked away and fixed her gaze on the green bulk of the mountainside on the far side of the loch.

Greville had come.

Quick heat pulsed at her core and she felt a sudden awareness of her own body, a wicked need to be touched, like a country girl with her first sight of a handsome officer at an assembly ball.

She had to look away from the loch and the boat and the bloody man and concentrate on her breathing. How dared he actually come here? When she could bear to look again, the yacht was now concealed behind the bulk of the headland and a dark mass of trees overhanging the water, even as Cressida realised that she could no longer hear the sound of voices from the inlet, or indeed any sound at all that would betray the presence of a boat so nearby: MacGuigan was lying in wait with a full crew of preventives.

Oh, Greville, use your head for once. As if guided by an invisible hand, Cressida picked her way down through the trees towards the loch, failing to crush overwhelming exasperation. Snatching up her skirts in one hand, Cressida removed her boots one by one in order to pick her way down the slope towards the pebbled beach in silence. So that was a pair of good stockings ruined as well as this gown. Breathing hard, she reached the small wooden boathouse, heart racing despite the fact that she couldn't be seen from the mooring. MacGuigan and his men would spot her, though, when she got that launch out onto the water, but it was a risk she had to take. He'd recognise the boat, all right, with the distinctive small brown lateen sail, but taking it out at this time was not a criminal act: someone from Drochcala would check the lobster pots most evenings around dusk before moving them to a new location and, as yet, no one had been out tonight.

She unlatched the boathouse door and strode over to the launch, hauling it across the floorboards with a rush of wooden hull grating against floorboard, so loud that she stopped to take a deep breath, steadying herself. You couldn't make an omelette without breaking eggs, and even at this moment, MacGuigan and his men might be rowing out towards that yacht with Lord Greville Nightingale in it.

Against Cressida's better judgement, she hauled the launch out onto the pebbles with a spray of muttered curses, almost up to her ankles in cold water before she had taken more than a handful of steps, even as she thanked providence for a high tide. Climbing aboard, Cressida shipped the oars and rowed away from the shore. She put down the rudder before stepping the mast and hauling up the little brown sail. It was odd how even after all these years every movement felt as natural as riding a horse. She'd spent hours out on the loch with Oliver in those girlhood summers, but this was not the moment for reminiscence.

The wind changed, and Cressida altered her course with another quiet volley of blasphemy. She would now have to tack away from the yacht, even as MacGuigan and his men waited, hidden on the mooring but ready and waiting for this to happen, MacGuigan with that fanatical light in his eyes once more. How had he known that there were free-traders expected? Cressida glanced over her shoulder. Pearlescent violet jellyfish bloomed close to the surface like a flock of otherworldly creatures as she sailed past the inlet leading to the mooring. She caught a glimpse of MacGuigan's cutter, low to the water. He had a lot of men with him, which was an evil sign, but that at least would slow him down.

The yacht tacked away from her, keen to avoid contact, but Cressida had foreseen that and gybed with a swift yank of the tiller, coming up alongside her instead. Her husband, Greville, leaned on the gunnels with his shirtsleeves rolled up to reveal lean, sun-browned forearms, eyebrows slightly lifted in a sardonic question he didn't bother to voice. Byron lounged at his side, drinking from a hip flask bound in waxed string, glancing from her to Greville and back again with ill-disguised mirth.

'Oh God,' he said. 'This is going to be exquisite.'

23

'Shut up, George.' Cressida spoke across him, and said nothing to Greville at all, serving him a dose of his own cold hauteur. Then she allowed her gaze to travel from crewman to crewman, taking in first John O'Neill and then Oliver Tait. The sight of O'Neill froze her to the bowels, and Oliver just met her sardonic gaze with the curt nod of a man who knew only too well that all of this was a bad idea, but had little choice about his part in it.

'May I suggest you get your load overboard if you want to see the end of the week?' Cressida asked. 'If they still hold the assizes at Inverness on a Friday, most of you will be hanged on Saturday morning. MacGuigan is waiting by the mooring.'

Eight men stared at her in silence, most of them familiar faces from her girlhood summers. Greville was otherwise engaged in scanning the loch-side and priming his pistol.

John O'Neill glanced across the thwarts at Oliver. 'I'd listen to her if I were you, Tait,' O'Neill said.

She'd deal with O'Neill later, somehow, not that she could really blame him for Rosmoney's machinations. There was no such thing as a former rebel, after all, English, Irish or Scots. She felt a quick, hot flash of anger at the way they had all relied on Lilias to keep Annis's guests off the path and away from the loch.

Cressida sighed. They all watched her, moonstruck. 'MacGuigan's on the running mooring: I suggest you move.'

'No, he isn't,' Greville said, peaceably, casting a quick glance over his shoulder at the glittering surface of the loch-head, beyond which the slate-roofed turrets of Drochcala rose up from behind a dark green sweep of Scots pine. 'He's over there.' Sure enough, the preventives' cutter sliced across the water with deadly speed, MacGuigan coxing his men with a series of hand-signals as they rowed.

'Now!' Oliver snapped, dragging one of the barrels from beneath a covering of burlap and heaving it overboard. The barrels were all roped together like lobster pots, the dog-head screws liberally coated with pitch: Tait was taking great care to allow nothing to foul the contents, then. Oliver thinks of everything, Annis always said. Either he'd anticipated the need to drop his cargo at sea, or the barrels contained something that somebody really didn't want to get wet. The men heaved the barrels overboard one after the other. They stepped around the snaking line with practised wariness. No doubt they'd all heard of, if not seen, a man, woman or child dragged overboard and straight to the bottom of the loch with that seaweed-coated rope tangled hard around one ankle. Then everyone moved in the same instant, and Cressida was dimly aware of strangled shouting across the water from MacGuigan's cutter. If he or any of his men had seen or heard the barrels go in, all this effort would have been for nothing. MacGuigan certainly wouldn't stop at sending a man to dive down after them. Cold instinct forced her to duck at almost exactly the same moment as Greville boarded the launch in one quick, fluid movement. All she was aware of was the salt-scented heat of his near presence and the faint, familiar aroma of his rosemary shaving water.

'Get down.' He spoke with quiet urgency, and now he was between her and MacGuigan's cutter, shielding her with his body and both arms around her in a protective embrace, and what in Christ's name did he think he was doing? A pistol-shot rang out, the sharp report echoing from one side of the loch to the other even as familiar, sulphuric yellow-tinged smoke rolled across the water. She felt the awareness in his body echoing the answering pulse of her own: battlefields and smoke and blood and dying men, and then the impact.

Greville swore quietly.

She turned around to face him, still in his arms; he'd closed his eyes now, thick dark lashes against sun-bronzed skin. 'You've been hit, you fool.'

'I know.' Only then did he release her and stand up again, with one hand pressed hard against his upper left arm, crimson blood blooming on the fine white linen between his lean fingers. He turned to address MacGuigan and his men in their rapidly approaching cutter with such a spray of soldierly invective that they stood silent and frozen to the last man. It wasn't MacGuigan holding the pistol but a younger lad, white-faced and shaking, his preventives' uniform jacket too big across the shoulders.

MacGuigan's cutter came up alongside the launch, which itself was alongside Oliver Tait's yachtful of Scottish smugglers and O'Neill. By now, they'd finished jettisoning their cargo and every one of them stood watching MacGuigan's men with perfectly manufactured expressions of insolent horror. Cressida watched as Greville let go of the wound and swung an oar into the cutter; this was no time to be a competent female: let Greville make use of what he was. Which he now did, to stunning effect.

'What do you actually think you're doing?' he said to MacGuigan in frozen aristocratic accents, and for the first time Cressida had a real idea of how Greville's men might perceive the indolent rakehell she'd married.

'It's what *they're* doing that I'm interested in, forbye,' MacGuigan said, squinting into the westering sun as he jabbed a finger at Tait and his men; O'Neill had retreated into the background, just as sullen, silent and salt-stained as the rest of Tait's men, with no trace of the leader about him. Byron had adopted the same persona: he must have been helping with the barrels and now stood with Tait's men, green strips of seaweed clinging to his forearms, and looking far more at ease here than he had done at the Craufords' dining table in London.

'I don't give a damn what they're doing. What induced you to fire upon a potting boat?' Greville spoke with alarming calm; arms folded as scarlet blood bloomed on his sleeve. Cressida tore a strip off the fine muslin hem of her gown and got up, balancing against the sway of the launch as she held the wad of frilled fabric to his wound, which needed pressure applying to it even if Greville was too busy asking difficult questions of MacGuigan.

Byron looked at her then with a warning writ clear across his face: where else did a woman learn how to manage a gunshot wound but in the train of an army? Irritated, she knew he was right, but what other choice was there? Inexorably, she recalled Greville's last mocking warning to her in London: *If everyone else finds out you whored your way across Portugal and Spain with half the British army, I'd imagine you'll become more of a liability than an asset. It's a risk, isn't it?*

Cressida pressed a little harder as she held the compress to the wound, but Greville didn't flinch, even though it must have hurt like the devil. This was what they were bred for, was it not? Hard men who could deal out pain just as easily as they were able to shrug it off themselves. A thick, unpleasant silence fell and for a moment all that could be heard was the tide lapping against three hulls.

'If it's a potting expedition then I'm sure Mr Tait will have no objection to my men taking a look at the yacht.' MacGuigan dealt out a wintry smile. 'Will your lordship be so good as to explain your part in it?' His gaze travelled to Cressida, resting on her for one moment too long.

Cressida stared back with bald aggression that in the baggage train would have seen her slapped, punched or worse by a man of MacGuigan's ilk, before retreating into unholy glee at the prospect of watching Greville deal with this. He did so, directing MacGuigan to search the yacht if he so chose, with a sarcastic enquiry about how long this would take, given that Lady Bute and her guests were now waiting on MacGuigan's pleasure before the household might dine. MacGuigan and his men boarded the yacht, stepping through the launch on the way, so that Cressida clung to the thwarts as the small craft rocked; a good half of the men nodded at her as they passed, some with a mumbled apology, every last one averting his gaze from the ruined state of her evening gown.

Oliver spat over the side of the boat when the last man boarded, his face devoid of expression, and Cressida hoped to God that they really had jettisoned all incriminating evidence. Hangings were wildly unpleasant at the best of times, especially if the victim of judicial execution was a man one had played knuckle-stones with as a small child. Overhead, a gull keened and wheeled above the loch. Apart from the sound of footfalls, everything was silent as MacGuigan's men went over Oliver's yacht like rats through a grain-store. Finding nothing, MacGuigan retreated, with a curt warning to Greville about taking care who he chose to convey him down the loch next time, as there were some habitual lawbreakers in this part of Scotland who might see him before a magistrate if he wasn't awake on every suit. Greville paid as little attention to that as he had to MacGuigan's insincere apology for the gunshot wound. They all stood watching as MacGuigan's cutter shot away across the loch, out towards the narrows and bound for the village of Droch Cala as it clung to the water's edge in a scatter of whitewashed stone buildings with moss-edged slate rooftops.

'What magistrate would even bother to hear a case

against a Nightingale of Crauford?' Cressida said, speaking into a potent, unpleasant quiet. 'His lordship is immune from the effects of justice. In the meantime, the rest of you may all thank me at your leisure.' She cast a look at Greville and then at Byron, who was now standing alone wearing a shuttered expression, leaning against the foremast, with the rest of Tait's men having drifted away from him, O'Neill included. And then all else was forgotten and there was no one but her and Greville on the loch, beneath the sky, both of them sitting in the launch, facing each other across the thwarts. With absent-minded grace, he held the wad of bloodied fabric to his wound, doing the fallen angel act that she recalled only too well from all the dawns they had shared before sleeping – ball after rout party after masquerade.

Cressida looked away across the green, silver-tinged surface of the loch, aware that Greville had followed her gaze to the pebbled shore of Eilean nam Fiadh, driven by the same instinct. As they watched, a young stag emerged silently from the tangle of birch trees, unnoticed by anyone else on the boat. Cressida caught her breath, only too aware Greville was now watching her with a darkling expression. An answering flare ignited within her at his presumption: how dared he judge anything she chose to do? He of all people. He got to his feet and moved with catlike ease into the yacht. Cressida shoved off with one of her oars and pushed the tiller away from her, turning back into the wind, which, thank God, had not died even if so much else had.

24

Half an hour later, Cressida had sailed to shore and hauled the launch back into the boatshed, collecting her boots on the way. The tide had by now gone out a little but she only had to drag the launch a short way across the pebbled shore and above a tideline of stinking ochre-yellow seaweed to the doors of the boatshed. A splash echoed in the half moment before Cressida realised that the yacht hadn't tacked again. The tide was high, so rather than sailing to the running mooring that MacGuigan had now vacated, Tait must be running the yacht up the loch-head and sailing right down to the iron gates of the garden itself, where a trench filled at high water among a network of beaches and natural inlets.

And someone else was swimming to shore. Watching between the tangle of birch branches, she glimpsed a dark head and a pale arm slicing the water. One of the passengers had climbed overboard, striking out up the loch towards the house: *Byron.* Of course he would make an entrance, sure of his audience as ever. In the water, his limp had never mattered.

With a swift glance out towards the loch, she took the path back to the house at a brisk pace, pausing only at the sound of a wet scrabble as Byron hauled himself ashore, and now faintly laboured breathing as he scrambled up the rock face to her right. Climbing hand over hand, he let out a satisfied gasp, as if he'd just spent his seed. Not someone who was used to moving in silence, but when had he ever cared to do that?

She recalled a long winter weekend at Newstead as a new bride, wandering alone in overgrown gardens glittering and white with hoar frost. At the sound of footfalls, she had on instinct stepped away from the narrow cinder path, crouching behind a lichen-covered wall. A fair-haired under-gardener hurried away from the potting shed with flushed cheeks, still adjusting his plain linen necktie. Moments later, Byron had followed with languid carelessness, because it made no real odds to him if anyone found out that he had been rutting his own staff.

You ought to be a damn sight more careful of Greenham's reputation, let alone his neck, Cressida had hissed at him, climbing back over the wall. *What if it hadn't been me?*

He'd laughed, linking his arm through hers. *But who on earth else would be hiding behind a wall in my garden like a naughty little girl escaping a thrashing?*

She'd found herself unable to explain even to him why she'd hidden at the sound of approaching footsteps; an echo from a nightmare had accompanied her on every long, dark night since that morning in the dusty library at Rosmoney when she had sat beneath her father's desk, waiting and waiting for him to come home.

You wouldn't understand, George, she'd said at length, fixing her gaze on the hard-pruned rose bushes lining the path, sugared with white frost.

He'd grinned at her, irresistible as ever, even though he did not understand and never could. *Oh, come now, what's really the matter, Cressy? Never mind my silly little peccadillos. Am I such a bad host that you are driven to entertaining yourself with solitary walks, or has Greville been neglecting you again? Honestly, the boy has no sense whatsoever. Don't say I didn't warn you.*

Without a sound, Cressida now edged away from the narrow path into deeper cover, concealed by bracken. Gaining the path at last, Lord Byron rose from the undergrowth like a male Venus Anadyomene, dripping seawater, a sodden lawn shirt clinging to the well-muscled expanse of his chest and belly, breeches plastered to his thighs. He wore a simple knotted scarf in lieu of a cravat, and soaking dark hair sent runnels of water down his neck. She remembered very well just how much effort it cost to maintain his appearance, but it was a job well done

And as Cressida watched in silence, George Byron smiled up at the summer night: the only man save Greville Nightingale and Arthur Lascelles who knew where she had really been in all those lost years. In truth, Byron was just as capable of ruining her this summer as she was of ruining him, and for her, this time it would be for ever. And then he turned the full force of his attention to her, droplets of water clinging to the ends of his dark lashes like so many tiny pearls.

Byron stepped closer and then cupped her face between his hands in a movement that felt so natural tears started to her eyes. 'Cressy, you look like hell. Do you think I'm here for the good of my health?'

He released her, genuinely offended by the state of her appearance. He spoke as if the entire adventure with MacGuigan had never happened; she brushed away the fact that Lord Greville Nightingale had just taken a bullet for her. 'Cleveland might be good value, but you know very well I find Annis Bute an untenable bore. She's bloody fashionable, but it sticks in my craw to give her the satisfaction of my coming here.' He allowed himself a delicate shudder. 'I was all for crying off but I came because I like you, Cressida, and by God you do need my help, but throw me a rope. Never mind what in hell's name you were doing out on the loch just now, but you're alone and unescorted on a loch-side path at six o'clock in the evening, looking like a baggage-train trull. What are you thinking?'

Cressida digested the fact that Byron had come here, in his own mind, to revive her reputation, when officially she had agreed to come here to engineer the opposite fate for him. Lascelles was always finding new ways to demonstrate not only just exactly how much of a shit he could be, but also how low he could really make others stoop.

'You came here because Caroline Lamb won't leave you alone and you're starting to find it embarrassing,' she said, ruthlessly, as Byron fell into step beside her. 'You're probably getting a bit bored of her, too, aren't you? I've always suspected she's not nearly as wicked and adventurous as she likes to make out.'

He laughed, shaking more seawater from his hair. 'You're terrible. Terrible and accurate. Caro has a habit of sinking into a vocal petit mort at almost the first touch, and it's predictable after a while. A word to the wise, though – if you want anyone to really believe you've been sauntering around the Levant with a train of servants carrying every last bandbox, don't deal with gunshot wounds as easily as you'd pin up someone's flounce, or put your own boat away in Scotland. Everyone in our circle knows your father taught you to sail, but even Rosmoney left that sort of thing to his servants.' He turned to her with another disreputable smile. 'Do you remember that night in Madrid?'

'Who could forget drinking champagne in an enemy-occupied city?' she asked, lightly. She had leaned on the cupola of the sun-warmed bell tower of the Cathedral, he standing behind her, hemming her in with one arm on either side of hers, and the warmth of his breath on the back of her neck as they looked out across the burning city. 'And was that a threat or a warning?'

He turned to her now with genuine hurt. 'Do you really believe I've the smallest wish to hold that over you?'

I believe that most men forget all honour when their own is called into question, and especially by a woman.

'Of course not, don't be a fool.' She leaned into him.

He frowned but relaxed at her touch, exuding a faint scent of brandy and starch. 'What were you doing out here, anyway? Are Annis's prosy guests too much for you already?'

Cressida smiled, making the usual calculation of what percentage of the truth she could afford to give away. 'You know what these house parties are like – there's no avoiding anyone at Drochcala. I walked Lilias Tait home. The silly girl feared a hobgoblin on the path, although I think she was more likely to encounter a drunken pack-trader if anything.'

As she'd expected, Byron was far more interested in himself than a female he'd never heard of, and made no comment. They neared the edge of the lawn where the formal gardens encircling the house gave way to a woodland loch-side path. 'I hope you don't mean to go into the house in that state?' he said, cocking one arching dark brow at her. 'It's all nothing but soap bubbles, Cress – form is what matters and very little else.' He looked her up and down, taking in her damp skirts of lavender silk, her dishevelled curls and her grass-stained boots. 'Before you ask, I've got two hundred in bank-notes but it won't get you very far if you don't look the part. What do you mean to do, set yourself up in Paris or St Petersburg? I warn you, if you've annoyed Lascelles' masters, they could get at you in either place and from what I hear they likely will.'

'New York, in fact,' Cressida said, crisply. Lascelles could afford to be so indiscreet with his closest friends; he and Byron and their friends must trust one another with their lives and their reputations, after all. She couldn't imagine placing such trust in anyone on earth, except perhaps Ines, with her youthful conviction that Cressida would manage everything.

'And when the money runs out, what next?' Byron spoke

with bored scorn, but she dared not let him feel the lash of her tongue when she needed him so much; she would not be safe until those bank-notes were safely sewn into her reticule.

'I'll be a rich man's wife or mistress by then.'

Byron looked at her with a flash of something approaching compassion in his cold, weary blue eyes. 'You're already a man's wife. Is a second son's portion and Greville's wages not enough to keep you in style?'

'Between you and Annis it feels as if I must take orders from an entire army about what I need to do to be considered acceptable again,' Cressida said. 'And don't worry, I've no intention of presenting myself in my cousin's drawing room like this. Do go inside, though. Annis will be beside herself about supper.'

He sketched her a mocking bow and Cressida sighed, giving him her hand. He raised it to his mouth like a connoisseur, brushing her fingertips with his lips so that a flash of heat shot up her arm. She withdrew then, stepping away, unable to help herself enjoying the outrage in his eyes. He'd got far too used to having those who piqued his interest exactly where and when he required them, but it was always better to leave him wanting. He left her then without a backward glance, making his careless way across the lawn, soaking wet breeches clinging to his magnificent arse and thighs; over the years, he'd perfected a slightly rolling gait to disguise his limp.

Cressida turned upon an instinct, her gaze drawn southward across the lawn she'd crossed with Kitty just hours before. It felt like days, even though she could still taste the champagne. Here, scythed green lawn dissipated into ferns and wild fuchsia among the Scots pine and silver birch that grew between the house and the loch, the boathouse just visible. The boathouse hadn't been painted since she was a child, still a dull rust-red.

Eventually, civilised garden lost the battle and the grass itself gave way to a tough, wiry cousin that thrived on a twice-daily soaking at high tide. Here, in the space between land and sea, the two bow-backed white pack-ponies grazed among the pines: in the stalking season, they bore deer carcasses, but for now they had nothing to do and one of them was lame, favouring a hind leg. And as Cressida watched, Lord Greville Nightingale emerged from between the trees in his shirtsleeves. Even from this distance she saw how untidy his hair was. Had they lost the wind coming down the loch? It would be so like him to take the oars, so bloody annoyingly competent. He stopped where he stood, watching the lame pony move towards him. Greville went to her, ducking his dark head to whisper into her tufted milk-white ear, then ran a hand along her flank and moved behind her, kneeling to lift up her back foot. The knife was already in his hand, the hoof swiftly doctored – a stone, perhaps. As she watched, he began walking up towards the house and Cressida realised he'd seen her and known she was there all along, but had chosen to ignore her presence.

25

With Ines's quick assistance, Cressida shed the damp and muddy lavender silk for another evening gown of emerald-green Rajasthani muslin and her sodden jean boots for soft silver slippers of fine embroidered leather. She sat down at the dressing table so that Ines could do something about the wild state of her hair.

'That poet came in right at the front door, would you believe, dripping wet and as good as naked.' Ines rolled her eyes at the pockmarked looking-glass: salt worked its way into everything at Drochcala. She untied the black ribbon, teasing out Cressida's copper-streaked curls. 'Does he have the money?'

'He does, and when I consider it your place to ask questions, you'll be the first to know, menina.' Cressida watched the fleeting change in Ines's expression in the mirror, aware that she'd failed to hide her own hesitation. The girl would find out sooner or later: 'Mr O'Neill was on the boat with Lord Greville and Lord Byron.'

Ines frowned. 'Your father's servant? I don't like it, mistress. What have any of these men ever done for us? We're better off without them, just me and you together.' Her eyes shone with unspoken emotion, and Cressida reached up and took the girl's hand, briefly squeezing her fingers.

'I think the Scots were carrying weapons or gunpowder,' Cressida went on. 'The dog-head screws on the barrels were coated with pitch: I've never seen anyone do that for brandy or whisky, free-traded or otherwise.'

Ines set down the ivory comb with a clatter.

'I won't leave you, you little fool,' Cressida said.

'If Lord Byron has come and he has money for you, milady, we could be gone from this place by morning,' Ines said. 'There will be a moon later: we could travel at night. I saw those maps on the wall outside Mr Tait's office – they show the whole estate and it looks like easy walking for us from the hills above the house, all the way to Lochinver. But if your father's servant is here, then where is your father? Five hundred pounds you were worth to him.' She broke off, watching Cressida's face in the mirror. 'We're not going, are we?'

Cressida forced herself to concentrate on the collection of pearl hairpins on the dressing table before her, white pearls against dark polished wood with a faint scent of beeswax polish. At the back of her mind, she saw the barrels heaped up in the Drochcala yacht, slick with seaweed, and the angry, resolute expression on Oliver Tait's face as he gave the order to jettison them all into the loch. O'Neill had worked hard along with the rest of the men as if he'd known them all his life, lifting barrels, stepping out of the way of coiled, wet rope, and Cressida couldn't begin to unravel the possibilities of Rosmoney's presence here: whatever the reason, it could be nothing good. *Five hundred pounds should suffice.*

Ines picked up the comb again and started teasing out the tangles in Cressida's curls, speaking around the hairpins in her mouth as she began to secure coiled ringlets. 'Well, if we're not going to talk about it and we're not leaving tonight, then have you decided how you mean to explain changing your gown between drinks in the drawing room and going into supper? The cut of this bodice will drive your husband to distraction, at least.'

A single look in the mirror bade Ines to concentrate on her work, and a few moments later Cressida stood like a mannequin as Ines smoothed the skirts of her gown, grumbling about the state of the discarded lavender satin. The dinner gong sounded as she fastened a simple gold chain around Cressida's neck, and then again, with a loud discordant clatter that was quickly silenced. Thank God she wasn't below stairs, given that dinner had been delayed now by at least an hour and a half. She left Ines to mutter about the state of her stockings and stepped out into the gloom. The oak-panelled hallway leading to her room was narrow and lit at this stage of the evening only by silvery light streaming in through a sash window at the far end. Unease shot through her: a sudden, certain awareness that, contrary to appearances, she wasn't alone.

'It's quite all right, don't be afraid.' Greville emerged from the room to her left, which Cressida realised was her own bedchamber, adjoining the dressing room.

'What are you doing in my quarters?' Briefly, Cressida closed her eyes and once again saw Greville facing her in the dressing room at Crauford House, leaning on the doorframe with all that arrogant poise, shirtsleeves still rolled up to his elbows.

You have not had nearly enough of my orders and strictures. You will not go to Drochcala this summer. You will not seduce George Byron or compromise him in any way, or anything like it.

He was close enough now that she saw him smile, with a flash of genuine humour. '*Our* quarters, my lady.'

Cressida caught her breath and closed her eyes. This felt more like Kitty's work than Annis's. 'I hope you enjoy sleeping on the floor.' Silently, she counted to four. 'How is your arm?'

Greville shrugged; anger crackled in the air between them. 'It was just a scratch. My man was in at Walcheren; he knows how to manage a wound.'

By now they had reached the top of the stairs, and a hum of conversation rose up from the drawing room below. At Cressida's side, Greville was tall and slim in his evening dress, broad across the shoulder, his dark hair still a little damp.

'Would you like to shed any light on why your cousin's irritable major-domo has a sideline in running black-market trade down the loch?' he asked, now infuriatingly casual.

'With pleasure,' Cressida said. 'I suspect that the Butes don't just turn a blind eye to smuggling on their land like most landlords. Can you imagine Annis Fane of all people learning of any such enterprise without taking her own cut of the profit? I would imagine that Oliver is expected to arrange any free-trading that takes place here to her satisfaction just as efficiently as he looks after the stalking parties.'

Greville watched her for a moment in the light of a branch of candles sitting on top of the polished walnut side table, raising one eyebrow. She'd forgotten how irritating this trick of his was. There had been a time when she would have told him everything, airing every last suspicion. Instead, they buzzed around inside her head like flies trapped in a cheese-safe.

'How did you leave your brother?' she asked instead.

Greville glanced at her with a searching, half-amused look as if he knew she was hiding something. 'Chas was still alive although probably regretting it, considering the lecture Crauford read him about frequenting insalubrious parts of London, as if it were his own fault he'd been shot. I left Crauford himself moralising and refusing to pay the next quarter of James's allowance after a letter from his dean enquiring after the state of his health. He apparently hasn't been seen in Cambridge since Michaelmas. And so naturally I left Jamie with his pockets to let and furious about it. The nursery quarters I abandoned to its usual mysterious chaos. What can I say? Very little changes in my family – it's still perpetual pandemonium.' Greville yawned. 'Not that it's any of my affair, by the way, but is there any particular reason why your father's groom was on that boat full of smugglers just now? Byron overheard the men talking about some free-trader they called the Gentleman on the *Kittiwake* – there were a couple from Fraserburgh who weren't speaking in Gaelic. I suppose they didn't realise he can understand Scots. I take it your father is here somewhere? It would be just like Rosmoney to give himself a nickname like that.'

At Cressida's side, overwhelmingly close to her, Greville smiled with arrogant ease.

'To be absolutely honest, Nightingale, I'm glad that I have simply no idea why O'Neill is in Scotland, let alone Drochcala, and I intend to keep it that way,' Cressida said.

He cast such a lordly look down at her that she had to restrain the urge to walk away. He leaned down, whispering in her ear, his breath warm against the delicate skin of her neck. 'I don't believe you've ever been absolutely honest about anything. Not a single day in your life. If you've been manoeuvring here with your bloody father, you'll live to regret it, my dear.'

Cressida's mind raced. She wouldn't think about the fact that Rosmoney was here but had made no effort to seek her out, let alone to apologise for selling her like a horse; in his own mind, it would all be justified, of course. Ireland had been quiet for years, and yet there were weapons moving, changing hands here at this lonely sea-loch; perhaps they came across the Irish Sea just as she had once done herself, running with the wind from Dublin to the port of Lochinver, where houses and wharves crowded from the hillside down to the sea in the shadow of Suilven. She had no wish to discover whatever foolish game Rosmoney was here to play, if indeed he was here at all. Instead, she smiled, sensing Greville's desire as she looked up at him; she had so seldom allowed herself to recall his face, the slant of his smile or the look in his eyes when he woke.

'Honesty has never been my strong suit, but I still have a good eye for a gown. Do you approve, my lord?' Greville probably thought he could tumble her in that guest bedchamber just to keep her in check. His glance lingered on her face before moving down to her décolletage. Her breasts rose from the confection of emerald silk, barely confined by stays and fine embroidered linens, and her nipples hardened as he looked at her. He felt this too, she knew he did, damn him to the sixth circle of hell.

'That gown?' Greville spoke looking down at her with his lashes lowered, and tension flickered around his jaw. 'It's the sort of wholly indecent confection that suits a woman best when it's up around her waist, as you well know.' Arousal flared in his dark eyes, entwined with such implacable anger and resolution that Cressida's body betrayed her. Greville's gaze rested on Cressida's face. 'Well, we can't remain here. They'll all be expecting something of us, after all. May I?' He held out his arm and Cressida took it, breathless not only at his faint scent of starch and soap, aware of the lean strength beneath layers of superfine and fresh linen. The sound of familiar laughter drifted up through the open doors of the drawing room: Byron. Cressida smiled: there was still time to put Lord Greville in his place tonight.

'I wonder what will be in the first gossipy letter Annis sends to England about you both?' Greville said. 'If you pull this off, Caro Lamb will scratch out your eyes, but at least it'll make the Little Season less sufferingly dull. I hate London in November. I wonder who Byron is charming now?' he went on, lazily. 'Cleveland or Annis? I'm not sure there could actually be a more sickening combination at the dining table.'

'Just make sure you don't get in my way,' Cressida said.

Greville turned, with a particular light in his eyes she had not forgotten, not in all these years. 'As you well know, madam, you're already in mine.'

26

Downstairs, Annis and Bute waited outside the drawing room. Bute was as elegant and amenable as ever, in his impeccably cut evening dress. There was something especially chilly and dangerous about Annis tonight, though, clad in her gown of oyster-grey silk, shining like a forged weapon.

'We all deserve to be horsewhipped,' Greville said, kissing Annis's proffered hand. 'I'm sorry.'

Cressida forced herself into a polite smile as she fabricated an excuse to Lord Bute about changing her gown.

'How unlike you to spill anything, my dear,' Greville said, clearly enjoying himself. 'I never knew you to be clumsy a day in my life.' His gaze now lingered shamelessly on her breasts, more presented for inspection than confined by the green satin of her bodice.

'You look ravishing either way, darling,' Bute said, with an amused glance at Greville.

'We should all get to the table,' Annis snapped. 'Goodness knows everyone has been waiting long enough.'

'Shall we?' Greville said to Cressida. He was going to lead her in to dine at Drochcala. Afterwards, they would go to bed as husband and wife. Briefly, she closed her eyes. He flashed her a disreputable smile for the benefit of the Butes and a bubble of fury rose within her: he'd better be content to sleep on the floorboards. They were still arm in arm, and she was too aware of his hold on her. He brushed her elbow with the edge of his thumb in a reassuring gesture and for a moment it was hard to breathe. They stepped into a candlelit dining room, where oil paintings in heavy gilded frames hung from chains against panelled walls limewashed in palest green and glittering with more gilt. Some of the paintings were Rosmoney's work; he had loved painting horses and dogs and if he'd stuck to that as a pastime none of them would be in this bloody bind now.

The young footman, Tam, led Cressida to a Queen Anne chair between Cleveland and Byron, with Kitty to Byron's left, which at least gave her the satisfaction of watching Greville's face as he went to a seat opposite her, between Annis and Bute. There was a kindling expression in his dark eyes in contrast to the calm good manners with which he held out Annis's seat for her, laughingly brushing off her apologies to the table about the uneven number of men and women.

'I'm afraid some of my guests lost their courage and cried off.' Annis's eyes bore a flat, calculating expression. 'Don't worry, Cressida. By winter, you'll be all the rage again, I'm sure. Don't you agree, Dominic?'

'No,' Cleveland said, with blunt finality. 'A girl's reputation is like her virginity.'

Annis smiled. 'Once it's gone, it's gone, you mean? I hope not.'

A howling silence descended on the table for thirty seconds that felt like thirty years.

'I'm sorry to make you so late,' Greville addressed them all with his easy charm, as though the exchange between Annis and Cleveland had never happened. He turned to Lord Bute. 'What on earth has got into Fraser MacGuigan, anyway?'

Bute frowned, pausing with a spoonful of saffron-scented bouillabaisse halfway to his mouth. 'The sheriff from Inverness had the wit to ask if he was actually in league with the free-traders, considering he never catches anyone. Nothing was ever proven, of course, but you can see how such an accusation would be bound to stir up bad feeling. There's been an enormous increase in smuggling traffic ever since Parliament banned all legal distilling early in the year, which was entirely predictable, in my view. MacGuigan has been desperate for, ah, a kill ever since.'

'The whole country has been on the brink of chaos since poor Lord Perceval was shot,' Cressida said. 'One feels as if the world has been turned upon its head, to think that such a thing could happen in London, at the seat of our own government.'

'Lord Perceval made some very ill-judged decisions about trade,' Annis said. 'We're bound for war in America as a result: I suppose he had many enemies who are pleased that madman Bellingham went to his length.'

'It's monstrous,' Lord Bute said, with an uncharacteristically quelling glance at Annis. 'I'm afraid that a murder at Westminster will only have made the free trade more frequent and fiercer than ever. Such people don't stop at smuggling brandy and claret. They carry information, too, I'm afraid, my dear, and you can be sure that the death of our prime minister will have every French pursuivant grubbing around like a pig after truffles.'

'How awful, my lord,' Cressida said, all innocence. Greville watched her over the dish of steamed cockles in herbed butter, looking seconds away from laughter. She vowed to school him for that later: he'd get himself killed at this rate. Either Bute knew nothing of the fact that his own steward was just as efficient at organising the free trade as he was at arranging stalking parties, or he was a far better liar than she'd yet given him credit for.

'Your dear cousin has chosen to serve Eris this summer, I see.' Byron spoke very softly at her side, his breath warm against her neck. She inhaled the reassuring scent of his shaving water, cloves and something warm and sweet: cinnamon? 'Look at the state of Greville.'

'I'd rather not. I had to do needlework instead of Greek mythology,' Cressida said, only half aware of Kitty and Bute doing their level best to establish a conversation about weather phenomena in the far north of Scotland. 'My father's revolutionary tendencies didn't extend as far as allowing me to study the classics. What was Eris the god of?'

'Goddess, actually – of chaos, strife and discord.' Byron glanced at Cleveland, whom Kitty was now managing with such an inexhaustible flow of polite enquiries about his estates that he had no choice but to answer her. 'Eris took great offence at not being invited to Helen of Troy's wedding, and consider what mess arose from that. What was Annis thinking, asking Dominic Lascelles to make up the party?' He smiled at her then, as if she were playing her unwitting part in a joke only he understood.

'Supposedly, we get the scandalous meeting over with here before I go back into society in the Little Season,' Cressida said, sitting back to allow Tam to place a rock-lobster on her plate with a pair of silver tongs. 'Anyway, what are you writing this year, George? More sex and rebellion?'

Byron raised a single eyebrow, cracking one of his rock-lobster's claws with the silver hammer. 'Please don't tell me how much you admired *Childe Harold*, even if you've read it.'

Cressida reined in the urge to tell him that she'd read both cantos of the epic published so far and that she'd found it both mannered and boring in equal measure. 'In truth, I think the best thing you've written this year was your speech in the Lords. *But while the exalted offender can find means to baffle the law, new capital punishments must be devised, new snares of death must be spread for the wretched mechanic, who is famished into guilt.* It's disgusting to introduce a capital penalty for men who smash the machines that cause their starvation.'

'I'm glad you think so,' Byron said. 'The months I spent in Nottinghamshire this winter were hellish because of it – whole families starving, and for what? The faster production of second-rate cloth so fragile they call it spider-work?'

'So you do have a sincere bone in your body after all.'

Byron let out a quick laugh just as conversation fell into a lull elsewhere, so that everyone else looked up, even Cleveland.

'Oh yes, quite the rabble-rouser, weren't you, George?' Cleveland said.

Byron raised his wine glass in a mocking salute, but a slight rush of colour spread across his cheekbones; they would have laughed and jeered as he delivered the speech. He would have hated that, she knew.

'But doesn't it pay to consider the grievances of the poor a little more seriously?' Cressida asked. 'On the day we left London, our carriage took four hours to navigate Pall Mall because of the riots. Wouldn't it actually serve us all rather well to consider why Lord Perceval's murder was greeted with such delight that it lit a bonfire of unrest? London is completely unsafe. He was the prime minister: we're not talking of some back-alley garrotting over a grievance between criminals.'

Greville ignored this, quietly conversing with Bute.

Cleveland shrugged with an elegance that reminded her of Lascelles. 'When have the poor ever been happy with their lot? And Perceval was killed by a failed merchant with delusions of grandeur. It's human to seek patterns in nature, but nature is both chaotic and unfair. There's nothing to discern. The killer is dead and justice has been served, of a sort.'

'So do *you* think it equitable or fair that the weavers who can't work now or feed their children must face the gallows for destroying the machines that replaced them, Cleveland?' Kitty asked, sharply, with the air of a woman who had held up her end of a soothing conversation for long enough. 'I wonder: what would you have done in their shoes? I know exactly what you did do in Lord Byron's boots: either you hadn't bothered to take your seat that day or you didn't speak at all.'

Cleveland grinned at Kitty across the table. 'Happily, I'm not in anyone else's shoes but my own.' He signalled for more wine and Tam obeyed as he was bound to do, pouring a thin stream of Rhenish into Cleveland's glass.

Annis smiled up and down the table. 'Oh dear! Far better, I think, dear Kitty, not to exhaust ourselves with the sort of questions better left for the consideration of our menfolk.'

'But isn't that part of the difficulty?' Cressida persisted. 'How will we go on if men with the privilege to sit in Parliament don't bother? No decisions will ever be taken.' She allowed herself the briefest of glances at Greville, who was watching over his wine glass with his dark, arching eyebrows slightly lifted.

Beside her, Byron raised his glass. 'You have the wisdom of the ages, Cressida. But even if all were emancipated – Catholics, working men, Black men, even women – I can tell you now that one solitary voice speaks in the House of Lords and that belongs to Mammon. Truth or justice play no part in any of it: only money. Most speeches can scarcely be heard against a backdrop of jeering and derision, and a more criminally corrupt nest of hoarding vipers I never saw.'

Cressida sipped her wine and relaxed into a warm alcoholic glow, even as she forced herself to resist the temptation to signal for more.

On Cressida's other side, Cleveland cracked open the claw of his lobster. 'You do look grim, Nightingale,' he said. 'What is it that irks you so much – is it women discussing politics or the sight of the mist and the loch that you find so insupportable? I remember so clearly that you, Byron and my young fool of a brother had a great deal to say about burning our tedious social mores to the ground and building all anew.'

Greville cracked open the head of his rock-lobster and ate the coral. 'I find a well-informed woman speaking of politics more edifying than a grown man of your stature fishing for an argument, Cleveland.'

Everyone stopped talking, and Annis frowned at Cleveland, as though he were a paid piper playing the wrong tune.

'Some do find the weather oppressive in this part of Scotland: it does incline to fog,' Lord Bute said, placidly.

Greville smiled. 'Cleveland does right to call me to order: I'll admit to being preoccupied. How does the chance of wind look tomorrow, my lord, in as much as we can ever be sure of it? Shall we get a sail in, do you think?'

'It's high tide at eleven o'clock tomorrow and *Flora* is already in the water – we can certainly try her,' Bute said, clearly relieved that Greville at least was inclined to play the same conversational game as he was.

'What about you, Cleveland?' Annis said, with a flinty smile. 'Do you sail? I seem to recall that your lovely sister has an interest in boats.'

For the briefest moment, open and obvious dislike pulsed between Cleveland and his hostess. Really, why *was* he not at one of his own estates? Or if not attending his young sister, why was he not at a house party of similarly unattached young aristocratic men and women from the demi-monde with gilded toenails and wide experience? Cleveland let the moment draw out; tension hummed in the air. Greville picked up a claw and cracked it open with a soldier's swift expertise.

'Georgiana likes it when I take her out on the water, Lady Bute.' Cleveland spoke with a cold edge, so experienced at withering pretension that he did it without even thinking. 'I oblige her as often as I can. Goodness only knows I'm a poor enough guardian as it is.'

Greville and Cleveland finally met each other's gaze across the table. In the candlelight Greville's liquid dark eyes were very still, signalling the complete dissolution of any adherence to conventional good manners. Cleveland stared back with a bland, polite smile. Stillness crept over Greville, his attitude of louche arrogance now gone: Cressida had seen men like this before, before battles, before hangings. Except that they were here at Drochcala, dining on bouillabaisse and rock-lobsters and steamed cockles and dishes of spiced green beans.

'Are you, though, Cleveland?' Greville said. 'You were always so good at entertaining –' he dipped his long fingers into a bowl of rosewater '– young girls.'

27

Cleveland set down his fork, breaking the silence with cold precision. 'You're lucky I don't call out unmannerly whelps, Nightingale. As ever, you stand in greater need of a whip than a duel.' He regained control of his temper with unsettling speed; Cressida had never seen him lose it before.

'Don't let me stop you attempting either,' Greville said, smiling easily. Cleveland was a good shot, but she knew quite well that Greville could shoot the ace out of a playing card from twenty yards. Greville, who had just deployed her past years of ruin, humiliation, penury and war to score points against an old rival.

She got to her feet, so lightheaded with anger that for the briefest moment the room spun around her in a blur of candlelit faces. 'That's quite enough from the two of you.'

The quiet was punctuated only by the crackling of the fire and the faint ticking of the bronze carriage clock that had always been on the mantelpiece. Greville looked at her, those dark brows slightly lifted again. Kitty sat very still with her lips pinched together in suppressed anger. Bute picked at his napkin with fretful misery, suddenly looking every bit of his threescore years and ten. Annis smiled, and Byron wore a pained expression, as though he had stepped in an open drain in his best top-boots. This was going too far, even for him. Cressida fought a wild urge to laugh. Then she pushed back her chair and walked out.

Closing the door behind her, Cressida leaned on it for a moment with her eyes closed, her breasts heaving against the emerald satin of her bodice: the clinging gown now felt ridiculous. In the dark, she saw campfires flickering on a bald Spanish hillside, breathing in the stink of a four-day-old battlefield. *Get a hold on yourself.* Then she turned and walked away at speed, her surroundings a muddle of lamplight, well-worn flagstones and familiar painted panelling. Roberts waited as usual in the great entrance hall, tossing Cressida an undisguised glance of appraisal, as if to ask what else she expected, nasty, forward miss as she was.

Cressida walked on with purposeful speed but no clear notion of where she was going, led only by instinct as though fleeing a French ambush. Past and present collided and if she stopped to help that woman wake her two young children, she'd end this night with her throat cut or left far behind. Cressida knew she'd hear that woman calling for help, and so many others, till the end of her days, but the army moved on, always relentless, stopping for no one, not even waiting for a woman to deliver a new baby, let alone for a mother to rouse her sick, exhausted children. There was not much place for honour on the march.

In the whitewashed back corridor Cressida stopped

outside the estate office and went in, aware only of a coal fire spluttering in the grate and the cut-glass decanters of whisky and brandy still laid out on a sideboard of ancient carved oak, just as they had been when she was a child. Whisky splashed her hand as she poured it into one of the small glasses filigreed with pewter, and she drank the whole measure. She poured another, even in the half second that she became aware that she was not, in fact, alone. She let the glass drop so that it bounced and rolled along the sideboard, inhaling whisky fumes even as she drew the knife.

'Do you not want water with the next one?'

She looked up to find Oliver Tait standing in his shirtsleeves behind the desk his father had used before him. Both hands rested on the battered green leather as he watched her. He lifted his eyebrows slightly at the knife, which she held level. Oliver raised both hands, his handsome features a portrait of concern. A half-drunk glass of whisky sat on the desk beside him, next to the heavy leather-bound accounts book and a chaotic heap of correspondence. It was just Drochcala. Only the familiar, pine-panelled estate office at Drochcala, here at this northernmost tip of the British Isles, with those watercolours of red grouse and the common rosefinch framed in chipped gilded oak.

'Jesus bloody Christ, don't surprise me like that, Oliver,' Cressida said. She was in Scotland, not in Spain or Portugal. All the strength went out of her legs, her head spun and she had to look down at her own white hands resting on the sideboard as she fought rising nausea. She was aware of Oliver coming closer, his hand on her arm. She breathed in his scent of starched linen.

'Here's a chair. Sit down.'

She sank into it, grateful for the embroidered cushion at her back, embarrassed at drawing so much comfort from the steady warmth of his touch. It was far too dangerous to let the past overtake her in this fashion. Oliver waited at her side for a moment and then went back to his own seat on the other side of the desk, never taking his eyes from her, even as he drew small, intricate patterns in the margin of the accounts ledger with a moth-eaten quill pen.

'Is something wrong? I heard raised voices.' Oliver glanced down at the accounts book with a small frown. 'I shouldn't say it, but I don't know what she was thinking, inviting your husband here as well as Cleveland. She'll get her fingers burned before long.'

'So will you. What the hell are you doing running black-market cargo down the loch? They'd hang you for that at worst, transport you at best, and hardly even bother with a trial.' Cressida drank the whisky he set down before her, savouring the alcoholic heat.

He gave her a cold smile. 'And now it's at the bottom of the loch, thanks to you and your husband. I'm looking forward to explaining that to my associate – and he to his, I shouldn't wonder. These aren't nice people.'

'Better your bloody cargo at the bottom of the loch than you at the bottom of the charnel-heap at Loch Lutharn gaol,' Cressida snapped, brutal. 'What a cesspool my family is. We seem to have quite the facility for destroying other people's lives. It's weaponry, isn't it?'

Oliver made a visible attempt at nonchalance. 'Whatever

it is, it makes no difference to me either way. I have my orders. I obey them and that's it.'

'It's the difference between being definitely hanged for treason or transported for free-trading,' Cressida said. 'Why don't you just resign your position and leave? You're educated and personable and you could bribe them into giving you a golden character. What possible reason have you to stay?'

Oliver watched her across the desk, unsmiling. 'Apart from the fact I have cousins employed at the same house and an infirm great-aunt living halfway down the loch?' His eyes narrowed with unvarnished hatred. 'Your cousin even gives orders for Lilias to warn people away from the loch at night. How do you think the law will view that? She'll be strung up with the rest of us, or find herself alone in Van Diemen's Land at best if she survives the convict ship. She's only just thirteen years old—' Oliver broke off, flushed with angry shame. 'And even if I left and took just Lilias with me, I've no way of supporting us. No one at the estate has been paid since well before the last quarter. The Butes are being dunned, too.' Oliver gestured at the heap of letters on the desk. 'These are just from Inverness and Edinburgh – wine-merchants, drapers, milliners: the lot. I can only imagine it's the same story in London.'

'It's Jamaica, isn't it?' Cressida said. 'Annis and Bute were starting to feel the pinch when I left in '09 but it's been five years since Abolition now. Four Winds isn't the licence to print money that it once was.'

Oliver stared at her; his mother had come from Four Winds, the Butes' Jamaican plantation. 'Odd how that happens when you have to pay people instead of buying them like cattle, and they're harder to come by in the first place. I don't know which I hate more, the slave-traders or the more patronising Abolitionists, who are always so surprised that I speak two languages and understand double-entry book-keeping. The ones who like to take all the credit for what freedom we've won are the worst.' Oliver's eyes flashed with banked-down fury, and although he was right, Cressida tried to snatch at another truth that she could only brush with her fingertips, like a ball of polished steel suspended in thin air, just out of reach.

'There's something else, isn't there?' Cressida said. 'You've been like a cat on a frying pan ever since I got to Drochcala.'

Oliver flinched, his jaw tightening. 'Your cousin has me over a barrel.' He spoke then in a rush, words tumbling out like water trapped behind a dam and finally released: 'There's been discrepancy after discrepancy in the estate accounts since January. Missing money, mostly from the rents. It's not vast amounts but it's enough to be noticeable.'

'And Annis knows?'

'Of course she knows. I'm responsible for receiving all the rent payments. I count it all down to the last halfpenny before it's all shipped off to the bank at Inverness with three armed men to guard it.' He flushed. 'When the first lot of rent went missing, I couldn't see how it had happened, not once I was certain I hadn't miscounted. I only knew someone was stealing after the rents had been collected, like skimming off the cream, and I'd probably be blamed.' Oliver looked her straight in the eye. 'I panicked and replenished the money from my own savings. I know it was foolish but I felt I had no choice. It kept happening, though, and then I had to tell her—' Oliver broke off abruptly.

'What are you going to do?'

He gave a quick, tight smile. 'I don't know. I'd leave if I could, but Lady Bute has made herself clear enough: she'll cry rope if I go. Even if I'm cleared of theft, at best I'll just appear incompetent. Who'd employ me? I've been through the account books and the cash itself as well as the bills and receipts more times than I can count, but they don't reconcile. The money's gone.'

'Have you tried to discover who the thief actually is?' Cressida asked, carefully.

Oliver stared at her. 'This isn't a case of some overexcited debutante stealing trinkets from her friends' mothers at house parties. People of my class and most especially of my colour are hanged or transported for theft. Lady Bute would make sure of that. Anyway, no one here has coin to spend, and servants aren't exactly blessed with many hiding places. We're talking of bags of coinage that weigh almost as much as a side of ham – far too much to fit into a small box beneath a servant's bed.' Oliver picked up one of the letters and let it fall onto the desk. 'When I confessed to Lady Bute that the money was going missing, she didn't look surprised. I think she's the one who has been taking it.' He shrugged. 'She's definitely not paying her creditors. It's probably some idiotic gambling debt she daren't confess to her husband.'

Cressida sipped her whisky, looking at the heap of bills on the desk beside the ledger.

Annis had many faults, but a passion for games of chance had never been one of them.

28

Cressida ignored the sound of voices drifting up from the drawing room: the time for playing at society guests had gone. Both her bedchamber and dressing room were empty: Ines must be dining in the servants' hall downstairs. Standing before the mirror, Cressida drew the pearl-headed pins from her hair, allowing tangled curls to fall in disorder down her back. In her evening gown, she raised the sash window and a sea breeze blew in from the loch, lifting her hair, cool fingers questing beneath her wrap as she listened to footfalls in the corridor outside, too heavy to belong to Ines. She watched the brass door handle turn, tamping down white-hot anger as she waited to deal with Greville. When the door opened, it wasn't her husband who came in but Byron.

He'd shed his jacket and stood in the doorway in his waistcoat and shirtsleeves, with the snow-white cravat at his throat. Moving with swift, angry economy, he walked into the room without asking her leave. Closing the door behind him, he walked over to her dressing table and let a roll of bank-notes drop, watching it land among the pearl hairpins and a necklace of gemstones that Ines had left out.

'Well?' Byron stood facing the mirror, leaning with both hands on the dressing table. When he spoke again, it was without turning to look at her, so helplessly balanced between humour and despair. 'How shall I restore your reputation? With a delicious fuck that everyone hears of? I'd be willing – it'd be worth handing my balls to Greville. Or perhaps I really should just make you my muse. That would probably do it. If you're going to go, Cressida, you should go. Take the money, take your maid or whoever she really is and leave. Annis is playing a dangerous game here of some mad design all her own and you know it as well as I do. Have you got anything decent to drink?'

Without a word, Cressida went to the walnut chest of drawers where Ines had unpacked her things, including the flask of twenty-year-old cognac. In a silence punctuated only by apple-logs crackling in the fire, she set out lead-glass tumblers on the silver filigreed tray and poured for them both. Still facing himself in the mirror, Byron reached out and took his, draining it. He turned to look at her at last with a bleakness in his expression she had seen before, in the early hours of the morning at Newstead but more often in soldiers walking away from battle.

Byron visibly gathered himself, with a humourless smile. 'If the Butes must aid and abet handsome, horribly inhibited smugglers, they could at least run some decent brandy. That stuff in the dining room is just insulting.'

'Leave Oliver alone,' Cressida said. 'The last thing he needs is that sort of rumour, and he doesn't even have the type of connections who can get him out of hot water. It's self-protection, not an excess of inhibition. We can't all be the brightest star in society's high firmament.'

'Don't be bitter, it doesn't suit you,' Byron said. 'I know I'm not wrong about Mr Tait, but unless I'm much mistaken his heart belongs elsewhere. And surely you have some idea of just how easily all that public regard for me might fall away? I'd accepted Annis's invitation before I knew you were coming to Drochcala. I had no choice.'

Cressida stared at him, but in her mind's eye they were back in that frozen garden at Newstead, when she had just watched him leave an outbuilding white with hoar frost, shrugging himself back into his heavy twill jacket as his gardener's lad walked away in the other direction.

'Which servant were you careless with?'

'Does it matter? Annis knows. She's blackmailing me, and I don't think I'm the only one. Why else would Cleveland be here?' He turned away, pouring them both a second measure of cognac. 'Oh to the devil with it, I suppose I'm drunk enough to bare my soul to you of all people.'

'I'm hardly in a position to betray your confidences.'

He ignored that. 'It wasn't a servant, either.'

Cressida caught her breath, recalling that moment at the breakfast table when Annis had turned to Kitty with such smiling malice. *Your cousin Jamie's quite thick with Byron at the moment, I hear.*

'You never did do half measures. When did it start?'

He gifted her with the smile that had always been so

difficult to resist. 'Jamie's father was a mentor of mine, of a sort. I went to stay with Tristan at Carver when I was eighteen, just for a few weeks. Jamie was a child then. He was precocious and indulged, as I'm sure you know, and I ignored him. Last winter I met him for the first time as a man. My God, that mind of his, Cressida.'

'And that arse,' Cressida said, drily. 'And that face. Let's not hedge around the fact that all the Nightingales are shattering to look at.'

'And ruthless. Jamie had the audacity to cut off the connection after that bloody awful night at the Craufords'. He said I was a hypocrite, that I didn't really want to change anything about our society. The boy is a firebrand, but he'll learn, just as we all did.' He gave her a twisted smile. 'He's right, but only because it's futile. I know it's a sin; by our rules it's a sin.'

'Who am I to judge? I've committed just about every cardinal sin there is nearly every day of my life for years and years. If we're going to hell, George, you and I, then at least we're going together.'

He let out an airless laugh. 'I've always suspected the company is likely to be better down there. Either way, Annis found out that there was more between Jamie and me than political debate. I always thought I cared about exposure because my mother was still alive, but it turns out I'm just as craven now that she's dead. At least when you fell you didn't take anyone else down with you. But most of the meaningful connections I've had in my life risk someone else just as much as they do me.'

'It's not cowardice to be afraid of becoming an outcast,'

Cressida said. 'I should know.' At least in death there was nothing more to fear.

He turned to look at her then, with a swift, considering gaze. He saw too much and always had. 'Chérie, you're still so young.'

Cressida leaned against the bedpost. 'Let's pray Fraser MacGuigan's at home asleep in bed. I wouldn't put it past him to send a boy down after that cargo. I'm sure he knows we dropped something more than a few lobster pots.'

'To hell with Fraser MacGuigan,' Byron said, relentless. 'Don't change the subject. That's two hundred in notes. Take it. Tait is sailing me to Thurso tomorrow. There'll be a trading packet heading south before the end of the week. Come with me: it's no more complicated than that. Whatever Annis is doing, bringing us all up here to play us off against one another, she's gone too far.'

Cressida looked out of the window, anywhere other than at him: the draw between them was animal and simple, and above all good humoured. Beyond the Scots pines and the beech trees, dim light spread across the surface of the loch. On the hillside above the house she'd inhaled her father's cologne: orange-flower mingled with something masculine and indefinable, a scent from that old century when men had worn their hair fairy-white with powder and had lived and died for freedom in Ireland, in Scotland, and she had ridden her pony in the hills beyond Rosmoney itself with only O'Neill to attend her.

Byron let out a swift sigh, as if in defeat. 'When are you going to tell Greville?'

'Which bit?' He'd always known her better than anyone, except perhaps Greville himself.

He subjected her to consideration that most people deemed him too frivolous to be capable of. 'Don't give me that. You're not the sort to go running to him with reports of Jamie's outrages. You need to be truthful with Greville and with yourself about what's between you, past and present, or the mess we're all in is only going to get worse. You and Greville have already brought your lives to ruin once. Are you going to do it again?'

Cressida closed her eyes, and in that moment she was back in Spain, at Byron's side at the top of a church tower, sharing a bottle of purloined champagne as they looked out over the scattered lights of enemy-occupied Madrid. The gown of plain linen and the respectable cap and the apron were rolled up in her pack, and she had worn silk once more, even if the hem was higher than it should be at the front and the narrow skirts accentuated a complication. With Lord Byron at her side, long ago, she had breathed in the drifting smoke of a thousand campfires as her hand travelled across her belly, as if to protect the fatherless child that had been growing inside her for six months now. A child that might have been the Duke of Cleveland's son or daughter. Or it might have been Greville's: some boy or girl with dark curls touched gold by the sun, and that smile punctuated by a single dimple, and that louche, elegant manner of leaning against a door to talk to her.

In the bedchamber at Drochcala, Byron looked down at her then; she never cried about this because what was the use, it was all well in the past, and yet now her eyes burned.

Taking her silence for the answer that it was, he took her hands in his and then slipped one around her waist; she followed him in the steps of a waltz, dancing to a slow beat that Cressida felt in her heart but could not hear.

'Come now,' he said, speaking softly, 'show me a merry face. Two hundred pounds, Cressy. Take the money and come away with me.' He leaned down and kissed away the single tear that had escaped; despite it all she knew very well he would have enjoyed taking her now with all the skill in his possession, only to look at her afterwards and find a ruined, tear-stained woman and not the unattainable intrigue he saw now. She turned away and rested her forehead on his shoulder as they moved through the steps of the dance, even as the door opened.

Greville stood in the doorway with the glow of the oil lamp in the corridor behind him, in a stillness and a silence that Cressida would remember afterwards as a moment preserved in amber. Then he closed the door and walked away.

29

Greville reached the top of the stairs and set down his glass of brandy on the occasional table beneath the window. The wound in his arm pulsed with slow, agonising regularity, even as he relived the sight of his wife in Lord Byron's arms, two lost souls dancing together in silence. *Shit.*

He couldn't help recalling the way Byron had looked at Cressida on the boat as she held the compress to his bleeding arm: that steady, warning light in his eyes. George Byron knew exactly where Cressida had been. The realisation had hit Greville with the force of a blow, costing him something to conceal. Cressida wasn't really at Drochcala to draw Byron into a scandal, political or otherwise, or anything like it. How could she, when he knew very well she'd spent her exile in the train of an army? Greville didn't know how Byron knew, or how in hell's name this had escaped Lascelles, but know he did. And Byron held that truth over

Cressida's head like the sword of Damocles, so what he had just witnessed between them was entirely sincere.

Take the money and come away with me.

Greville drank off his brandy in one. She'd looked after herself long enough. Why was she really here at all? Whatever the reason, Byron offered her a route out of this mess. Doubtless the attraction would pall when they needed more money. In another world, in another time, Greville would have given her two hundred pounds as inconsequential pin money to buy gilded feathers for her hair and a scandalous nightgown that revealed more than it concealed. Anger was pursued by shame.

It was hard to escape the conclusion that Cressida had come to Drochcala so that she could equip herself to leave him behind for good. Used and pursued in London, the far north of Scotland was a much easier place from which to disappear for ever: New York, St Petersburg, Gothenburg. A thousand cities. Once she'd gone, there would be no more chances. And he'd taken Cleveland's bait and let his damn bloody temper run away with him once more. Had he learned nothing?

Greville flinched, leaning against the white-painted panelled wall as he recalled the swiftly concealed expression of betrayal on Cressida's face when he'd dealt that childish coup de grâce to Cleveland: *You were always so good at entertaining young girls.*

Drochcala was eerily quiet: it was a house party – the whole place ought to echo with laughter, music and a hundred different conversations. Instead, they'd dined in silence punctuated by the subdued clatter of cutlery against porcelain. Annis, Byron and Kitty had withdrawn before the dish of lemon syllabub and the heap of golden hot-house grapes brought up from London were even removed. Leaving Bute to exchange pained conversation with Cleveland, honour had demanded he apologise to Cressida, even if it were too late. That would have to wait.

A cold slick of fear slid down Greville's spine, the sort a man only felt when there was a threat to those he was honour-bound to protect. A disastrous night at a fashionable house party by anyone's reckoning, this, with the hostess and half of her guests already retired before ten o'clock. This mismatched gathering made no sense, and the clue to it all lay with Annis. Annis Fane had the social instincts of an eighty-year-old dowager. She didn't make mistakes. Greville's lips twitched into a faint smile at the prospect of asking Annis why she was strong-arming her own estate manager into running black-market cargo up the loch.

Greville obeyed instinct and followed the corridor to the front of the house, stepping away from the bare waxed floorboards at the top of the stairs and onto deep Rajasthani carpet in the wide, well-lit hallway that led to the master bedrooms. The house was still unsettling in how quiet it was, but then again these houses always were if you ventured upstairs when all servants were finally sitting down to eat. The Butes' treatment of their staff was skinflint at best: according to Somers they had dined for two days now on the remains of a maggoty side of beef that must have made its first appearance at Annis's own table in London almost a fortnight before. Even Crauford ensured his staff ate well, even if he couldn't help extolling the virtues of a plain diet for the lower orders.

Greville loped towards the large double doors at the end of the wood-panelled corridor lit by candles in brass wall sconces. The walls here were a pale shade of cream that thickened to yellow where heat from the candles drew linseed oil out of the paint. Greville stared at the flames, inhaling the unmistakable scent of death. All he could hear was his own breathing, his heartbeat pounding in his ears.

You're imagining it, you bloody fool. This happened from time to time, just as it must do for anyone who'd spent any amount of time in the vicinity of a battlefield. You'd smell it again: that meaty, rotten reek, with the hint of sweetness.

Greville drew his pistol then, going like clockwork through the procedure of loading and priming, walking at a steady pace towards the double doors at the end of the hallway. The smell intensified. It was the soldier in him who opened the door, standing back, taking a quick look into the room. The housekeeper stood with her hands pressed to her mouth, her tartan sash skewed at an angle, her eyes wide with panic. Greville laid a steadying hand on her arm, looking past her at the long, grey shape on the floor. Annis had been wearing oyster-grey satin at dinner. Stepping into the bedchamber, Greville was prepared for the stench of bodily fluids and walked over to the window, throwing up the sash. Even so, he had to take in a few deep draughts of fresh, salt-scented air before he could turn back to face what had once been Annis Fane, Countess of Bute. She lay contorted on the floor beside the bed, still in her evening gown. The room reeked of blood, vomit and human effluent, with that sickly sweet hint of decay that must have been in his imagination because she couldn't have been dead for more than an hour or so.

Greville went to Roberts, who stood shaking violently, her eyes wide and staring. 'When did you find her like this?'

'They'll say I killed her,' Roberts said. 'They'll hang me.' Tears streamed down her face like sheeting rain in November, but it was all fear without a shred of grief for her mistress. Quite understandable, all things considered. 'They'll all know I had a reason to wish she was dead, but I didn't do it, I swear.'

'What reason?' Greville said, focusing on Roberts for a moment instead of what remained of Annis Fane.

Roberts was panicking now, too distressed to dissemble. Greville handed her his handkerchief, which she pressed to her mouth, her bone-white fingers still quivering. Taking a deep breath, she gathered herself, words spilling forth in a rush: 'It may not seem much to your lordship but I take pride in my work. It took me twenty years to become a lady's maid, working my way up, and she has me up here waiting at table, fetching and carrying downstairs, even if it is all my own fault.' She drew in another long, shuddering breath, looking him dead in the eye now. 'I've not been paid for six months. *My old friend Roberts*, she always says to me, promising they'll look after me. So it's been bed and board with only a promise of my wages, and I put up with it until my sister Betsy's girl was turned off without a character with her master's brat in her belly—' Roberts broke off, making a visible effort to compose herself. 'And so I pawned Lady Bute's earrings – just a small pair that she didn't even like, and I never thought she'd miss.'

'But miss them she did?' Greville said. It wasn't going to be easy to single out one person who hated Annis enough to kill her. 'It will be quite all right, just tell me when you found your mistress like this.'

'No more than a quarter of an hour ago,' Roberts said, clutching at the handkerchief. 'We'd all that minute sat down to eat when Tam came in to say that her ladyship had gone upstairs early. She hadn't rung, which was odd, but I knew I'd have to come up and undress her.'

'And just as you'd at last taken the weight off your feet,' Greville said, glancing at the carriage clock on the mantelpiece: it was a quarter to ten. He was going to have to look at Annis now. He must take a hold on himself and just do it. She lay bent backwards like a mackerel, stretched out on the Turkey rug with her arms at odd angles he'd still see long after he'd left this room and all evidence of the manner of this death was quietly tidied away. Poison: it was obviously poison. Clearly something that produced spasms and contortion rather than anything next door to opium. Whoever had done this wanted Annis to die without a semblance of dignity.

Greville forced himself to turn and look at Roberts, who made an obvious attempt to steel herself.

'Wait here – in the dressing room if you'd rather. I'll fetch Oliver Tait – he's got a sensible head on his shoulders. We can't have this going through the servants' hall like a dose of cholera before Lord Bute is told.'

Greville left her, closing the door behind him, leaning

on the wall outside the master bedchamber for a moment. Unless Roberts was a consummate actress, she wasn't the killer. Shock and fear rather than guilt were writ clear upon her face. But someone had poisoned Annis, and Greville felt a horrifying sensation of relief: the stifling, wicked tension concocted by the dead woman had now evaporated, even if only to be replaced with the promise of the rope for someone almost certainly still within the walls of Drochcala itself.

30

Cressida left Drochcala by means of the scullery, listening to the low hum of conversation from the servants' hall as she passed, breathing in the starchy scent of boiled early potatoes. With the roar and clash of battle in her ears, Cressida stood outside in the laundry yard as cool night air kissed her skin. Closing her eyes, she listened to the tide lapping against the shoreline at the bottom of the garden. Once Byron had walked out without looking back, leaving her alone in the bedchamber she was meant to share with Greville, Cressida had changed her clothes, slipping out of the emerald silk and fastening herself into the comfortable gown of pale blue linen, swapping embroidered silver leather evening slippers for the jean boots that were still damp.

Alone, she made her way to the plantation of fir trees behind the house, turning back on an instinct: a cold, intense prickle of awareness between her shoulder blades.

She looked up at the large first-floor window that presented a view from the landing outside the master bedroom. Two big geranium plants on the windowsill inside partially concealed the shape and form of the observer, but even at this distance and in this Highland summer half-darkness Cressida knew that it was Roberts who was watching her, standing unnaturally still by the window.

There was nothing to be done about that now, and she was no longer a debutante escaping Annis's strictures about masquerade balls that you had to buy a halfpenny ticket for and where the punch was laced with arrack. Cressida let herself through the gate and out onto the path strewn with pine needles, now well on her way up the hillside. What remained of the light filtered down through the trees, illuminating her path, but even without it Cressida knew where to tread, relishing the challenge of the climb, blood pumping through her body as her muscles worked. Half an hour passed as she climbed, making her way methodically up the path she had last followed in Oliver's company. Far below, to the west, Loch Iffrin glinted in the last of the summer light. To her right, the heather-jacketed hillside reared up against a clear night already pinpricked with stars. The windows of the bothy glowed golden, lit from within, and with the ease of long practice Cressida moved more quietly the closer she got so that she stood outside the door with her jack-knife in one hand, listening to the low hum of undisturbed conversation within. Reaching for the old iron doorknob in silence, she stood with her back to the wall in case they fired a shot straight out of the door: she wouldn't have put it past either of them.

Cressida walked into the bothy to face her father, Rosmoney, and John O'Neill sitting at a small table, illuminated by a single lamp as they examined papers laid out before them. Her father was dressed in ancient dark twill but hadn't overlooked his boots, which were polished to a shine as always.

Rosmoney directed a freezing glance at O'Neill. 'Oh, for God's sake,' he said. 'What did I tell you? Sheer bloody carelessness.'

O'Neill, of course, could say nothing, but Cressida did: 'It was scarcely Mr O'Neill's fault. I'm sure it was the last thing he expected, finding Greville and Byron on that free-trading run. My joining them wasn't exactly planned, either.'

'Don't permit me to hear sarcasm from your lips again, my dear.' In the flickering lamplight, Rosmoney spoke as though she were still the ten-year-old he had left behind all those years ago.

'Very well. Tell me what you're doing here, then, and why, before I alert the whole household to your presence, including my husband,' Cressida said. 'I do hope you enjoyed spending that five hundred pounds, Papa. Is it gone already? Was your Mrs Winters just another lie, or has she gone off to find herself a better marital prospect?'

Rosmoney got to his feet then, sinuous and sudden as a striking snake. He hadn't noticed the jack-knife in her hand and Cressida moved quickly, backing her father up against the whitewashed wall with a strength and speed that took him by surprise, to judge by the flare of alarm in his eyes.

She held the blade close, so that he could feel the touch of cold steel against his throat even as she breathed in cologne mingled with sweat, a jarringly familiar scent that tugged her back to the stable-yard at home, where she would run out to greet him when he came in from the gallops.

Looking past her, Rosmoney glared at O'Neill. 'Can't you bloody do something?'

O'Neill sat frozen at the table. 'But it's Lady Cressida.'

'It most undoubtedly is,' Rosmoney shot back, now with a flash of humour. 'Don't look at me like that, my girl, like your mother when she was in one of her moralising moods.' He smiled at her then. 'I'm sorry, darling, but you're far more like me than your extremely proper Mama, the Lord rest her soul.'

'You know nothing about me, not really,' Cressida said, so furious that her voice shook. 'Tell me what you're doing here before I put a little more pressure on this knife.'

Rosmoney sighed, as though she had just interrupted him poring over some important papers in the library. 'What do you want to know? I'm hardly going to tell you everything, am I, so you may as well forget that. We'll be here all night.'

'Unless I gut you like the pig you are, my lord,' Cressida said, smiling sweetly. 'There's a stinking mess at Drochcala that looks likely to lead a lot of good people to the gallows, so I knew you had to be involved somehow.' That hit, although the flash of wounded emotion in his eyes was so quick it would have been easy to miss. He recovered fast; he was immune to shame and lived in a world of his own confection in which his every betrayal and excess was completely understandable – she understood that now.

He smiled, with that old irresistible light in his eyes. 'Cut my throat if it pleases you, a linbh,' he said. 'I suppose it would be a fool's errand to make the point that the more you know, the more danger you find yourself in. What do you want to know?'

'Where the weapons are coming from, to start with.'

That actually silenced him for a moment, even as she held the knife to his throat. He shot another filthy look in O'Neill's direction, who stared resolutely down at the table and looked as if he would rather be anywhere but here.

'Don't blame your servant,' Cressida went on, conversationally. 'And don't bother trying to deny it. On the one hand it was foolish to take on Greville and Lord Byron as passengers, but on the other their presence was a useful cover. I once went up the River Tagus with the men and the weapons, though, Papa – did you know that? No one sealed the barrels of rum with pitch, only those holding gunpowder. An excess of caution, one might say. One might do the same for weapons. I'll ask again: where did they come from and where are they going?'

Rosmoney faced her with another glimmer of humour. 'Annis always complained that you were not disciplined enough but I never could bear the thought of anyone taking a switch to you. I don't like to admit it but on balance she was right.'

'Oh, shut up,' Cressida said. 'And if it's any consolation, she found other ways.'

'Clearly not effective enough, my dear.'

Cressida smiled. 'Save yourself the trouble of wasting all that charm upon me, Papa.' She allowed the blade to graze the shaven, suntanned skin at his throat.

Rosmoney sighed, as far as he was able without allowing

the blade any closer to his neck. 'It's actually muskets and powder, straight from the magazine at Enniskillen. I transfer it here to another agent. It all goes down to northern England. The weaving towns have been ready to rise up since before Lord Perceval was shot.'

Irresistibly, Cressida recalled Lascelles facing her and Greville across the guest bedchamber at Gordon Square.

No one knows if that gunshot was the first of a full-blown revolution.

Cressida paused. For a moment, her throat was so dry with fear and shock that she couldn't speak. This wasn't real: it couldn't be. 'And who takes them there?'

'I haven't the smallest notion who moves the weapons on from here, angel. How should I?'

'*You're* shipping weaponry from Ireland?' Cressida stared at him. 'You've been in the pay of the British government for more than a decade. God, that's absurdly dangerous. It's actually just absurd. What does the War Office and Lord Liverpool have to say to that? Papa, you're in the Committee of Secrecy's pay – what are you playing at? They'll hang you at Newgate for this.'

Rosmoney just smiled at her, with an incalculable expression in his laughing dark eyes. 'I always say that what the man doesn't know can't hurt him, angel. Now just don't put me back on that pedestal again, will you? I don't do well there at all.'

31

Greville ran down to the end of the garden, making for the stables. Oliver, so he'd been told, had abandoned the servants' table early to check on the horses. He could only pray that Roberts had the sense to stay put: it would be a kindness to Bute to contain this until he'd been told. Greville stopped on the cinder path, staring out at the loch-head where grass tumbled down into white sand, all overgrown with drifts of pale pink thrift glowing in what remained of the light: he couldn't forget Roberts's spiteful smile, telling him and Cleveland how she'd seen Lady Cressida walking away from the gardens towards the plantation and the hillside beyond. *I thought as it seemed a strange time for a walk, my lord.*

Take the money and go, Byron had told her.

Greville battled a futile urge to go after her, alongside an unnerving sense of unreality: how could the loch look so peaceful, and the wide pale sweep of beach away to the west so serene? This felt like one of the vivid dreams he sometimes had after a battle, but neither brandy nor a lit candle would banish this. In a household full of civilians who couldn't be trusted to organise their way out of a burlap sack, someone had to manage a hell's breakfast of this magnitude. He recalled the expression of naked nihilism on Cressida's face, just moments after they'd made love in Chas's dressing room at Crauford House. Surely the question wasn't what Cressida was capable of, but just how little she cared what happened to her?

Greville shook himself like a dog coming out of the loch. He had to take hold of himself. Somers absorbed servant-hall gossip like a sponge and he knew that Annis had struck Cressida across the face outside the dining room. Poison was a woman's weapon, but Cressida had the look of someone who would do the job with their bare hands if she did it at all, in much the same way as he preferred to organise the task himself. Again, that soldier's instinct whispered a quiet warning, this time to open the stable door in total silence. Which meant that Greville was faced with Oliver Tait kissing a tall, sun-bronzed and long-limbed young man clad in salt-stained breeches and a fisherman's jacket of heavy twill, his honey-gold hair stiff with salt. Tait had one hand in Jamie's fair hair and one on his arse. Oliver saw Greville first. Slowly, Jamie turned around.

Jamie put a hand on Oliver's arm and then moved to stand in front of him, a lover's protective gesture. 'It'll be quite all right. Greville—'

'Shut up.' Greville spoke with such soft savagery that Jamie actually listened, even as Greville recalled with a jolt the way Oliver Tait had looked at him across the bar in the Loch Iffrin Tavern just hours before, for all that it now felt like days. *Tait had recognised him.* He and Oliver Tait had never laid eyes on each other before but Oliver clearly knew Jamie, who was Greville's cousin not only legally by adoption, but also by blood-ties of illegitimacy.

'Are you an actual Radical, James?'

Jamie shrugged so that Greville really had to restrain the urge to clip him around the ear. 'Something has to change: surely you can see that? Without a free and fair society, we're nothing. The poor in this country are treated like animals.'

'Then I beg you will tell me why the bloody hell you're up to your neck in a mess that will like as not send most of the Butes' servants to the gallows for free-trading? They're not larking about playing at smugglers and getting sent down from Cambridge, are they?'

Jamie flushed then. 'They were free-trading anyway. I wouldn't expect you to understand the rest.'

He was the Gentleman, not Rosmoney after all. It explained those long, otherwise inexplicable absences from Cambridge. It even doubtless explained why Chas, with his casual resemblance to Jamie, had been shot in London: Jamie could easily have crossed the wrong man, playing this sort of game. And above all, it explained why Oliver Tait had looked at him, Greville, with such clear recognition in the Loch Iffrin Tavern. Tait was up to his neck in the Gentleman's trade in black-market weapons, too: weapons that now waited at the bottom of the loch, although not too far down, almost as easily retrievable as a line of lobster pots.

Greville didn't wait for an answer, which was just as well

because Jamie didn't look even close to presenting him with one.

It only needed this. Greville measured out each word with ice-cold clarity. 'Let's try this again: who in the devil's name is paying you to ship weapons up this loch and where are they going?'

Jamie gave him a pitying look. 'Do you really think I know who's paying me? The chain of command has to be kept secret, Greville. Anyway, I don't keep the money,' he continued, without a hint of remorse. 'I'm doing it because it's the right thing to do: I gave everything to the benevolent fund for the weavers last time. I just cut through the Pentland Firth and then go down past Fraserburgh and south to Morecambe,' Jamie went on, as though this were nothing, and not a mission of unhinged danger.

'There's a war on. How do you know those weapons aren't going to end up making their merry way straight across the Bay of Biscay to the French army in Spain, let alone the information that's probably carried with them?'

Jamie looked momentarily chastened at that.

'I keep telling him it's a fool's errand,' Oliver cut in, with restrained anger. 'But he never listens.'

'No, I would imagine not. Where did you get the boat?' Greville asked. 'Did you steal it?'

Jamie gave him a scornful look. 'Of course not. I take the *Wren*. No one ever sailed her after my father died. She was just mouldering alongside the quay at Blyth, and she's pretty tough for a yawl of her size. I'm not doing anything the Norsemen didn't do.'

'Of course. And where is she now, if I might ask?' Greville

said, now fighting twin urges to laugh or hit him across the stables. The fucking Norsemen.

'Only about four miles away, on the quay at Sangobeg,' Jamie said, impatient. 'I walked over: word is Fraser MacGuigan's been patrolling up and down the loch here for days, and if he's not here, he's poking about at Loch Eriboll.'

'I don't even know what to say. Christ.' Greville stared at his cousin for a moment, examining Jamie's face once more for any sign of remorse or regret. Seeing neither, he resisted another urge to clout him. 'Next time you want a little excitement in your life, can I suggest you do it in the name of King and country and join the army?'

Jamie smiled at him, but his eyes were hard. 'Why would I want to serve the King? Thousands of his subjects are starving and yet nothing is done. Why else do you think I'm doing this? No one of our class cares about injustice and they should: it's disgusting, the way you all sit around screwing each other's wives and stuffing your faces like force-fed geese, looking down on everyone else who doesn't quite meet the standard.'

'Shut up,' Greville said, ferocious. 'All I've got to say about this is at least you've given each other something of an alibi. Tait, come with me now. James, I'll deal with you later but you'd better come into the house. This is a mess.'

'An alibi?' Oliver's voice was toneless with shock, not that Greville blamed him for that. He didn't care to judge men for who they chose to bed, not as long as all were willing and none of it concerned his wife. Greville was no greenhorn, either. He knew quite well that some like Arthur Lascelles preferred other men all their lives, never taking up with women. But all the same, actually getting caught with another man could see Jamie and Oliver in the stocks, pelted with filth, or even on the gallows: they both needed to be a damn sight more careful.

Not trusting himself to say another word, Greville jerked his head towards the door in an unspoken order. Following Oliver and Jamie outdoors into an azure-tinted Highland night, Greville's mind raced as he sorted through twenty years of memory: remarks made by great-aunts and friends of the family when the Nightingale children were brought up to the drawing room. Some of those comments had been nothing but harmless throwaway observation, others more pointed, even whispered.

Goodness, isn't Jamie the image of Tristan? (That had always merited a frozen silence.)

Are not Chas and Jamie precisely like peas in a pod, with that pretty fair hair?

Lord, Greville is your image, Sylvia! Crauford always had far more of their father about him, did he not?

Greville scarcely favours his papa at all.

Jamie, on the other hand, was the image of his natural father. Their fathers, natural and legal, had been brothers. Any resemblance between him and Jamie was quite understandable – had Greville actually resembled his own father much at all.

Greville knew quite well that he had never done so.

You have only his hands, Sylvia always used to say, holding out her own for Greville to kiss. And yet place her alongside him before a mirror and the resemblance was strikingly clear, for all that his mother was a woman and he a man: the long, curved mouth, those tilted eyebrows. Even the single dimple was identical.

Jamie did look exactly how Greville remembered his libertine, fair-haired uncle Tristan, so different a man to his own quiet, thoughtful father. But in that stable, Greville saw for the first time what Oliver had seen in the Loch Iffrin Tavern: as a grown man, Jamie also clearly resembled him.

Greville wondered how much time they had before everyone else saw it, too.

Part Four

An Axe Laid to the Root

32

The night Annis Bute died, everyone except Lord Bute and Cressida kept a vigil in the unaired drawing room, where all the candles in polished brass sconces upon the walls had been allowed to burn down to nothing. It was a wake of sorts: Cleveland lay stretched out asleep on the chaise longue, still in his evening clothes save for his boots. Not a soldier, Greville thought with a strange, detached sense of amusement. Byron reclined in a wing-armchair, his legs crossed at the ankle. He stared straight through Greville, the cut direct. Jamie sat leaning against the log basket for most of the night, awake too, but only just, his hair thick with salt spray and arranged by the wind. Kitty slept on Greville himself, curled up on the chaise with her head on a cushion in his lap. Cressida, meanwhile, had returned to the house sometime after dark, offering no explanation for her absence. Greville let Kitty give her the news, and it had been Kitty who left Cressida alone with Lord Bute, who that night refused to see anyone else except Mrs Scudamore.

Greville recalled the morning afterwards in only snatches of polite, forced conversation, and the summer light of the far north streaming in through the tall, unshuttered windows as if in defiance. Annis's death dwarfed Jamie's appearance and Greville could only be grateful that no one except his sister was surprised at the ill-timed late arrival of another Nightingale. Everyone fell into deathbed habits: Kitty and Cressida served tea to the priest and the kirkwarden from Leirinmore, all the while discussing when the mackerel would shoal and if the weather was likely to turn: the fishermen said there was a storm on the way from Cape Wrath.

An army surgeon home on leave was also fetched from Leirinmore and confirmed the cause of death to Greville and Cleveland in a low-voiced conversation that took place by a bright fire in the bedchamber where Annis had died. A ruddy, capable surgeon in the Black Watch, Gunn looked very much as if he wished himself on the battlefield: anywhere rather than here. Annis had been laid out on the bed and her jaw bound with a wide white strip of muslin, which was just as well considering how the dose of poison had contorted her face in a howling, unheard scream. Pennies now closed eyes once alight with laughter, calculation and mockery: she was dead, actually dead, and this was no fever-dream, even if Greville was starting to feel distinctly below par, hot and cold every other moment, the wound in his arm throbbing with distracting regularity.

'Strychnos nux-vomica is my best guess, I'm afraid, to judge by the effects – and an enormous dose at that.' Gunn showed them both a cracked glass found beneath the bed.

'Lady Bute had a fondness for a dram of very fine cognac before retiring, according to her woman. The decanter and a glass was always kept here, on her dressing table. It looks very likely that Lady Bute consumed the poison in her cognac and was overcome before she even had the chance to ring for her woman to undress her. I suppose there's no way of discovering who might have had the opportunity to slip into her bedchamber?'

When Gunn had gone, Greville turned to Cleveland. 'Whoever did this couldn't have chosen a worse way for her to go. She must have been in unimaginable pain. The difficulty will be to find out who didn't have reason to inflict it.'

Cleveland yawned and stretched, catlike. 'Well, I couldn't bear the woman, but I didn't kill her. That's Lascelles's style, not mine. Depending on what time of night she died, at the very least you, Byron, Bute and I can swear to each other's presence in the drawing room. And I think Bute's the only one of us who didn't actively dislike her. Kitty's easy to account for – both she and her maid can attest to each other's presence. Cressida, on the other hand, is a different story.' He turned to look at Greville then with unsettling perspicacity. 'Are you all right?'

'Of course I'm all right,' Greville lied. 'Why did you come to Drochcala?'

Cleveland gave him a swift, searching look. 'Rubbish. You and Lascelles were always cut from the same cloth – right down to wearing hair shirts, I see, although he's by far a better liar than you are.' Cleveland spoke next without shifting his gaze from what had once been their hostess.

'I came because there was an obligation,' he said, shortly. 'Annis took the opportunity to remind me of it when it suited her, which it did this summer.'

Greville ignored a wave of exhaustion, sleep having evaded him altogether. 'What did she want? Money?'

'That, and my presence here. If what I'm about to say is ever repeated beyond this room, I will find out, and I will ruin you: I'm here because of our sister. Mine and Lascelles' sister.'

Greville said nothing, giving Cleveland all the rope he needed.

'Georgiana is only sixteen years old, and she has spent much of her life at Kielder Castle.' Cleveland allowed himself a tight smile. 'Probably too much of her life, because I was so rarely there myself, and when I was I can't say I exercised myself a great deal about her welfare beyond securing the very best in tuition and the most proper of companionship. But Georgiana didn't need an Italian governess: she needed a friend.' He paused, into an echoing silence. 'She found that without my help, in the son of a local fisherman. Beyond a certain mutual infatuation, I believe that the relationship between them was innocent, even as they grew older. One night, Georgiana and Tom got into difficulties sailing on Kielder Water. The mast broke, and although they managed to reach the shore, they were both soaked to the skin and Georgiana unwell with an attack of asthma. They did manage to reach a posting-inn not far from Windermere. Unhappily, it was also where Lord and Lady Bute changed horses on their way up to Drochcala to keep Christmas.

'I knew she wouldn't hold her tongue for nothing,' Cleveland went on. 'I'm sure it's no news to you that the Butes sank far too much into their Jamaican interests, or that Bute's father gambled away most of the rest in the sixties. I don't know what Crauford was thinking: I'd allow no brother of mine to marry a girl associated with prospects like that, even if they were only her guardians. And those interests in the Caribbean are much less profitable since Perceval championed Abolition, but the Butes' desire to keep up appearances never wavered, did it? Obviously, profiting from enslavement is far more genteel than becoming involved in trade or the City, and they have no son to marry into money. When Jamaica no longer paid, Annis chose blackmail.'

Greville digested the fact that Cleveland had a moral compass after all, and one that swung in much the same direction as his own. 'Annis had us over a barrel, too – I daresay you can broadly guess why. Evidently someone has saved us all the trouble of dealing with her.' He couldn't ignore the growing certainty that Cressida, with her tattered reputation and her peculiar disappearance, was going to emerge from this as Annis's most likely killer – perhaps even more so than Oliver Tait.

'When Bute has recovered from the first shock of grief, he's going to want this investigated,' Cleveland went on. 'You may as well know that I've no intention of dumping my obligations to Annis Fane on some provincial magistrate and I advise you not to do the same.'

Greville felt the old hot anger kindle. 'I'm not going to allow a servant to swing for this: it'll all have to be dealt with somehow. And this provincial magistrate of yours is actually Bute himself.'

Cleveland gave him a thin smile. 'Of course he is. Unless we can find a satisfactory explanation for Annis's death, it'll surely go before the sheriff. That's Lord MacCrae. This is no case of petty theft or feuding peasants taking it in turns to burn each other's thatch. It would be reprehensible to persuade Bute that it will be in his own immediate best interests never to share all this information Annis had gathered with MacCrae, wouldn't it? An old man in his condition, after such a shock.'

'Beyond the pale,' Greville agreed, and with no further discussion he and Cleveland moved as one and went through Annis's dressing room where her bottles of strawberry leaf tincture and Gesso's milk were still laid out on her dressing table. At last they reached Bute's oak-panelled bedchamber, where their host sat at a small escritoire by the window, dressed in his nightgown and an embroidered banyan that had probably cost him more than one of the enslaved men or women cropping sugar on his Jamaican estate. Greville crushed a surge of hatred: better not to show that yet. Bute didn't look around when they walked into the room, absorbed in staring at the sheaf of papers spread out in disorder before him.

'Awful how the numbers don't tot up right the more you stare at them, isn't it?' Cleveland said.

Bute reached convulsively for his glass of brandy before turning to face them. 'Oh, it's not really figures, thank goodness. It's all such a dreadful affair,' he said, as though they were discussing an act of God, like a child succumbing to the measles. 'I'm afraid I never had any head for business, and my dear Annis always used to handle this sort of thing. I must admit, I never did quite understand the purpose of this particular investment and now it's all rather uncomfortable and embarrassing, to say the least. Now she's gone I haven't the least idea what to do about it.'

'I should turn it all over to Mr Tait, my lord,' Greville said.

'Oh no, that wouldn't be at all appropriate. Oliver is quite wonderfully intelligent – they are, you know – but this is nothing to do with estate management. I'm afraid it's a private affair rather beyond Mr Tait's understanding.' Bute smiled ruefully even as Greville registered what he had just said: *they are, you know*, as if Oliver and Somers were both less than human. Did he believe the same of Kitty?

'Perhaps we can help?' Cleveland said, with the speed and precision of a striking adder.

Bute gave them both a vacant smile. 'I should be very grateful for that, and I'm sure I can count on your discretion. It's really all so unfortunate – worse even than just being involved in trade. I'm hopeless with correspondence and paperwork – Annis advised me to burn all this, but that feels grubby, as if we had something to hide. She never knew I kept it all.' He let out a burst of braying laughter. 'Well, I could just never understand the worth of the investment: you see, it's not as if the Bellingham fellow had a sound head for trade as far as I could ever make out. He was actually thrown into prison in Russia, you know, over something to do with duties, which, as a merchant, really ought to have been his affair to understand. Annis insisted the investment would be worthwhile. She was quite clear about that: Bellingham's next voyage was certain to be a great success that would benefit us all, that's what she said to me. It would be well worth the investment: she was sure of that. We paid the Bellingham fellow an awful lot of money and then of course he shot the prime minister.'

Even Cleveland had nothing to say.

'I can see the difficulty,' Greville said. 'How awkward to have a business connection with the prime minister's murderer.'

'I mourn the man, but I can't say that I mourn his policies,' Bute said, inconsequentially. 'I only pity Lady Perceval and the children, I must admit. I quite understand how they must be feeling.' When he next looked up at Greville and Cleveland, his face was wet with tears.

33

In the kitchen at Drochcala, Cressida warmed herself at the great black range, unable to forget how Rosmoney had lied to her face just hours before and with her knife to his throat. Even then, she still hadn't seen it in his eyes: Jamie Nightingale was so unmistakably a Nightingale that there wasn't a chance her father hadn't known who he was.

Ines stood at the table with a long hot-pressed linen apron tied over her gown, carving a large ham and issuing scathing instructions to Jamie himself about how to butter the loaf of brown bread before cutting each slice. Roberts had been given some tatting to do for her nerves, as Mrs Scudamore would have it, and sat like a black crow with the basket of rags in the battered armchair by the big kitchen window.

Jamie was making Mrs Scudamore and Ines laugh with a long, involved story about the pigs at Summercourt escaping into the walled garden last summer, but he stopped smiling the moment Greville came in, as well he might.

'Set to work, James?' Greville said, amiably. He spoke without a hint of malice, leaning on the doorframe, but Cressida had heard experienced officers use that tone before with recalcitrant younger staff, and Jamie's eyes glittered.

Mrs Scudamore glared at Greville, accusing. 'We'll none of us be touching any cooked food for a day or so yet, not for all the carbolic soap between here and Edinburgh, so it's just as well Mr Nightingale has shifted himself to help, unlike some people.'

Greville gave Mrs Scudamore a look that bordered on chagrin, tempered with a smile that made the colour rush to her cheeks. 'A wise choice, mistress.' His gaze flickered towards Cressida. She nodded almost imperceptibly, and he added that they wouldn't keep the boy long. Greville held the door open, and Jamie had no choice but to follow him out: a masterful handling of the situation, Cressida had to admit, even if Greville did look pale, his lips a little compressed, whether by dint of the wound in his arm, a lost night's sleep, or the sheer effort it must be taking not to howl at his cousin.

Walking in silence down the stone-flagged corridor, they met Kitty in the small, little-used parlour at the back of the house. Kitty's eyes were hollow with shocked exhaustion, and her morning gown of printed poplin had been haphazardly pressed. Bute had missed his chance to impose fashionable good taste in here, and so Cressida watched Greville and Kitty take it in turns to quietly eviscerate Jamie against an incongruous backdrop of floral-patterned silk wall-hangings and tapestried Queen Anne chaises longues littered with overstuffed embroidered cushions.

'Have you quite finished?' Jamie asked, when Kitty paused for breath.

'Don't bloody talk to Kitty like that,' Greville snapped.

Jamie made an obvious effort to control his temper. 'Listen, I understand your views, but it's clear you don't respect my position at all. Someone has to take action against the utter atrocious cruelty of this government and they listen to neither reason nor importunity.' He glared at Greville and Kitty, who was watching him with her arms folded, flushed with an angry, uneven patch of colour on each cheek. 'I don't know how either of you can stand there and talk such rubbish about change without revolution when Cressida's father played his part and lost everything for his trouble. I'll take my leave now, if you don't mind.'

'You will not,' Cressida said, and Jamie stopped where he stood.

Kitty smiled.

'I must lift that cargo. It's expected—' Jamie broke off, clearly opting for the position that none of them were to be trusted with Radical plans. 'You three of all people I hoped would have some sympathy for the cause, but I might as well be explaining myself to bloody Crauford. I don't understand you.'

'That much is obvious,' Cressida replied, choosing her words with care, even as she was aware of Greville watching her. 'Jamie, listen to me. You don't need to tell me about the cruelty of our government: I grew up in a country where I saw evidence of it daily. My family have been in Ireland since the Norman conquest, but when you look at the circumstances it's not that difficult to understand why we were never really accepted by the Irish: we stole their lands and their way of life, we prayed in a different church. Nevertheless, my father wanted change, for Ireland to be united as one, setting her own rules for her own people. Rosmoney became the man he is today because the United Irishmen were infiltrated like every other rebel movement since the dawn of time. You can bet your life that since Lord Perceval was shot, every single government mole in every single rebel group in England is waiting for the order to encourage his fellows into an atrocity that will only deliver them all to the gallows. The same will be true of the Radicals you're arming. True rebellion is like a game of chess: don't allow yourself or others to make a move that will end in checkmate. If you can't see that's exactly what you're enabling here, then I don't know what to tell you.'

Jamie had been listening in angry silence; now he looked at them each in turn, his gaze resting longest on Cressida, no doubt proud of himself for not telling them all that he knew exactly who had brought those weapons across the Irish Sea. 'I feel sorry for you, I truly do.' He turned to Kitty next. 'And don't think I'm not aware why you're here, meddling away on Sylvia's behalf. Why can't you just leave me to arrange my own affairs? You could have at least asked me before playing into the hands of that absolute bitch upstairs on my behalf. I'm really not surprised she's dead.'

Leaning against the mantelpiece, Greville turned to Kitty with a calm, enquiring expression that fooled nobody.

'Oh, *Lord*,' Kitty said, exasperated. 'Jamie, did you ever stop to consider that the reason I'm here has less to do with you and more to do with Sylvia? Try to understand the notion that not everything is only about you.' Stalking over to the door, she opened it, looked down the deserted corridor and closed the door again, then rested against it for a moment with her eyes shut.

'Go on!' Jamie hissed. 'Tell them. I'm not ashamed.'

'Oh, do be quiet!' Kitty said. 'I've heard just about enough from you for one morning. Have you no care at all for Greville's feelings?'

'Don't hold back on my account – Cressida knows all my faults,' Greville said with infinite patience. 'If it helps, I've already come to the conclusion that Jamie and I have the felicity to be brothers, rather than cousins. I suppose our mother had an affair with Tristan: it would be exactly like both of them. It explains a great deal, including why you're here, Kitty, instead of at Straloch with Alasdair and the children. Annis was blackmailing our mother, too, I suppose, and you came here in her stead when she wasn't able to leave Chas?'

Cold unease prickled between Cressida's shoulder blades: the truth about Jamie's parentage clicked into place like a jigsaw piece. Now that she knew what to look for, his resemblance to Sylvia and to Greville himself was startling, and unsettling in how that likeness had been there all along, if only they had known what to look for.

'You know what Annis is like – was like,' Kitty said, before Cressida had the chance to walk out. 'She adored watching people. If anyone was likely to ferret out the truth about you, Greville, purely by observation, it was going to be Annis. She didn't get us all up here to blackmail us about Papa not really being your father, though. Why should she?

There can't be many top ten thousand families without a cuckoo in the nest. As long as the heir has the right father, no one really cares much about the others. Tristan was your father, yes, but Mama is Jamie's mother, too. She almost left Papa when Jamie was born.'

All that could be heard was a log shifting in the grate, throwing out a shower of tiny sparks which Greville absent-mindedly trod out.

'What an absurd farce,' he said. 'If it hadn't ended with Jamie enacting melodramas, it would be a straightforward comedy.'

'You can hardly talk,' Jamie retorted, white-faced with suppressed frustration. 'You didn't have to put up with twenty years of people whispering behind their hands about who your real mother and father were.'

'I'm sorry,' Greville said. He poured brandy from the decanter into four crystal glasses. 'That part of it makes no sense to me, either. Sylvia had already presented my father with one bastard to pass off as his own; why on earth she couldn't have just done it a second time like everyone else, I have no idea.'

'Because Papa wasn't in England when Jamie was conceived.' Kitty took the glass he passed her. 'He was on a diplomatic expedition to Russia. There was no covering it up. You're too young to recall, but I'm not and neither is Crauford: Mama disappeared for almost a year. It was put about that she'd gone to Austria to take the waters, but in reality she went to Tristan at Carver Hall and had the baby there. Tristan's circle at that time was so scandalous that there was no chance of her meeting anyone she knew, and there were enough secrets at Carver that Tristan's friends never betrayed her, whether out of affection or self-protection.'

'It would have been affection,' Jamie snapped. 'You didn't know them.'

'In fact,' Kitty went on, ignoring him, 'Mama was in love with Tristan. When Papa came home from Russia, he went up to Northumbria and persuaded her to come home. You and Jamie are brothers: you share the same mother as well as the same father. Annis worked it out years ago in that way she has of ferreting out exactly what one least wants her to know. She used to say what a shame it would be if it ever came out, and how everyone understands about the odd bastard under one's roof here and there, but if it had got out that Sylvia nearly left Papa and spent almost a year actually living at Carver Hall, she'd be ruined and so would the rest of us. For a start, even George Byron's circle has nothing on Tristan's.'

'I didn't kill Annis,' Jamie said abruptly. 'I would have liked to, but if I'd done it I wouldn't have chosen poison: I'd have held her down and drowned her in the loch.'

'Steady now,' Greville said with such calm authority that Jamie fell silent.

'Either way, let's hope we can convince Lord MacCrae of that when he comes down from Inverness,' Kitty said. Greville did nothing but fix his gaze out of the window at the silver waters of Loch Iffrin, now lost in thought, and Cressida knew she had to walk away from this family, before their loves and their disasters drew her in for ever to a position among them that she did not deserve.

34

Cressida paused on the threshold of her bedchamber, listening to Greville's shallow, uneven breathing. She took two quick, quiet steps into the room and found him stretched out on the floor at the foot of her bed in all his long-limbed grace. How like him to fall asleep in the wake of a revelation that would have floored most men. She stood watching, unable for a moment to look away: he lay on his back on a bedroll that Somers must have laid out before the fire, stripped to the waist but still in his breeches and boots, as if he were expecting to get up and fight, and unaware for now of how she took in every inch of his form. Dark blood had already soaked through the linen bandage, but his arm was a sculptor's study in muscle and form: surely looking at him like this was just a harmless small pleasure?

Cressida allowed her gaze to fall from Greville's arm to his naked chest, torso and belly. Four years ago, he'd had the lean strength of a rich young aristocrat favoured by the gods, trained only by riding hard and sparring in the boxing salon he favoured. Now there was a new edge to that strength. The Greville she'd known had taken pleasure in satisfying his every want.

'You still look like a fallen angel, you fool,' she whispered into the darkness, dropping into a crouch at his side. The uneven rhythm of his breathing betokened feverishness. Somers must have drawn shut the heavy velvet curtains, but thin grey sunlight slanted in through the crack, illuminating a faint sheen of perspiration on his forehead. She fought a half-forgotten desire to trace those winged dark brows with her fingertip, but he woke anyway, opening his eyes to meet her own, even as he flexed the long, strong fingers of one hand, reaching for the knife sheathed close to his waist so that it would have been concealed beneath his evening jacket. The liminal half-waking expression cleared from his eyes, and he let the hand fall by his side.

'Cressida.' There was an edge of humour in his voice mingled with threat, and she was overwhelmingly aware of his size and strength. If Greville was a clear danger now, what would he become when he learned she'd found Rosmoney? She'd taken a step closer to understanding the lethal mess Jamie was in, and had not told him.

'You should be asleep,' she said, instead. 'You'll go home by weeping cross if you're not careful. I'm sorry about your mother and father.'

Greville watched her steadily. 'That sort of dirty great secret is never as much of a shock as everyone thinks – at least not to the people it concerns. At any rate, so will we all go home by weeping cross if we go on like this. I don't think there's a person at Drochcala without a motive to kill your cousin, and the last thing we need here is the sheriff.' He stretched then, wincing as he moved his injured arm, crooking the other behind his head. The sight of his dark underarm hair sent a shock of intimacy through her, even as she was certain that Greville himself knew something he had chosen not to share with her. He looked up at her again: 'I wish you weren't here. I wish you weren't part of this.'

She didn't quite manage to keep a thread of anger from her voice. 'I've been in worse fixes, Greville.'

'And I wish that wasn't true, not that wishes are much use to anyone other than children.' Greville got up then, moving with a little less grace than usual because he was favouring the wounded arm. He crossed the room to the large window and drew back the curtains before leaning on the window frame, facing out towards to the loch. His shoulder blades rose elegantly from the lean, muscled expanse of his naked back and she had to catch her breath. It shouldn't hurt like this to look at him, whatever he was keeping from her.

'It's my fault,' he said, at last. 'You should know at least that I accept it.' He turned to face her. 'Every last insult that you've suffered for the past three years might as well have been at my own hands. I swore before God to protect and honour you, and instead I drove you straight to Cleveland and from there into what can only have been a form of hell.'

Cressida sat on the end of the bed, like a puppet with the strings cut away. Now it was her turn to make wishes: how dared he do this, here and now? 'Why didn't you come after me? I always did wonder that. I thought you'd reclaim your legal property, if nothing else.'

What if he had come after her? What if she'd never set foot on that troop ship with her Michael, or not without Greville at least? What if Sylvia and Kitty had succeeded in packing her and Greville both off to Summercourt to let their mutual fury scorch itself out behind closed doors? Had her baby lived, he or she would have been rising three years old now, either Greville's child or Cleveland's cuckoo. It struck her that Greville would have probably found it within himself to love a cuckoo, or at least to treat him or her with the careless kindness he showed to all animals and children.

Greville watched her now, very still, with the afternoon sunlight and the loch behind him. The window was ajar, and she breathed in the faint scent of exposed seaweed as the tide began to turn. 'I didn't come after you because on that occasion anger and stupidity overrode my pride. I'm sorry for it. And if you want the truth, actually I'm still furious with you. I don't even know the half of what you did, what you faced. And even then I'm still not as angry with you as I am with myself. But you don't need me to rescue you any more – if indeed you ever did.'

His face was cast into shadow by the light streaming in behind him, so that it was hard to read his expression.

'You've been looking out for your own survival since the day Rosmoney left Ireland, have you not?' Greville went on. 'Dealing with his idea of a pleasant, rational mode of living must be second nature to you by now.'

'You're feverish,' Cressida said. 'Did that man of yours

even clean the wound before he bound it?' She refused to think of how Greville had enveloped her in his arms on that launch; she wouldn't waste a single moment on the memory of how he had taken that bullet on her behalf as though it were more natural than breathing.

'He bled me, and I've felt devilish ever since. Cressida, where is your father?'

She had trusted Rosmoney in that bothy last night, believing him as he lied straight to her face. Trust was too dangerous a game to play now, with anyone. Greville said nothing, at least mercifully quick to realise that he would get no more secrets out of her, just as he showed no signs of sharing whatever he was keeping from her. He was hiding something: she sensed it, almost an invisible presence in the room. Instead, Greville sat beside her on the end of the bed, swearing quietly as he reached around to loosen the pin in his bandage. She removed that pin herself, sliding it out of the fabric. Greville caught his breath as they touched, but whether this was because of the discomfort or the flash of heat as his fingers brushed hers, she couldn't say. The gunpowder had been wiped away, and dark bruising now flowered in its place. Cressida sent for boiled water and clean linen, ignoring Ines's look of warning as she glanced from husband to wife and back again before retreating to the safety of Mrs Scudamore's kitchen.

Cressida left Greville sitting on the bed and took feverfew and honey from the battered roll of canvas she'd carried from the dusty apothecary shop in a shady Lisbon back alley all the way to Badajoz. She took the can from her pack and set water to boil at the edge of the open fire, crouching down to turn the can with the blade of her knife and the old iron spoon she'd found in a ruined house near Talavera. When the water had boiled, she dressed the wound with honey and bandaged it again.

They had settled into silence and neither spoke as she shook dried feverfew flowers from her leather pouch into the seething water, brewing a tisane with willow bark and some of the honey drizzled from the end of her knife, which she went to wipe on her apron until she remembered she hadn't worn one for months. Nudging her can away from the glowing embers to cool on the hearthstone, Cressida got up and found Greville still watching her, leaning on one of the bedposts with the old velvet canopy above his head.

'You work like a bloody soldier.' The anger in his voice was undimmed; he would never forgive himself or her.

'No, Greville. I work like the soldier's wife I lived as.'

'You're my wife,' Greville said, with an expression in his eyes of such fury and come-hither that if she didn't leave the room now, they'd both regret it.

35

Cressida made at first to walk past him; he wasn't going to stop her. 'Your tisane is ready and should be cool enough to drink.' Her dark eyes gleamed in the lamplight. 'I suggest that you do so, before fever sets into that wound.' In a whirl of sudden movement, she bent to pick up the steaming can from the fire's edge without flinching at the heat, holding it out to him with an air of command.

'Your concoction be damned. I wouldn't put it past you to lace it with arsenic.' Greville was unable to quell a flare of satisfaction at riling her, even as he wanted so badly to take her in his arms, even if he could never make amends, even if they couldn't take that most childlike of first steps and actually trust one another. Her cousin had funded the prime minister's killer, and yet how did this fit with the way Annis had died? In another time and place, they would have discussed that from every angle, dissecting every possible implication, he as ever a little in awe of her calm, methodical intelligence.

'I suppose you think I killed Annis as well,' Cressida said. 'Are you so afraid of me, my lord?'

It was the scorn in her expression and in her voice that made Greville lose his temper, so irrevocably that he didn't even register a sense of satisfaction at the brief flare of alarm in her eyes. 'Believe me, my lady, there are many ways I've wished to use you since you ran away from your cousin's ball. But I've never been afraid of you.' With an inclination of his head, Greville took the can from her hands, ignoring the bolt of heat as her fingers brushed against his. He drank the tisane in one draught, sweet and faintly herbal, and then set down the can on the mantelpiece with a decided click of tin against slate.

'I'm pleased to see you've learned a modicum of common sense.' Cressida turned away, walking towards the door, leaving behind attar of roses and the lavender-water scent of her hair.

If she wanted this, then let her have it of her own volition.

'Are you going to walk away again?'

She turned back to face him, chestnut curls escaping from her coiffure, her skin luminously pale against the dark blue linen bodice of her gown. How many times had she lain down to sleep on the march, content with a rain-soaked ditch or a burned-out nunnery when she was his own wife and he ought to have been pleasing her on fine linen sheets, all this time?

'You know what will happen if I don't,' she said, steadily. 'What else would you have me do?'

'I would have you come here,' Greville said.

She stood before him, her ears strung with pearls that

glowed in the gathering darkness. 'How on earth can this possibly help either of us?' She smiled, with a glimmer of her old humour. Now there was no hint of flirtation.

Greville let out a breath. He allowed himself to really look at her then, to relish the strong curve of her waist and the rise of her breasts. 'Because you still want me, and you haven't forgotten all the things that I can show you, and all the things that I can do for you, and how much you enjoy serving me the same.' If nothing else, they could have this, even if it was just for one last time.

'You're still not troubled by modesty, I see.'

'But either way, you and I are long overdue a proper reckoning, are we not?'

It had always worked this way between them, neither one giving an inch of quarter: parry, strike, a bloody hit. Greville held out one hand as though he were leading her in to dance. After a heartbeat of a pause, Cressida took his hand. With a single authoritative tug, Greville drew her closer, a step in this dance that she was only too willing to take. He kissed her with bruising force, her long fingers entangled in his hair with a punishing tug that sent him feathering her neck with kisses so that she let out a pent-up gasp. He would have her calling his name by the time he was finished; she would be his once more, really his, even if only for now. This would be no savage, regretful flyer against a dressing room wall. Greville meant to take his time. He ran his hands down her back, over her rear, pushing up the skirts of her gown and teasing with his fingers until he felt the liquid heat of her need through the outrageously fine linens she wore; he took vicious pleasure in her willing response, her hands all over his naked back.

She was lying to him. Even now, she was hiding from him the catastrophic secret of her father's real intent here at Drochcala, protecting a man who scarcely deserved the name of father, and yet how could he blame her? Had he served her a better turn? Greville kissed Cressida's neck again, lower this time, lower still, until with one ruthless tug he freed her breasts from the linen bodice of her gown and the fine lawn beneath her short stays. Her skirts had slipped back down again, catching against her petticoats, but he would soon divest her of those.

He spoke softly into her ear. 'I've wanted to do that for a very, very long time.'

'Good.' She had to catch her breath. 'I hope the thought of it kept you up at night.'

'You're damnably improper.' Greville picked her up then, hardly feeling the protest of agony in his bandaged wound, kissing her even as he walked to the bed with his wife in his arms, after all this time.

She looked up at him from a heap of pillows in lace-edged linen slips. 'Oh, for God's sake, do your worst, Devil.' With the tip of one finger, she drew a circle around his left nipple, and Greville ducked his head and devoted himself to her white breasts, which at long last were all his to enjoy once more, for as long as he pleased. Cressida laughed and trailed one fingertip along the brushstroke of dark hair that led from his belly button beneath the waistband of his breeches.

'Oh no, you don't.' Greville held both of her hands

above her head, her slender wrists loosely but irrevocably imprisoned, knowing she'd like that, the sensation that for once she did not have to be in control because he was. He remembered exactly how to please her, making short work first of her skirts, and then of her self-possession, so that at last he looked down at his wife as she lay among disordered linen sheets, turning her face into the crook of his elbow as she tried not to cry out, and when that failed, she laughed up at him with a flash of anger, her cheeks brushed with those golden freckles and now flushed with desire.

'That ought to give them all something to talk about.' Her hands moved then with consummate skill that had always been innate; they'd for ever spoken this language when words failed. She'd learned from others as well, a thought that drove him to take such pains with his wife that he knew she'd be left unsatisfied by an encounter with anyone else, up to and including George Byron. When at last they were both spent, Cressida lay in his arms on the wide bed, resting her head in the hollow below his clavicle. Greville absently traced a line between her shoulder blades, breathing in the scent of her hair.

He turned to face her, separated only by inches of crumpled linen.

'Sometimes I wonder if we would have had children.' He didn't look away, taking in the dark auburn arch of her brows, the curve of her mouth. 'Did you?'

Silence stretched between them. Cressida spoke first, he supposed with a need to hurt him. 'I would imagine that you've left a trail of little bastards from Lisbon to Badajoz, but we'll never know, will we?'

All they could do was watch each other across a distance that, despite all this, was impossible to breach. At first he thought she would get up and walk out, but in the end, Cressida just turned her back on him and Greville allowed himself to plummet into a dreamless sleep at last. Afterwards, he came to regret that more than almost anything else in his life.

36

Not long afterwards, but long enough, Greville woke at Somers' touch, one hand gripping his shoulder before swiftly letting go. Cressida was gone, the expanse of bed linen beside him now cold to the touch.

'Sir, you'd best come downstairs.' Somers spoke in a low voice, pregnant with all the warning that Greville needed.

In the drawing room, there was no sign of Bute. Greville felt a wave of cold revulsion at the thought of laying eyes on his host, and if Gunn had either sense or compassion, he would have dosed the man with enough laudanum to fell a drayhorse. Instead, Greville found Kitty and Byron at the small mother-of-pearl-inlaid table pulled close to the fire. They were sharing a decanter of port and another of brandy with Cleveland, the bloody man's fair hair gilded in the firelight. For one crazed moment, Greville saw double. A second slender, fair-haired man sat at the table with them, his back to the door, clad in a jacket of charcoal twill with an exquisite set across his lean, muscular shoulders. Greville took a hold of himself: there was only one Cleveland. The second man – cut from the same very expensive cloth – was his brother, Arthur Lascelles.

For once George Byron didn't look as if he were enjoying the tension but rather sat with his fingers steepled on the tabletop. He cut Greville completely, not even looking at him.

'Would anyone like to explain?' Greville said.

Cleveland leaned back in his chair, eyebrows slightly lifted. 'I'll leave that to my dear brother.'

Lascelles spoke without turning around. 'Get a chair. You're going to need to sit down.'

Greville lounged against the fireplace. 'I'll survive.'

Lascelles waved one gloved hand at the nearest decanter. 'I'd have thought you'll want one of those, at least. To begin with, you and I must go back to Spain, Greville. Wellington is on the move again. As for the rest, it's sensitive.'

It was always like this: the army came before everything. Lascelles clearly knew something was in the air, not that he could speak of it here. Soon Greville would be scouting ahead of the lines with his men, guiding Allied troops away from ambush by the French, lying in foxholes with his rifle again. Kitty's expression was unreadable.

'Go on,' Greville said. 'We're all out in the open here; I don't think we've a skeleton left in the cupboard between us.'

Lascelles gave him a quick, calculating glance and not for the first time Greville felt the cold force of his intelligence probing through his mind like the questing articulated legs of a spider in deep, velvet darkness. 'Fine, if that's how you wish to play it. There are several matters that Greville and I must deal with at speed before we go back to Santander.' He turned to Kitty. 'For a start, I'm afraid your brother Charles has been arrested on suspicion of inciting sedition. He's not well enough to be moved, of course, but the house is being watched.'

'Poor Crauford and Marianne.' Kitty let out a cry of shock, as though she'd just been struck a physical blow. Greville rested one hand upon her shoulder with a brief squeeze.

'You must go home first, Greville,' Kitty said. In the candlelight, her long-lashed eyes looked enormous, glittering with reined-in emotion. 'You can't leave Crauford and Mama to manage this.'

'Did you know Chas had those sympathies, Nightingale?' Lascelles asked.

Before Greville could answer, they both turned to the door on instinct and watched Jamie come in.

'If they've arrested Chas, it's because they should have arrested me,' Jamie said, closing the door behind him.

'It only needed this, did it not?' Cleveland said, looking bored.

'Don't look at me like that, Grev,' Jamie went on. 'It's not as if I don't know what Lascelles does out in Spain; everyone knows that the Corps of Guides deals in intelligence. But if you think I'm just going to let Chas be accused of all manner of treason just because he was mistaken for me, you don't know me at all, and I don't care if Lascelles knows it or not.'

Kitty rested her elbows on the table and put both hands over her face. Byron placed one arm around her shoulders and she sank into his embrace: as ever, he was attuned to the needs of the nearest woman.

'You might have a little consideration for your cousin's feelings, however, James.' Byron was as languid as ever but Jamie coloured at his words.

'You can hardly talk,' he said. 'For all your hot air about rebellion and religion and changing the bloody world, and hypocrisy, why don't you ever actually do something to bring about change? One speech in the House of Lords and I suppose you think that's your job done—'

'When this juvenile display is at an end,' Cleveland interrupted, 'perhaps my brother will be good enough to tell us why he's really here.'

'It's the house party of the year, Duke,' Byron said, in a careless tone of voice that Greville had only ever heard him use when dangerously angry. Ignoring Jamie, Byron poured a brandy for Kitty. 'Don't worry, angel, one day all this will be nothing more than an anecdote.'

'I rather doubt it,' Kitty said, but she drained the glass of brandy all the same.

Greville watched Lascelles across the table; he was as immaculate as ever and despite having dressed for the countryside in twill rather than superfine, he looked as if he'd stepped out of White's less than five minutes before. All the same, Greville caught the faintest hint of woodsmoke and fresh air: Lascelles had spent more time outdoors than one might at first guess.

'Let Jamie finish,' Greville declared. 'You were big with

news when you came in. We can unravel this mess with Chas at our leisure. What is it?'

Jamie folded his arms, glancing out of the window at the black waters of Loch Iffrin. 'That preventive's here – MacGuigan,' he said. 'Lilias Tait saw him patrolling near the mooring earlier this morning, and now he's at the house. Tait's holding him off, but Mrs Scudamore says she's sure MacGuigan doesn't believe him.'

Greville caught Byron's eye just before he managed to conceal his fear: here was a scandal that some of this house party would not survive, with fame and public adulation no protection.

'If that's the local preventive and he's lifted that cargo already, you'll have to kill him to keep this quiet,' Lascelles said, as though they were discussing how best to deal with a rat problem. Greville knew in that moment Lascelles was talking about more than a few barrels of free-traded cognac: he understood about the weapons, too.

Kitty rose then, holding up both hands for silence, her hair dishevelled from Byron's embrace. 'Don't any of you say a word. Not a word. I don't even want to know why it's a point of concern that the local preventive officer has arrived at this house, but I'm going to the kitchen and I'm going to tell Fraser MacGuigan that his wife has gone into labour at Leirinmore.' She glared at them all, one after the other. 'Mrs MacGuigan nearly died last time and they lost the baby, so I'd be willing to wager that he'll go, and you'll get at least one or two hours to do whatever it is you need to do, and I hope to goodness I never know what it is.'

She went out, closing the door behind her.

'I don't want to know, either,' Cleveland said.

Greville smiled at them all. 'No, Cleveland, you really do not. We're going to retrieve that cargo of weapons,' he said, watching Cleveland roll his eyes, 'and before Fraser MacGuigan comes back to look for it himself, we're going to drop it in the North Atlantic where no one will ever find it, do you understand? To hell with your armed uprising, Jamie, and your ideals: give those men guns and you may as well escort them to the gallows.'

One, two. Greville counted beats in the silence before he spoke, watching how Jamie exchanged a swift glance with Byron, who just shrugged.

'Harder than it looks to rebuild society from the ground up, James, is it not?' Byron said, pushing up the sash window. 'I hate to be childish, but if MacGuigan's already in the house, I rather think this is our best way out. I can't bear men like him, mealy-mouthed self-righteous puritan arseholes.'

Greville hadn't seen Cressida since the moment they fell asleep in each other's arms; for now, he could do nothing but ignore the growing, ugly sense of misgiving.

37

At Drochcala, Cressida awoke an hour before Greville into an unfamiliar sensation of calm, relishing the warmth of his presence beside her as the past faded away. She was no longer a child left alone at Rosmoney as English soldiers scoured the countryside for rebels. She was safe with Greville here in a way that she had not been for years. He lay sprawled on his back, naked beneath the sheets, with one arm flung above his head, which was turned away from her to reveal the beautiful line of his unshaven jaw. Unbidden, her mind drifted back to the way Rosmoney had smiled at her in the bothy and the sensation of safety ebbed away, leaving cold unease.

I'm sorry, darling, but you're far more like me than your extremely proper Mama, God rest her soul.

In almost the next breath, Rosmoney had lied without shame – or rather he had omitted the truth about why he was here. She'd been such a fool, indulging in that moment of real relief: shipping weapons across the Irish Sea, her father was still the true rebel hero she'd always wanted to believe in, not just a well-connected aristocrat who had run away from the brutal aftermath of a failed rising, leaving his fellow rebels to be hanged and shot in front of their terrified wives and children and their homes burned, and his own daughter left alone at Rosmoney for her only surviving relatives to deal with eventually.

In the bothy, Rosmoney had only said as much as he needed, letting her fill in the gaps by herself, just as she had allowed Annis and Bute to do at Bute House in London. *The most successful lie is a bedfellow to the truth.* Yes, Rosmoney was shipping weapons across the Irish Sea that were ultimately bound for English rebels in the weaving towns, aided by Jamie Nightingale. But if Rosmoney were motivated by the same cause of bringing down the English government, why had he still been at Drochcala, hours and hours after sending the latest cache of weaponry down Loch Iffrin for Jamie to collect?

Why, in fact, had he not disappeared to fight another day, as any rebel would?

Cressida closed her eyes: she had been such a fool. It would hurt to leave Greville now, but with trust between them so impossibly out of reach, there was no choice. This was her mess to unravel, not his.

A quarter of an hour later, Cressida left the house through the scullery once more, with Lilias Tait staring after her, still holding the tankard she had been washing at the stone sink. That wasn't desirable, but there was little enough she could do about it now. Climbing hard, running up the path where she could, Cressida wished for her old clothes – the skirt of heavy cotton, the shawl and her boots: the flimsy linen gown clung to her arms, offering scant protection against an angry grey mist that had settled on the peaks behind Drochcala.

When she reached the bothy, just over an hour later, there was no smoke coming from the chimney. Inside, thin grey light slanted in through cracks in the single shuttered window. A heap of dry wood and kindling lay stacked near the hearth and a rusty iron tinderbox sat on the crude stone mantelpiece; Oliver would have seen to that, ready for a stalking party that had never stopped here. Rosmoney had a leather flask of small-ale, which he passed to her without a word; he accepted her arrival with no comment. Thirst had already taken hold after the scrambling hike, so Cressida drank half her share of the flask, cool, sweet ale slipping down her throat. She had to force away a memory of Greville's smile as he lifted her in his arms, blaspheming under his breath as he registered the pain radiating from that gunshot wound.

'Where is O'Neill?' Cressida asked.

Rosmoney shrugged. 'I sent him on ahead. All this is looking a little untidy.' He waved one hand dismissively, as though he were talking about the prospect of a new arrangement in the shrubbery. 'I do wish you hadn't come.'

Side by side, they stood at the unglazed window, looking down the bracken-choked hillside to Loch Iffrin below. The *Kittiwake* was out, her white sail a pale splash against a backdrop of dark water, and Cressida knew that Greville had gone to retrieve the weapons, with or without Jamie's help. From this height, Eilean nam Fiadh was a burst of vivid green against the waters of the loch, and Cressida thought of the deer moving quietly through the trees on their island, in their own place and perfectly at peace.

'I don't know why the deer stay on that island. Do you think they remember the stalking?' Cressida spoke as if to herself. 'There's nowhere they can go to escape. It must seem safe but it's a prison.'

'It's all for the good, all for the greater good at least,' Rosmoney said, not looking at her, and she knew he wasn't really talking about the deer any more but his own actions, always so excusable. As they watched, the white sail of the *Kittiwake* moved at a dream-like pace across the loch, moving into the lee of Eilean nam Fiadh, between the island and the shore.

'Queer they're going back that way,' Cressida said, when what she wanted to do was ask him what he had done. 'They'll never get through that channel on a single tack.'

At her side, Rosmoney went still, smiling a little. Following his gaze, Cressida saw why: a naval cutter had sailed up the loch-head, slicing across the dark water. She'd woken in Greville's arms for the last time, drinking in that blissful half-waking moment in the knowledge no one could possibly harm her as she lay curled against his side. She'd fallen asleep with her back to him, but in sleep they'd found one another once more, as if it were all so simple as holding one another in the night.

Side by side, she and Rosmoney watched the naval cutter go about, sailing with deadly purpose. For a long time, neither of them spoke. Someone, somewhere had sung a little tune, bringing the full might of the British government down upon Loch Iffrin and Drochcala.

'It's quite sharp of the British, really,' Rosmoney said. 'They've always been good at springing traps like this for those of a Radical persuasion: I should know, having been caught in one. You see, what all this does is create the appearance of a wider rebellion in the wake of Lord Perceval's murder.'

'Thank you for the explanation. I don't think I could quite have grasped it otherwise,' Cressida said, mildly. Had he ever believed in anything at all except himself, even a free Ireland? Perhaps that had been a game to him too, best left behind as soon as inconvenient consequences began to pile up, like burning villages and summary executions. 'It's a shame about my husband's cousin, though, isn't it? He's so young. Barely even twenty.'

'We'll both be quite safe, of course,' Rosmoney said, ignoring unpleasant truths just as he had always done, and Cressida knew he'd engineered this: that her father was an integral part of this trap, part of the machinery of the Committee of Secrecy. 'I've a yawl anchored off Rhiconich. With a fair wind, we'll be in Dublin by the end of the week.'

We.

'Before you were born,' Rosmoney went on, 'I always wanted to sail from Westport instead and go north, right up around Cape Wrath. I'd have sailed to the Arctic Circle if I could.'

Cressida fixed her gaze on the cutter, which was now hunting westward across the loch, aware of the pistol holstered at her waist and the knife sheathed at her garter, the leather scabbard cold against her stockinged thigh. There was absolutely no chance of escape for Greville and whoever had gone with him to lift Jamie's illicit cargo.

In that moment, the sudden, unmistakable call of a grouse rang out, just yards away from the bothy, wings beating the air with a sharp crack like wet laundry shaken out.

Rosmoney smiled, nodding. 'They'll have disembarked some of the men at Rhiconich – a wise move to send some of them overland. Marines, you know.'

'They've got Drochcala surrounded by royal marines,' Cressida spoke, battling a vivid sense of unreality. No soldier on a mission of this nature would pass by the bothy without further investigation: there was nowhere to hide.

'Papa,' she said, 'can you explain to them who you are?'

38

A little earlier, Greville, Lascelles, Byron and Jamie walked down the length of the lawn to the furthest reaches of the loch-head in grim silence, picking their way across salt-soaked grass and pebbles slippery with stark orange and ochre seaweed. They left Cleveland and Kitty to fend off MacGuigan's enquiries with Cleveland's eleven generations of ducal scorn and Kitty's Banbury tale about Mrs MacGuigan in childbed. Greville ignored the discomfort as seawater soaked through his boots. They boarded the *Kittiwake* with varying degrees of elegance, and Greville untied her painter from the iron ring mounted in the gravel, wading out a few steps before hauling himself on board: that would be the end of this pair of boots. What an idiotic thought when they were unlikely to see the end of the month without at least one of them on the gallows, at best. What remained of his reputation would be up in smoke. Greville was surprised how much he cared, surprised at how much he wanted, in truth, to take Cressida back to the Peninsula as his wife. He wanted to go with her to balls in ancient walled Spanish cities and watch her ride out on the hunt in winter, and to lie with her in the darkest part of the night. He wanted to give her the life she deserved, so that she could at last lay down her weapons.

Jamie had wordlessly taken the oars and started to row at a steady, angry rhythm. Byron stood holding the shrouds as they put up the sails, looking out towards the open ocean, now actually enjoying all this with an irritating degree of relish. Lascelles sat at the prow, staring out across the loch, and Jamie glanced at the luff of the sail, noting a series of wrinkles near the mast. Greville watched with cool amusement as Jamie trimmed the sails so that the yacht shot across the loch, close-hauled: the boy could sail, at least. The morning had worn on and sun burned through the mist, warming the back of his neck as they tacked across the loch, at last approaching the hidden inlet where they'd dropped the cargo.

Lascelles got up and stepped across the daggerboard, ducking beneath the boom as he came to sit beside Greville, who moved to make room for him.

'Rosmoney is here – there's more to this than we knew in London.' Lascelles spoke to Greville in quiet Portuguese, just as they neared a shoreline of tumbled black rocks.

'You do surprise me,' Greville replied in the same tongue. It would be a long time before he was able to forget Lord Bute looking up at him and Cleveland with tears streaming down his face, not because he'd paid a delusional merchant with a wife and children to kill the prime minister, but because it was all so embarrassing. Lascelles hadn't arrived at Drochcala this morning at all. He'd been watching them all for days, living on the hillside like a guerrilla scout with the scent of woodsmoke in his hair, perhaps even inside the house, too.

'I hate it when you're sarcastic,' Lascelles said. 'If I'd have known we'd end up in a bind like this, I'd have hanged your wife in Spain. There's far too much treason in this for my liking—' He broke off at the expression on Greville's face, raising both eyebrows. 'It's like *that*, is it?'

'Never mind. What about her father? Is there any such thing as a retired rebel?' Greville said. Byron and Jamie were arguing about the exact location of the cargo drop, the frozen entente cordiale between them temporarily forgotten. The Butes' involvement in funding the murder of a prime minister and Rosmoney's presence at Drochcala nagged at Greville like sections of a patchwork quilt that refused to tessellate. No matter how many times he tried to match together the edges, they would never fit.

'Very likely,' Lascelles said. 'But Rosmoney's no rebel. He was under orders. It took me four days to get an audience with Lord Liverpool and even then it was involuntary on his part, shall we say. He was surprised to find me in his library.'

'You got into the private library of the Secretary of State for War and then threatened him?' Greville laughed and swore in the same breath.

'It's absurd, the lack of communication between my unit and the more official channels,' Lascelles said, aggrieved. 'I look after my men – which for the sake of argument in this case means you and Cressida, and I suppose him as well.'

He shot a look at Byron, who was still standing artistically by the mast, holding on to the shrouds.

'Not that he knows, strictly speaking, that you were using him like a punch doll in your very own puppet theatre,' Greville said.

Lascelles ignored that. 'Listen, we know it made no sense to hang Bellingham so quickly, not unless somebody wanted to ensure he never discussed where the money he lived on came from before the murder: call it a double execution. And if it led a few Luddites and Radicals to the gallows, all those respectable pillars of society who paid Bellingham's way in London could hardly complain.'

'The Butes were up to their necks in that,' Greville said, watching Lascelles carefully. 'But how does a consortium of avaricious mill-owners and aggrieved slave-owners paying a delusional merchant to shoot the prime minister get Radicals hanged?'

'Come on, Greville,' Lascelles said, squinting over his shoulder at the loch-head shrouded in mist. 'Perceval had a lot of enemies in government, and they don't like rebels any more than he did. The movement of weapons is a trap, a fiction from start to finish. It was designed to spark unrest and create the illusion of a Radical uprising in the wake of Perceval's murder when there was no such thing. And Annis Bute went too far, like a greedy little child eating a plate of sugar-plums as well as all the cake. If she'd stuck at only aiming for a change of policy and making life easier for slave-owners by arranging Lord Perceval's death like an opera breakfast, we'd probably still be blessed with her company. But she was blackmailing all of us as well, which risked everything else. To be honest, if I hadn't killed Annis, I strongly suspect Rosmoney was under orders to do the same and would have gladly saved me the trouble. From his point of view, and that of the War Office and the Committee of Secrecy, her greed and manoeuvring threatened the security of their entire operation.'

Greville stared at him, tasting salt upon his lips. 'Dear God, Arthur. When we get back to Spain, what are we actually fighting for?'

'Money, as usual? And if Annis had stopped at siphoning money from her own estate to fund a murderer, I might have been able to let her live.' Lascelles smiled then. 'Probably not, though, considering what she tried to do to my sister. The thing is, if Annis didn't want to be poisoned in her bed, she shouldn't have threatened to ruin otherwise blameless young people guilty of one small mistake, or attempted to blackmail the family of a man with no discernible moral compass.'

Greville stared at him, salt spray drenching his face as the wind picked up.

Cressida hadn't trusted him enough to share the truth about her father; if she had, they could be working together now, not battling in separate futility: she should be here with him, safe with him no matter what ugly storm raged around them. For a few sacred hours last night, all that mattered had been the warmth of her body beneath him, her strong, slender legs wrapped around his waist, and the scent of her skin, and the faint hint of chamomile and lavender in her hair, all before the cold hard intrusion of obligation and reality.

'Is this the place or not?' Jamie asked, with brisk hostility.

'I don't know if you and Lascelles have quite finished jabbering in Portuguese yet, but if you want to pull up that cargo, I'd as lief we did it before MacGuigan comes out to play again.'

Byron glanced at the shoreline, animated with the excitement of it all. 'Not yet. Six feet or so closer to the rocks, and then go about. The prow was level with that spit where the small beech trees are growing.'

Jamie put the yacht head to wind and Lascelles uncleated the anchor, dropping it overboard, hand over hand. Jamie stripped off his jacket and sat down in the thwarts to haul off his boots, stretching out one long leg and then the other. They were alone on the loch save for a small potting boat in the far distance with a rust-red lateen sail that stood out against the grey sky, and Greville felt a pulse of cool relief. It was now or never. Jamie slipped into the water with a quick, elegant vault over the bows that barely rocked the boat. He came up for breath with the fine linen shirt plastered to his chest and then dived like a porpoise. He emerged once, flicking back his hair and blowing out a spray of water; he shook his head, then dived again. Greville, Byron and Lascelles watched the loch in silent tension and Greville felt the unmistakable slow prickle of danger between his shoulder blades; he couldn't even be sure they were in the right place. It would have been so easy to misjudge their distance from the shore as MacGuigan's lad fired his shot. He'd shielded Cressida with his body then, enveloping her in his arms so that he breathed in her familiar scent of rosewater and Marseille soap; he felt her loss now more than he had ever done before.

Jamie dived for a third time and emerged right at the prow, spitting out water and holding the end of a line tied in a monkey's paw and black with pitch. He swung a leg over the side of the boat and Byron grabbed a handful of his sodden shirt, heaving him on board. Jamie flushed, disentangling his legs from the tiller, daggerboard and jib sheet, and immediately began hauling in the line, hand over hand. A gull wheeled overhead, a splash of white against the grey sky, sending up a wild keening that bounced from one green-mantled loch-side to the other.

'What about your arm?' Jamie said to Greville, panting with effort.

'What the devil about it? Just heave,' Greville snapped. Sunlight glanced from the surface of the loch, and out towards the loch-head the water went dark with flashes of the small waves that as children they had always called white horses; the mackerel were shoaling and moments later the black shining flank and fin of a porpoise emerged, then more: hunters and the hunted. It was backbreaking work, and before long, they all began to breathe with harsh, urgent economy, sweating into their waistcoats; they had all long since stripped off their jackets, Greville with a suppressed, furious wince. Crimson blood showed on his rolled-up sleeve, blossoming through layers of bandage and fine linen. He glanced over his shoulder to see that the potting boat had hauled anchor and drifted off to the north, running before the wind; even at this distance he could make out that someone had propped the lateen sail out to one side to make the most of the wind. At the very least, there was some. What if they lost the wind entirely and had to row back to the house with a single pair of oars?

Men had hanged for far less than this.

'*Now!*' Greville ordered, and the yacht leaped forward across the water as Byron took the tiller, steering her into the wind once more, even as Jamie edged past to haul up the last of the anchor-chain, coiling and cleating it, as well as the seaweed-coated line, the heap of barrels glistening in the weak sunlight.

'I don't like it,' Byron said, hauling in the jib sheet a little to trim the smaller sail with surprising efficiency, his muscled forearms bare to the elbow. 'I don't bloody like the fact there's no one out here. It's too quiet.'

'There's little enough we can do about that. Anyone who is minded to had best just pray.' Lascelles squinted into the sun as a skein of cloud slid away. There was nothing they could do but sail.

39

They tacked down Loch Iffrin with the tide against them. Greville adjusted the mainsheet; he'd long since taken the tiller from Byron, who seemed to know that if Greville wasn't steering the boat, he'd do something worse with his hands.

He kept a keen eye levelled down the loch, taking care not to look at Jamie, who sat watching the black waters of the kyle sweep past with a wooden expression. Were Jamie and Oliver Tait lovers, in as much as men like Jamie and Lascelles and sometimes Byron ever could be together? The irony didn't escape him: Lascelles had dragged him up here to keep a weather eye on Byron, holding his interest in Jamie over Greville's head. Instead of making a fool of himself over a poet, Jamie had been swiving a strait-laced estate steward whose unwillingness to smuggle black-market cargo only matched his competence. And that was when he wasn't singlehandedly running cargo after cargo of stolen weapons across the Pentland Firth. On balance, Greville thought, grimly, he'd have preferred to hush up a scandal with Byron. Jamie's relationship with Oliver meant more than a tumble in the stables, that much was clear. Greville couldn't help recalling Jamie's fiery, protective expression when he'd surprised them both in the stables, and the way Jamie had stepped forward as if to shield Oliver from harm, as well as Oliver's obvious exasperation at Jamie's constitutional addiction to danger. How they had parted, knowing this cargo would likely lead to ruinous scandal if not the gallows.

They sailed north-west until Loch Iffrin spread into the black, glittering waters of the North Atlantic. Another school of porpoise played along the bows of the yacht, Jamie watching them with a quick smile of pure unalloyed joy.

'There's a boat.' Byron's voice was sharp, nerves stretched to breaking point. Greville followed his gaze down the loch and saw the navy cutter slicing through the water from the direction of Sangobeg.

'My word, someone has been busy,' Lascelles said, with laconic fury, which Greville was glad of because until then he hadn't been sure whose side Lascelles was actually on.

'Drop the lot of it. Get it in the water, now,' Greville heard himself say, and they all moved at once, jettisoning one barrel after the other, the wound in his arm throbbing in slow waves of pain all the while. The naval cutter was a fair distance away; Christ alone knew where it had come from. Now at least the barrels were all gone, rifles, pistols and ammunition from the magazine at Enniskillen all making their final slow journey to the bottom of this cold northern ocean, neighbour now only to spider crabs and graceful pods of white beluga whales.

Jamie crouched at the tiller now, turning her back into the wind as Lascelles watched the naval cutter, fingering the holster of the French pistol he'd raided after Talavera. Greville caught a glimpse of blue jackets and a white sail. *Shit.* They had the advantage of wind and tide, with the navy cutter having to beat against a wild wind that shifted and changed like a malignant spirit haunting Loch Iffrin. Jamie caught the advantage of each change in the wind on every tack. He seemed to feel no fear, even as he was white-faced with anger. The naval cutter was much lower in the water and sailed with less expertise, but even so this would be a close-run thing. Cloud thickened, descending so that all was cloaked in grey mist, and cold gobbets of rain fell even as they sailed so close to the wind that waves crested over the railings.

'If we make it back to the loch-head, they'll find us anyway,' Byron said, with the rain in his face. 'They'll come to the house, and Lady Bute has been dead for less than twenty-four hours. It's like playing choose your own route to the gallows: murder or smuggling.'

'Cleveland will deal with it,' Lascelles said, but for once even he looked rattled.

'Ready about.' Jamie yanked the tiller towards him as the boom swung around, the sail filling with wind once more, and Greville tightened the jib sheet. The yacht shot down the loch, flying into the mist with the naval cutter in hard pursuit, the distance between them briefly shortening as the cutter made the best of a gust.

'Eilean nam Fiadh,' Jamie said, reading the loch and the precise angle of the wind against his cheekbone. The granite bulk of the island rose out of the water, capped green with young beech trees, heather and ferns – a chance, if nothing else.

'You can't be serious,' Byron said. 'We'd as good as besiege ourselves. All they'd have to do is hunt for half an hour and they'd have every last one of us.'

'That's not what Jamie means,' Lascelles said. 'Listen.'

'It's less than twenty feet from the island to the mainland,' Jamie went on. 'There's a small natural harbour around the other side. It's not much more than a cleft in the rocks. We anchor her there, where she'll be clearly visible to that cutter, and then we swim ashore to the mainland. It's a sheer climb, but I know those woods. We'll come out not far above the track that leads back to the house. If we can get back to the house before that cutter reaches it, we may at least have a chance.'

'In the absence of any better notion, it will have to do.' Byron's tone was acidic. 'I didn't have a trip to the gallows planned as part of my summer, strangely.'

Jamie shrugged, reading the wind and the pooling tide, and tacked again. The mainsail and boom swung across the boat so that they all either ducked or moved their seats again, distributing their combined heft to trim the boat. Against the mist-shrouded horizon, the naval cutter was now the size of Greville's hand and growing slowly but inexorably larger with every moment. They may not have been found with the incriminating evidence, but this was the smooth, slick operation of a well-oiled machine. Greville allowed his mind to linger for a moment on Cressida, and the way she had cried out his name in the dark of the night, asking himself if that would be enough to save them now that she had gone.

Part Five

They say all lovers swear more performance than they are able and yet reserve an ability that they never perform, vowing more than the perfection often and discharging less than the tenth part of one. They that have the voice of lions and the act of hares, are they not monsters?

Cressida, *Troilus and Cressida*, William Shakespeare

40

A quarter of an hour before, Cressida counted in silence as she listened to the even rhythm of her own breathing. Crouching at her side against the wall furthest from the door, Rosmoney gave her a quick smile and held up four fingers; he was actually enjoying this. To judge by the soft footfalls she could now hear, they were surrounded by at least four men, perhaps more. A thread of light streaked in between rotting shutters, strong sunlight burning away the mist.

'Come out and show yourselves.' The voice rang out strong and clear, echoing down the fellside, the voice of a well-bred Englishman.

'Papa, you stay here,' Cressida said. 'I'll go out first, and then you can explain you're under orders.'

Rosmoney turned to look at her with a flash of the genuine anger she had so rarely seen. 'Use the sense you were born with. It's far too great a risk.'

'I don't care. I'll go,' Cressida said, telling him the truth that she had told no one else.

He was coward enough to let her do it, she knew that. But this time Rosmoney just watched her, as if he saw her then for the first time.

'I think not: you've so much still left to live for,' he said, and Cressida didn't tell him that when she closed her eyes at night, she still saw the child wrapped in rags, perfectly formed but born too soon, with a cap of dark hair that might have been gifted by Greville. It was common, though, for infants' hair to rub away and grow fair, guinea-gold.

Rosmoney was already on his feet.

'Papa—' she said quietly, even as the soldiers outside called out again. *We know you're in there.*

He relinquished her arm and she felt his hand grip her shoulder. 'Do as I tell you,' he said, 'do you understand? It'll be a simple matter to explain. Wait here.'

Rosmoney walked to the door then, and softly, quietly, Cressida sang for him as she had done long ago, a rebel song in the language she had learned from his servants, but with never the right to call her own. As she watched, her father kicked open the door, admitting a savage burst of daylight, with his hands held high in the air as he walked into a hail of musket fire.

First of all, Cressida couldn't move, couldn't even draw breath in the clouds of thick sulphurous smoke. Rosmoney died before he hit the flagstones. Blinded by smoke and choking on the familiar stink of spent gunpowder, Cressida felt along the damp stone wall for the windowsill, and every moment stretched to an hour. Her mind was clear as she placed her hands carefully on the sill and hauled herself up onto the ledge with strength she hadn't been close to possessing in that world of gilded teacups, champagne, and open deceit. Then, Cressida let herself fall out into the daylight, onto the wiry fellside grass. Rummaging in her skirts, she drew the small pistol from the holster at her waist, loading and priming it ready to fire, half choking on the bitter taste of gunpowder as she bit off the end of her cartridge and rammed the ball down into the muzzle. She ran, hard and fast, with tears streaming down her face for her father at last, after fourteen long years, but even before Cressida chanced a look over her shoulder, she saw that a young marine had spotted her and was now loping along in easy pursuit, just like a sighthound after a rabbit.

Cressida stopped and turned around to face him, breathing hard. Even starting to explain was next to impossible. He smiled at her, just the type of young man you might meet in a dowager's drawing room at Christmas, seeming to see straight through every last scrap of linen she wore.

Cressida scanned the fellside behind him: there was no sign of the rest of the men, who must have gone into the bothy after her father. She could run, but this boy soldier would be faster. Cressida lowered her hands in the barest of half moments and shot him in the leg. He went down with the shock, but not before firing at her. Cressida felt a burst of sickening agony in her ankle, even as she breathed in the stink of gunpowder again, and all was lost in the smoke.

Alone on the fellside, she crawled hand over hand across tumbled grass and heather, traversing outcrops of scattered rock spotted with patches of grey and ochre lichen, even as black mist intruded all around the edges of her field of vision. With her sight fading, she smelled the woodland before she was really aware of it, pine sap and leaf mould. Stones pressed into her bleeding palms, digging into her knees, and it was as hard to draw breath as it was not to allow the skirts of her gown and petticoats to tangle around her legs. Nausea surged through her, unstoppable, and she vomited up green bile, having nothing else left. The marine had aimed his pistol at her right ankle: what was left of that would swell and rot. Either that rot would poison her blood or she'd face the surgeon's saw so that she lived to meet one of those men, like Rosmoney, who carried out the most secret wishes of the government with knives and garrotting wires in dark streets at night; men who had long since sold what was left of their honour.

She thought of Greville, and the way he would rest a hand on Kitty's shoulder. How must it feel to be Kitty, absolutely sure of another person in that way? She needed Greville now, but he'd soon enough know that she wasn't the woman he thought he'd married, that she had in fact been a mother too, for however short a time, and God only knew that woman was bad enough.

She'd as lief die under the sky, in a place of her choosing, that was all.

The marine was in pursuit. He staggered out from between a stand of young birch trees, his hands and face black with gunpowder. Even with blood streaming from his thigh, blooming red on his pale grey breeches, he was quicker on foot than she could ever be now. She had lost the pistol and now had only the knife sheathed at her thigh.

Cressida snatched up her skirts and drew it all the same, and he grinned at the sight of her bare stockinged legs. Crawling to the nearest tree, Cressida hauled herself upright, clinging to the solid trunk even as the sharp scent of pine sap hit the back of her throat. Clutching the knife, she blinked away that encroaching darkness, but it was little use. She'd never set both feet to the ground again, let alone walk again or dance. The marine approached, swaying like a man drunk.

'I hate doing this,' he said, raising the pistol, and Cressida wished he hadn't smiled, even as the shot rang out and the air filled with choking sulphuric gunpowder smoke. The last thing she saw before darkness closed her eyes was the perfect scarlet hole blooming in the centre of the boy's forehead: and he was just a boy, really, after all. The last thing she heard was Greville's familiar voice in her ear – *Don't you dare leave me* – just as she'd always imagined.

41

Greville went down the hill at a jolting run with Cressida in his arms, leaving Lascelles, Jamie and Oliver Tait to deal with the dead soldier stretched out on that blanket of rust-brown pine needles. Lascelles had turned to him on instinct in the half moment before he raised the pistol and fired.

Greville, don't. Remember the court martial. You're a better man than this—

No, I'm not. Greville squeezed the trigger as he spoke.

Now he cradled the dead weight of Cressida's body. Her face was sweat-streaked, turned into his chest in a gesture of trust that crushed the breath from his lungs. The high arch of her brow was obscured by gunpowder, and he tried not to think of her executing a perfect *pas de tout* in his mother's ballroom, long ago. He could only be grateful she was unconscious because so many bones must have shattered in her right ankle. If only he were not so afraid that she wouldn't wake up: sometimes it happened like that, if wound-fever didn't take hold. Just the shock of a gunshot wound was sometimes enough to stop a heart, and carrying her like this he couldn't check her pulse or brush the knotted auburn curls from her pale throat. All he could do was pray in silence as he sometimes did before a battle.

Afterwards, Greville would remember that journey downhill in a blur of shattered images: vivid green beech leaves against the sky as they reached the edges of the wood, dark leaf mould at his feet and golden-yellow chanterelle mushrooms growing at the tree roots. He gathered his wits when he reached the servants' quarters at the back of the house, bearing her in his arms through an empty laundry yard and into the scullery, carrying her now when she needed him, as he should have done for years. Mrs Scudamore came first, followed by the footman Tam MacCannell and Lilias, even Roberts, and Greville heard himself giving orders as if to his own men, as all other sound drained from the world.

He carried her through the great stone-flagged hall, where Cleveland stood quietly eviscerating a group of eight exhausted royal marines, who had come to the front door with Byron, who was still soaked to the skin and leaning against the wall watching the scene with an unusually martial light in his eyes. Cleveland turned as Greville passed, with the briefest of nods. Greville found that he didn't care about any of it, or what might happen to them all once the gunpowder smoke had cleared; he just made for their own bedchamber, running up the stairs because Cressida was bleeding freely. He knew she was still alive because he could hear her breathing now, fast and shallow, but that was no good, because men breathed like that when they bled out and died. She was cold, too, and Greville knew too well what that meant. Mrs Scudamore and Ines spread an old linen sheet across the bed before he laid her down at last.

'Hold her hand!' he said to Ines and Lilias. 'Talk to her.' He'd not let her think she was alone and friendless, not this time. Greville had cut away what remained of Cressida's jean boot by the time Lascelles came running up the stairs with Oliver and Jamie, and Greville was grateful for someone else who had seen a battlefield. The next half hour passed like battles sometimes did, in a jumbled series of staccato moments: blood, bandages, hot water, until there was nothing to do but give her laudanum and wait to hear if Gunn had already returned to his regiment or if he was still on leave with his mother and wife at Leirinmore.

With Mrs Scudamore's arm around her shoulders, Cressida turned her face away from the cup of laudanum tisane that Ines held to her lips, speaking to the girl in Portuguese that only Greville and Lascelles understood.

'You know I can't drink that stuff, menina, not now,' she said.

'You must, mistress, you're feverish and it's best you sleep it through,' Ines said, with none of her usual pert manner.

Cressida closed her eyes, and Greville understood that of course the women of the baggage train kept their guard through the night, too: what other choice did they have?

He took the cup from Ines's hands and spoke in Portuguese to his wife. 'You've finished your watch. Rest now, meu querida.'

*

Cressida woke to find her bedchamber in darkness, alleviated only by moonlight shafting in between the curtains. Dull, aching pain radiated from her ankle and moving her foot even just a little made her feel sick, so she lay still, unable to examine it for herself. In that moment, she felt beyond reach of harm and only understood why when she turned her head and saw Greville sprawled in the armchair drawn close to her bed with his long legs stretched out beneath the window. She remembered Annis again, and her father raising both hands in the air before they shot him down; she was not safe at all, because any magistrate worth his salt would take one look at her chequered reputation and reach for the black cap, if they bothered with such gothic displays in Scotland before handing down a sentence of death. Either way, she'd hang this time, one way or another, earl's daughter or not: the news-sheets would enjoy that. Greville stirred as she woke and took her hand, and the sense of loss crushed her chest and throat so that she wasn't able to speak.

'You wouldn't hold my hand if you knew all the things I've done.' She tried for a smile.

'I'll be the judge of that. Do you think I'll just sit here and allow an opinionated, vexatious woman like yourself to tell me what to think?'

'I can't imagine a tyrant like yourself would allow anyone to tell you what to think, even if she were an amiable, well-disposed young woman of reputation.'

'Which you have never been.' The laughter went out of his expression. Greville rested his elbows on the edge of the mattress and raked both hands through his hair, looking up at her with his brows raised a little.

'I'm going to assume you don't know that we dropped the weapons in the sea and George Byron insisted on escorting their captain up to the house so he and Cleveland could personally excoriate the man for disturbing a household in mourning.'

'It was neatly designed,' Cressida said, and she told him how Rosmoney had sprung a trap for the poor and the starving on the orders of Lord Liverpool and the Committee of Secrecy. 'The whole thing is a ruse, built to catch men like Jamie and whoever handled the guns and ammunition, let alone whoever received them at the other end and planned to use them.'

'I know,' Greville replied. 'Lascelles got wind of it and came to warn us; I suppose it's good to know there's still some of the old Arthur left in there. You're a little feverish, you know.'

Cressida closed her eyes. 'How lowering to be so very dispensable.'

'You're not dispensable to me.'

She smiled then. 'You can marry some woman of birth and sense and beauty, and in all likelihood we'll never cross paths again, unless at one of those chaotic balls fuelled by brandy and hysteria like there was after Talavera,' Cressida said.

'To be honest, my blood runs cold at the thought of you at such a ball, if I knew I couldn't have you afterwards,' Greville said, sidestepping the rest of their history as though it were irrelevant. 'And, my dear, you seem to forget that for me to marry again you'd have to die, which Gunn assures me you're unlikely to do. He says you've a constitution of iron, which I could have told him. And if I hadn't been so grateful to him for saving your foot, I would have.'

She wanted to reply that it didn't matter if she walked or danced again or not, because neither dukes nor respectable aristocratic women were charged with murder when she was available, the disgraced daughter of a rebel, informer and spy.

'You do realise that I'm the most likely person here to be suspected of killing Annis,' Cressida said. 'You know what that means, don't you?'

'Of course, but to start with you're my wife, and they don't hang Nightingales. Secondly, Lascelles killed Annis, and so her death will be recorded as misadventure. The government doesn't like it when men start shooting in the House of Commons, even if the people who organised and paid for it are really very respectable.'

Cressida stared at him, and then let out a short crack of laughter.

'You could divorce me, though,' she said. 'And you probably should, considering that I lied to you by omission I don't know how many times.'

And because I bore a stillborn child in Portugal, and I don't know whether you were the father or Cleveland.

'What, and allow you to serve up your tender mercies to some other poor soul?' Greville said, with a certain look. 'I don't think so. Now drink this, before you talk yourself into a real fever.'

Cressida took the cup of tisane that he held out, drinking it in easy stages.

'You must be feeling low,' Greville went on. 'It's quite unsettling to see you adhering to a simple sensible request.'

'Don't get too used to it,' Cressida said, grateful that his hand found hers in that moment, so that he clasped his long, strong fingers around her own, and all she need think about was the warmth of his touch.

Greville woke in the armchair at Cressida's bedside, aching all over, to find Kitty briskly drawing open the curtains in a way that reminded him of their old nurse. 'Wake up, dadash,' Kitty said, deploying the Persian term of endearment she used for none of her other brothers. She wore a tartan wrap against the morning chill, the Alasdair colours bright against the pale linen of her gown. Greville stretched and cursed as his sister stepped away, allowing Ines to set a cup of steaming coffee down on the bedside chest of drawers. Cressida was already awake, damn them all, and likely had been for some time, because she was sitting up with a shawl tucked around her shoulders, and Ines had tidied her hair. She should still be resting, but instead she watched as Cleveland came in with Lascelles, both of them equally well put together for the hour of the day, which was irritating until you remembered the cold-eyed termagant of a father that they had both bowed to at four o'clock every afternoon for the short duration of their childhoods. The Lascelles were followed by Byron, en deshabille in his embroidered banyan, and Jamie, dressed with meticulous attention to detail. Somers and Oliver came in, too, and Somers closed the door behind them all, impassive as ever. As Oliver stepped past Jamie, the backs of their hands touched so briefly that anyone less sharp-eyed than Cressida would have surely missed it: so this was how the land lay, and may heaven keep them both.

'Cressida, you damn well mustn't scare us like that again,' Jamie said, sounding for a moment like the young boy she had once nursed through a fever with melodramatic novels and too much ginger wine. 'You must be so uncomfortable and bored. I'll sit and read to you if you'd like it.'

Cressida smiled at him. 'What a charming thought, a chroí.'

Jamie frowned at her. 'You really are tired. Greville says you only ever speak in Irish when you're exhausted.'

Cressida caught Greville's eye and he smiled at her; they were the only two who knew when she lost herself and called out in that language. Even so, he sensed a slight, sudden distance, as if she had just withdrawn into herself, but there was time enough to deal with that, or so he thought. Later, and not for the first time, Greville would come to wish that he had granted his wife his full attention in that moment.

Kitty smiled with the sort of iron resolve that one only really saw in women who regularly managed young people not yet at their majority. 'Of course Cressida is tired, my dear. I'm sure Lord Bute would be very pleased with your company, Jamie. Mrs Scudamore thinks that he would be far better for the companionship of his girls, but as they are not here, I'm sure you'll do your best to comfort him. I always think that youth is the best tonic for tragedy.'

Jamie looked up and noted the expression on Greville's

face. He bowed, dropping a cousinly kiss on Cressida's forehead before he went out. Somers closed the door behind him and removed the cloth from a tray of ham sandwiches he had set down upon the table near the fire, beside the Delftware ewer and washbasin. There was a jug of coffee, too, and a decanter of whisky which had already been liberally applied to Greville's coffee, scalding down his throat.

'It's Annis's death that frightens me,' Kitty said, finishing off a sandwich and handing the plate to Lascelles. 'Even if it's passed off as a suicide, we all know that someone at Drochcala actually killed her. Everyone here had reason to loathe her, but how on earth do we know they won't do it again? Surely that's far more difficult to deal with even than being accused of smuggling weapons to rebels, which I need not remind you all amounts to treason, or the fact that Greville killed a British soldier in cold blood. And we all had a reason to silence Annis.'

Greville didn't miss the look of extreme misgiving that Cleveland gave to his brother in the moment that Lascelles smiled and helped himself to a sandwich.

'I can tell you now that no one in this room has any cause to fear Annis's killer, now or ever.' Lascelles consumed his sandwich in just two bites. 'I stood and watched and made sure she was dead, which was remarkably unpleasant. But one has to be humane about these things.'

Cleveland stared at him. 'As we've said, I'm sure Gunn will be pleased to record the death as misadventure.'

'Whether he likes it or not. I sent a bird last night with the orders for Chas' release,' Lascelles went on. 'We all have the Dowager Lady Crauford to thank for the fact that the entire mess was kept silent in London.'

When Byron spoke, his tone was measured and caustic. 'Thank goodness for that.'

42

Ines was arguing with the innkeeper's wife over the quality of the claret, and so Cressida sat alone by a leaping fire of apple-logs with rain hammering at the shuttered windows, grateful that the Green Dragon was as quiet a place to change horses as Greville's mother had always claimed, not that it would do her any good to think of the Nightingales now. They were some days south of York, and having left Drochcala while Greville was at last asleep, Cressida still had no real final destination in mind, even though several weeks had now passed on her slow journey south. She swirled what remained of the claret around in the bottom of her glass, remembering how Byron had stared straight through her at Drochcala, a direct cut no one could deny she deserved. She had his two hundred pounds, but now she'd lost his regard, there really was no one. *Don't be a fool*, she told herself, swallowing the dregs of the claret, which stripped her gullet like home-brewed daffy. *This isn't the first time you've been alone, this isn't the first time you've had to set out with bank-notes and nothing else. At least this time there is money.* Things had been worse: she had done worse.

This wasn't the first time she'd been without Greville, even if she couldn't walk without a stick.

Ines came over, big with news and triumphant; she opened her mouth to speak and then closed it again after glancing at Cressida. How could she ever surrender herself to Greville once more with a secret between them that was so painful she couldn't even think of it, let alone speak of it? She only had to close her eyes briefly to squat once more at the side of that mountain road with the scent of pine needles and wild thyme and wet mud on the air, and a woman from another regiment holding her hands. She'd never even known the other woman's name, but she could still see her work-chafed hands. Cressida remembered the silence when it was all over, too, and then the bundle in her arms, so still, too soon.

'Mistress!' Ines said, filling Cressida's glass again. 'Do you attend?'

'I do, you impertinent little baggage,' Cressida said. 'I ought to turn you off without a character.'

Ines suppressed a smile, with difficulty. 'Mistress, listen, I said to that woman with a face like a dog's behind that she must needs put away this rubbish she feeds to her guests, because there is *such* an equipage outside in the yard, the like of which you have never seen. Although I suppose you have, at one time in your life, but she'll have to bring up the good stuff from her cellar now. The post-boy said she was as fine a mort as he'd ever seen, proper well minted, he said, who won't be putting up with jack-sauce.'

'I'm glad to see your English is coming along, my girl, because it certainly is improper,' Cressida said. On instinct, she reached for the knife as the door opened, forcing herself to clasp the claret glass instead and to think about where on earth she was going to start a new life in the morning.

The innkeeper's wife bustled into the taproom from the back-kitchen, elbowing the post-boy out of her path with a brisk clip around the ear. 'How many times have I told you to stay out from under my feet when we have— Good evening, milady. We have such a snug fire here, which I beg you to warm yourself at, on such a blustery inclement night as it is. It's not much of a summer, I would call it.'

'Quite, and you can find us some champagne, if you please.' Sylvia Crauford swept into the parlour in a fur-trimmed travelling cloak, throwing back the abundant hood to reveal a heap of curls tinted newly gold by the skilled hand of her personal apothecary. Kitty Alasdair came in behind her, clad in a much more subdued cloak of dark blue superfine with embroidered frogging in the military style, with a small shako pinned to her dark crown of braids, and wearing every minute of a long journey with her stepmother writ upon her face.

Cressida looked up from her empty glass to witness Sylvia's imperious order for three glasses. Kitty took a seat and consulted the travel guide that lay before Cressida on the table.

'It says here the eels and the fruit pie are very good. We'll have that, I thank you. Mama arrived at Drochcala just after you left, Cressida.'

Sylvia settled herself in the chair beside Cressida and bestowed a smile upon the innkeeper's wife, who was hovering in anticipation of gossip. 'How fortunate that we should meet my daughter-in-law upon this road. My son, you know, has gone back to the Peninsula to rejoin his regiment, taking my nephew with him, who has just purchased his commission, as well as a servant from poor Lord Bute's estate, and we are all feeling their absence horribly, as I'm sure you understand.'

'Oh yes, ma'am,' the innkeeper's wife said, a little less sure of herself now. 'My sister's boy has been out since last April, and it is a trial to think on when we might all see him again.'

'You're quite right: it's a great burden upon one's mind, is it not?' Sylvia said. 'My daughter-in-law will be much the happier keeping me company in the countryside, at least until we can all divert ourselves in town again, and I daresay I shall be, too. One always fares better with a little honest occupation, do you not think?'

Cressida ignored a darkling look from Ines. She would just have to explain to Sylvia why she'd had to let Greville go. Sylvia must learn to understand, and to bear it, as she must do the same. The innkeeper's wife bobbed a curtsey and swept off to call for champagne, trailing the sulking post-boy behind her, who cheered up a little when Kitty tipped him fourpence.

Cressida despatched Ines to unpack their bags, leaving her alone with Sylvia and Kitty. In the quiet parlour at the

Green Dragon, with apple-logs crackling in the grate, she could at last admit to the secret that, despite all her courage, she had kept from Greville. When she had finished, Sylvia sat back in her chair, speaking in French lest they should be interrupted.

'That's just what I said to him in London,' Sylvia said, briskly. 'Exactly what I said, was it not, Kitty? That there was bound to have been a child of questionable parentage, and you were so unable to face that obnoxious manly pride that I have been trying to coax him out of for the best part of four and twenty years. I'm very sorry, darling. I lost three myself and Kitty two, and it never gets easier. One just gets used to it, and a good remedy I have found, where it may be arranged, is to have another.'

'Mother!' Kitty hissed. 'That is not always possible, nor even desirable. Ma'am, I wish you will have some sensitivity, at least.'

'Well, that's as may be,' Sylvia said, unchastened. 'But all the same, you know what Greville is like when he's in a truly awful rage, or most likely you don't, for I'm sure he'd never show you such a display. I thought he was going to hit Crauford across the room all those years ago when he so much as breathed that perhaps it was all for the best that you had gone, not that I can blame him, if I'm truly honest. Kitty, perhaps you may leave us for a moment, my love.'

Kitty went outside, leaving Cressida with Sylvia, who pulled off her kidskin gloves and took Cressida's hands in her own. 'Your poor fingers, my dear girl,' she said, 'are so cold. You have no mother and, for all my faults of which

I have many, I am the nearest thing to it that you do have, God help you. So now you will listen to me.'

And so Cressida had no choice but to listen to Sylvia Nightingale, and to repair her face as best she could with a handkerchief from Kitty's reticule when she came back in with the innkeeper's wife, who was bearing a tray of champagne and glasses, and a few thin slices of caraway seed cake on her best gilded plate in case they should fancy something to take the edge off their journey.

43

Four days before Christmas, Cressida climbed the snow-covered ramparts of the hill fort behind the dower house at Summercourt with a basket over her arm, now able to manage the climb without her walking stick. She had come ready with a hip flask and a pair of secateurs to cut holly and ivy for Sylvia Crauford's mantelpieces. Eddying snow blew in her face as she stopped to look back down the valley at the grey bulk of the church and the village huddled along the old Roman road. The road ran straight as a die through the landscape, flanked by cottages with lamp-lit windows glowing like strings of fair-folk lanterns. In the village, they called this hill the old camp. In Cressida's view, these earthworks had been made or stolen by Roman soldiers. Master tacticians, they knew how to use the ground, and sweeping views of valleys and plains reached out to all four points of the compass. And yet what was the use in wasting her time thinking of armies and tactics and warfare here? The most exciting conflict at Sylvia's house took place in the servants' hall, where Sylvia's butler had a long-running feud with her housekeeper. Cressida suspected the battle was fuelled by frustrated desire and had placed quite a substantial bet with Sylvia that war would continue to be waged over the state of the linen until Sheringham made an honourable woman of the widowed Mrs Reston.

She turned back to see that Kitty had caught up with her, striding up the hill armed with a stout stick. Her children and the younger Crauford siblings had gone a little further west around the ramparts, calling out to one another as they collected mistletoe and holly, and for once since the eve of St Nicholas's Day she and Kitty could be private – almost an impossibility in a house crammed with Nightingales in the weeks before Christmas.

'Cressida, how long are you going to stay here with Mama?' Kitty said, not unkindly. 'What are you going to do when the rest of us have kept Christmas at Summercourt and flown the coop? By the end of January, it'll just be you and Sylvia again and, say what you like, I'll never believe that you're content with her life in the country.'

Cressida laughed. 'It's just as well that you, Chas, Alasdair and the boys and all the children are staying with us. At breakfast, Chas swore that he'd commit fratricide if he had to listen to Crauford's moralising any longer than necessary.'

'Sylvia makes a party of every evening,' Kitty said, 'and the truth is, Crauford and Marianne are quiet souls, aren't they? Come on, you know they're both happier at Summercourt without the rest of us, playing chess and discussing next year's planting.'

'I only hope their children are as retiring as they are, otherwise heaven help them all,' Cressida said, watching pale clouds chase one another across a yellow-tinged winter sky pregnant with more snow.

'Stop trying to alter the subject,' Kitty said, with a sharp look. 'How long will you stay out here in this backwater before you get bored enough to do something awful? Sylvia won't be back in London until at least March, and you won't convince me that you can stand another three months of gardening society meetings or musical recitals in stuffy drawing rooms.' She looked away, then, obviously steeling herself. 'Has anyone heard from Greville?'

'Not for weeks.' Cressida opened her hip flask and took a draught of sloe gin. 'He can't really communicate anything to us in case it's intercepted by the French: you know all of the Allied troops in Spain have been in retreat. Jamie and Oliver are doing well with Greville's regiment, I hear, but all this time Greville and Lascelles will have been scouting ahead of the route into Portugal. No one knows where they are.'

'And yet every drawing room in England is populated by experts,' Kitty said, as a red kite wheeled above them. 'Consider it: just last night, the vicar was adamant that we'd only lost a few hundred men in the last retreat, whereas Crauford maintains it's in the tens of thousands. It's incredibly tiresome.'

Cressida didn't reply; spotting Kitty's boys and the younger Nightingales pelting each other with snowballs on the ramparts of the hill fort, she wished she could still run and join them.

*

Later that evening, Sylvia's drawing room was bright with candlelight. Painted shutters were drawn closed across the tall windows, held fast with brass clasps, and the hearth was garlanded with ivy woven with dried oranges, so that the scent permeated the room along with the warmth of candlewax and pine sap. Along with Kitty, Sylvia had gathered a court of local ladies around her to gossip and play *bouts-rimés*, as if there were nothing better to do with one's life than swap scandal. Kitty's kindly husband, Alasdair, gamely led a discussion among the men about the possibilities locally for salmon fishing, and how they compared to his native Scotland, where he would much rather have been, although he was far too well mannered to betray that. Chas and his younger siblings and cousins clustered around the walnut table, engaged in a raucous game of fish with the vicar's son and his formidable freckled cousin, who kept accusing them all of cheating, justifiably, in Cressida's estimation.

'Come on, Cressida,' Chas called out, laughing. 'Stop trying to pretend you're interested in my mother's word-games. We need you to defend us against outrageous charges.'

'Aren't *you* supposed to be able to do that?' Cressida retorted. 'I don't know what else they're teaching you at university, if you can't argue and debate – I pity the first Luddite you defend in court if you can't put up a fight against poor Miss Beardsley.'

Miss Beardsley laughed, holding up her hands. 'If you Nightingales don't stop cheating, I swear I'll go into hysterics.'

'Don't do that,' Cressida advised. She drained her third glass of champagne, steadying herself as she got up, and yet certain in the knowledge that she couldn't stay inside for one moment longer. She had to escape to breathe.

The stable-yard was cold and quiet, the cobbles slick with a thin layer of frost, so that Cressida was glad of the wooden pattens that she'd slipped on over her boots by the scullery door. Leaning on the gate, Cressida tugged the shawl around her shoulders and gazed out across tumbling fields towards the moonlit church. Sensing that she was not alone, a trickle of fear slid down her back. *At last.* What else did one expect, uncovering corruption and betrayal in the heart of the establishment that went so deep it had even silenced Arthur Lascelles for five minutes?

Even as Cressida made the choice not to reach for her knife because it would be quicker that way, she understood that in fact she didn't need to. Instead, she turned to face Lord Greville Nightingale crossing the stable-yard towards her in his greatcoat. She caught a glimpse of braiding: he was still in uniform, unusually gaunt, and the breath caught in her throat.

'We must stop meeting like this,' she said, with all the cold distance she could muster.

Greville's reply to that was swift and uncompromising:

he lifted her in his arms so that she sat on the gate wrapped in her shawl, and then he kissed her hard on the mouth, pushing away her tears with the edge of his thumb. Finally, he pulled back and absent-mindedly kissed her on the forehead as though he had been out cutting wheat in the fields for a day, and not guarding a starving retreating army with his rifle.

'If you're going to attempt the cold, uncaring ice queen, you'd do better not to weep. Are you drunk?' he said, conversationally. 'I wouldn't blame you if you were. I always used to go wild with boredom here as well.'

She should pull away, she should tell him about the child and watch him walk off in disgust, but her face was now pressed against the front of his greatcoat and he teased a curl of her hair with his fingertip in such a way that heat pulsed at her core. 'How in the devil did you get here?'

He held out one hand and she took it, allowing him to help her down from her undignified position on the gate; the ankle had healed well, but she dared not risk leaping down in the way she once would have done.

'My mount threw a shoe about four miles away – I left him with Vaughan at the toll-house and walked. I'd as lief go on Shanks's pony straight here than walk back another four miles and rouse the smithy.' He kissed her again, running both hands down her back to her rear, pulling her close. 'Cressida, whatever it is you're trying to save me from, can you please do me the honour of kindly not?'

'In that case, can you do me the honour of listening to what I have to say?' Cressida said. 'Greville, we didn't have time to discuss anything at Drochcala, not really.'

'No, you were too busy nearly dying, and terrifying me, and then absconding before we'd had the chance to talk properly,' Greville said, calmly. 'I've been sent home on leave. Do you think I never knew you at all? Do you think I didn't realise you were holding something at a distance, from yourself as much as from me?' He let out a breath, looking away. 'My love, we were apart for years, and you lived in the train of an army, entirely on your wits. Do you think I don't know what you must have had to do to survive?'

'You might want to walk away from me when I tell you the whole.'

'You can tell me anything you please, but I promise I'll never do that again.' Greville watched her for a moment. 'Will you come inside with me? I mean, will you come away with me, because you were born to be an outrageous adventurer, and quite frankly the thought of you sitting here playing propriety for just long enough to ask for a respectable divorce is not something I'll countenance. But will you come inside first? Because there are things that I've been longing to do to you, and for you, since long before I boarded the ship.'

Cressida's answer was simple, even as she kissed his smile. 'Yes, Greville.'

Author Note

Writing a historical novel has been intimidating at times, especially one which includes such a well-documented war and Britain's first-ever true celebrity. *My Lady's Secrets* is a work of fiction and a figment of my imagination, but some of the events in the book really happened, like the murder of Lord Spencer Perceval and Lord Byron's speech in defence of the frame-breakers. For anyone interested in the lingering mystery surrounding the real motive of Lord Perceval's murderer, I strongly recommend you read *Why Spencer Perceval Had to Die* by Andro Linklater. Linklater acknowledges his debt to Mollie Gillen, whose painstaking research in the Public Records Office revealed the telling details of Bellingham's final financial transactions.

Cressida's life as a camp follower was inspired by my work on a heritage programme for military spouses with the charity Waterloo Uncovered, researching the lives of the ordinary soldiers' wives and children who accompanied the Allied army all the way from Portugal to France in the Peninsular War. They led extraordinary lives which are still little known and probably less well understood. Unlike their counterparts further up the social scale, very few first-hand accounts by these women are easily available. If you would like to find out more about them, in the words of one of their own, I'd recommend reading the diary of Catherine Exley, which is published by Brandram. Hunting for evidence of lives that were treated without much consideration at the time is sometimes like searching for a needle in a haystack, but if you're interested in genealogy and have ever stumbled across a British ancestor born in Spain or Portugal in the early nineteenth century, they may well have been following the drum. Peter Snow's *To War with Wellington* is a fantastic history of the Peninsular War and all the events that led up to the Battle of Waterloo. Ordinary soldiers spring to life on the page, with some unforgettable characters among them.

Lord Byron, to my knowledge, was never used in the way I describe in this novel, and Jamie's mission to ship weapons to Radicals, set up by Lord Rosmoney, is also a work of fiction, but the British government was certainly not averse to using spies, informers and agent provocateurs to infiltrate and destroy radical groups. If you'd like to read more about Britain's radical past, I recommend *Black and British* by David Olusoga and *Staying Power* by Peter Fryer. Lord Rosmoney himself is also a fictional character, although he was inspired in part by Lord Edward Fitzgerald, who supported the United Irishmen in the rebellion of 1798. As part of the Anglo-Irish aristocracy, this was an incredibly unusual position for a man of Fitzgerald's background to take, just as it would have been for Rosmoney.

Cressida, Greville and their friends and family took on chaotic, messy lives of their own as I was writing this book. Keeping track of their excesses against a complex backdrop of battles and political instability gave me a few sleepless nights. All that remains is to sincerely apologise to any readers who may have discovered the sort of lingering mistake that made them throw the book across the room. I hope that the rest of you enjoyed this adventure in the Regency, a period of such wild excess and horrifying despair that I can never quite escape its spell.

Acknowledgements

I would like to thank my editor, Rosie de Courcy, who is always up for an adventure, and is just as spellbound by the Peninsular War as me. I'd also like to thank my colleague Sarah Dhanjal and all the truly incredible military spouses who took part in Waterloo Uncovered's Hidden Histories: Women of Waterloo programme as I was writing this book. You know who you are, and you are all incredible. Special thanks are due to Sacha Coward, who once told me that with this book I had invited him to dance, and gave me the confidence to look Lord Byron in the eye. Huge thanks to Ian and Shirley-Anne MacMillan for discussions about Irish words and rebel songs, to Lisa Glass and Emily Paterson Morgan for their thoughtful responses to an early draft, and to Will Llewellyn for once again checking the sailing bits for me. Thank you so much to Evelyn Clegg for creative and thoughtful assistance with Gaelic place-names. Drochcala is exactly the sort of name the Butes would have given their house because they liked the sound of it, without understanding the true meaning of Droch Cala (Bad Harbour). Tapadh leat, Evelyn. Dr Ciarán McDonnell kindly answered my questions about the Irish Rebellion of 1798 and Irish military service, and any mistakes or misapprehensions are completely my own.

My Lady's Secrets is dedicated to Lucy and Alec Birkbeck, and I would like to thank them here for so many years of excellent times in Scotland, which went a long way towards inspiring the location of this book and gave me a place where my imagination could run riot at a time when we were all stuck at home. You guys are always so much fun.

Writing a book is the work of many hands, and thanks are due to my agent, Catherine Clarke, and the wonderful Bianca Gillam, as well as the whole fantastic publishing team behind putting this book in your hands: Amy Watson, Ayo Okojie, Zoe Giles, Holly Humphreys, Clémence Jacquinet, Jo Liddiard, Nicola Bigwood and Tamsin Shelton.

About the Author

KATY MORAN is the author of *Game of Hearts*, *Wicked by Design*, *Scandalous Alchemy* and *My Lady's Secrets*. Katy is fascinated by the glamorous world of high society in the past but drawn to darker, grimier corners of history where her own ancestors scrubbed floors and polished other people's shoes. She has worked on many arts and heritage projects, including Hidden Histories: Women of Waterloo with the charity Waterloo Uncovered, which examines the lives of camp followers, women and children who followed the British army to war in the early 1800s. Katy lives in the Welsh Borders with her husband, three children and four miniature sheep. You can visit her website katymoran.co.uk or follow her on X @KatyjaMoran.